Praise for *The Rise and Fall of Miss Fannie's Biscuits*

"Hang on for the ride of your life as retired detective Foster Bates and amateur Detective Fannie Yoder attempt to untangle this hilarious web of mystery and join forces to determine who actually 'Dunnit.' I've known both Martha Bolton and Wanda Brunstetter for quite a few years. And 'devious' is the last word I would describe either one of them. However, they are VERY capable at creating some devious, manipulative, and deceptive individuals—characters who bring great drama, mystery, and intrigue to a story! That's exactly what these two award-winning writers have done in their first collaboration on 'Rise and Fall.'"

– Dan Posthuma, music producer and the president/producer of Blue Gate Musicals. Over his 40-year career, he has received numerous Dove awards and several Grammy Award nominations.

"If you're in the mood for a cozy mystery that stirs up laughter, a generous scoop of drama, and a dash of romance, *The Rise and Fall of Miss Fannie's Biscuits* is your next must-read! With a baking contest gone awry and a cast of quirky Amish, Mennonite, and non-Amish contestants, Fannie and Foster's latest whodunit is a perfect recipe for pure entertainment."

– Suzanne Woods Fisher, bestselling author of *Anything but Plain*

T0282071

THE RISE AND FALL
— OF —
MISS FANNIE'S
BISCUITS

— A —
COZY AMISH
MYSTERY

WANDA &
BRUNSTETTER

New York Times Bestselling Author

AND MARTHA BOLTON

BARBOUR
PUBLISHING

For more information about Wanda E. Brunstetter, please access the author's website at the following Internet address: www.wandabrunstetter.com

Cover design: Kirk DouPonce, DogEared Design

Model Photography: Richard Brunstetter III

Published by Barbour Publishing, Inc., 1810 Barbour Drive, Uhrichsville, OH 44683, www.barbourbooks.com

Our mission is to inspire the world with the life-changing message of the Bible.

Member of the
Evangelical Christian
Publishers Association

Printed in the United States of America

"Be strong and of good courage, do not fear nor be afraid of them; for the Lord your God, He is the One who goes with you. He will not leave you nor forsake you."

Deuteronomy 31:6

CHAPTER 1

Sugarcreek, Ohio

After a long day working at her quilt shop, Fannie Miller was ever so glad to be home. Her feet hurt from being on them for a good many hours, and she was tired from answering so many customers' questions. Sometimes it seemed like the experienced quilters had more questions—or at least things they wanted to discuss with her—than those who were just beginning to learn about quilting.

Fannie removed her shoes and stockings then hung her outer garments on the wooden rack near the front door. After fixing herself a cup of tea, she sank onto the couch with a weary sigh to read the local newspaper. "Ah, that feels much better," she murmured, taking a deep breath and placing her bare feet on the coffee table. It always felt good to get out of her shoes so she could wiggle her toes and allow her foot flesh to cool. Shoes were not only restricting, but her feet were more apt to become sweaty within the confinement of shoes and stockings. Ever since Fannie was a child, she'd enjoyed going barefoot, and even now, as a grown woman who had recently turned forty-three, Fannie preferred going barefoot to wearing shoes. Of course, that wouldn't look too professional if she ran around the quilt shop wearing no shoes. And she wouldn't go out shopping, attend church, or be seen at other social functions in bare feet. But in the privacy of her home, Fannie saw no reason not to give her feet the freedom to walk around without the captivity of shoes. Now that spring had sprung, bringing warmer weather, whenever Fannie had the chance to be in her yard, she could enjoy going barefoot and walking on the soft, green grass.

Fannie wiggled her toes a few more times to get the kinks out and sipped some tea before opening the newspaper. Like she always did when reading the paper, Fannie thumbed through the first several pages, stopping to read anything that caught her attention. There on the third page was a big write-up about the Tenth Annual Tuscarawas and Surrounding Counties Baking Contest. The event would be held at the Carlisle Inn in the Dutch Valley complex, right here in Fannie's hometown. Fannie had been there previously for a quilt show, and she knew for a fact there was plenty of parking outside the building and easy access to enter. In addition to the lovely rooms for guests to stay, the inn had a conference center that accommodated up to 250 people in theater-style seating, or 208 people for meetings with straight tables and chairs. The facilities also had full audio/video capabilities, mounted television monitors with full connectivity, and an excellent sound system. There were also communication tools, including flip charts and internet access.

Fannie figured that most of the people who entered the contest would stay at the inn or some other nearby facility. But since Fannie lived in Sugarcreek, if she entered the contest she would not be in need of overnight accommodations but could rest comfortably in her own bed at night.

Fannie had entered every year this event had been held, but she'd never won first place. This year, however, Fannie was hopeful that, thanks to an old recipe passed down from her aunt Selma, she might actually make it to the finals. During the last nine years of entering the contest, Fannie had made Pumpkin Custard Pie, Applesauce Cake, Sour Cream Apple Pie, Pumpkin Bars, Rhubarb Cake, Banana Nut Brownies, Zucchini Bread, Gingerbread, and Shoo-fly Pie. The judges had smiled and said that her entries were good—just not good enough for first place.

"I truly hope this year will be different," Fannie said aloud. "Aunt Selma's Buttermilk Biscuits are the best around, and I should have tried entering them sooner."

Fannie's mind wandered back to a time when she was a young girl and her aunt had given her a lesson on biscuit-making. . .

———

"Now, Fannie, dear. . .please pay close attention to everything I am going to say and do."

Fannie, who had recently turned twelve, moved closer to the kitchen counter, where Aunt Selma stood with a sifter in one hand.

"The first thing we do is sift all the dry ingredients together." The tall, dark-haired woman gestured to the large, stainless steel bowl sitting next to the measuring cups and containers of dry ingredients she had already set out. "Fannie, would you please measure out two cups of flour and pour it into the bowl?"

Fannie did as her aunt requested, and then she stepped back quickly when a dusting of flour hit her right in the face. She reached for a paper towel and wiped the flour away.

Aunt Selma chuckled and continued to instruct Fannie on how much baking powder, salt and baking soda, to put in with the flour. Next came the shortening and buttermilk.

With the exception of the dusting of flour, Fannie thought the process of making biscuits seemed easy enough, and she enjoyed being in her aunt's cozy kitchen.

After the shortening had been added, Aunt Selma cut it into the dry ingredients with a fork. "And now," she said, with a twinkle in her eyes and a broad smile on her face, "for the most important ingredient of all." She picked up the measuring cup that had been partially filled with buttermilk and poured it into the bowl.

Fannie watched with interest as her aunt stirred the batter. It looked kind of sticky, but Aunt Selma obviously knew what she was doing, so Fannie wasn't worried about it. She had eaten a good many of her aunt's tasty biscuits, and every bite had always been delicious and left Fannie wanting more.

Things went bad when Aunt Selma told Fannie to place her hands in the flour she'd poured into a separate bowl and then take some of the dough out and form it into a biscuit with her hands.

Fannie's attention was drawn to a big fly on the wall near the sink, and she stood there staring at it until her aunt said, "Go ahead and do as I said, Fannie."

Fannie reached in and took out a chunk of dough. For some reason, it felt gooey and stuck to Fannie's fingers. She wrinkled her nose. "Eww. . .this feels yucky, and I don't know how to get it off my hands!"

In her usual patient tone, Aunt Selma pushed a small bowl that had a little flour in it toward Fannie and said, "I guess you weren't listening to everything I said."

Fannie tipped her head to one side and squinted. "You told me to take some dough out of the bowl and form a biscuit."

"That is true, but I also said you should place your hands in the flour I poured into the bowl over there." Aunt Selma gestured with her head. "And then I said you should gather some dough and form a biscuit."

Fannie's face burned with the heat of embarrassment. She should have paid closer attention. "Wh—what should I do now?" She turned her hands palms up and held them close to her aunt. Fannie figured it was a hopeless case and Aunt Selma would say that Fannie would never learn how to bake biscuits.

Instead, Aunt Selma helped Fannie wipe the dough off her hands and told her to start over again. It took several tries, but with her aunt's help, she finally formed a biscuit that looked halfway decent and placed it on the baking sheet, along with the ones her aunt had already made.

———

The clock on the mantel over Fannie's fireplace chimed six times, bringing her thoughts back to the present. It was almost time to start supper. Only, Fannie wasn't the least bit hungry. The only thing she had on her mind was the baking contest—and which of her recipes she would use to enter this time.

Since that first day when Fannie had learned how to make Aunt Selma's buttermilk biscuits, she'd made them dozens of times over the years. Sometimes the biscuits would rise perfectly, and sometimes they fell, but Fannie kept practicing until her biscuits turned out well, with just the right texture and moisture. Fannie thought they were every bit as good as Aunt Selma's, and whenever she had served them to guests, she'd received numerous compliments. Of course, she never let their comments go to her head. That would be considered *hochmut*—prideful—an undesirable trait among most Amish.

Yes, Fannie told herself, rising from her seat. *I will enter Aunt Selma's buttermilk biscuits in the contest, and I hope with great success.*

Full of renewed determination, she gave a slow shake of her head. *There will be no burned, crumbly, or hard biscuits made in my kitchen, because thanks to Aunt Selma's teachings, I have mastered the fine art of making the best biscuits in town. I am certain to win that contest!*

———

Glancing at the clock on the far wall of the Three Sisters Bakery, Faith Beiler cupped her hands around her mouth and hollered, "It's five o'clock, Hope! Could you please put the CLOSED sign in the front window so we can go home?"

"I'm on it!" Faith's middle sister called in return.

Faith's youngest sister, Charity, stepped between them with one hand held high. "It is time to close the bakery for the day, but none of us can go home yet." Her thick lashes fluttered, emphasizing the depth of her pretty blue eyes.

Faith tilted her head to one side and back again to look straight at her sister. "How come?"

"Because we haven't decided what we should make to enter in the upcoming Tenth Annual Tuscarawas and Surrounding Counties Baking Contest," Charity stated with a note of excitement in her voice.

"Oh, that's right," Hope put in, pushing a strand of her light brown hair back under her white, cone-shaped head covering. "And I remember how the three of us decided earlier today that we wouldn't go home until we came up with something we all agreed upon."

Faith heaved a sigh and leaned against the front checkout counter. "I'm really feeling *mied* from being on my feet most of the day, but I suppose we ought to follow through with our plans."

"I'm tired too," Hope said, "but if we're going to enter the contest, then it's important that we come up with the right entry so we will have plenty of time to practice making it."

"Let's all take a seat, which will allow us to be off our feet while we discuss the potential prospects." Faith gestured to one of the small tables where their customers often sat when they wanted to enjoy a cup of coffee with their favorite pastry.

Once the sisters were seated, Charity spoke up. "I think we should enter one of our delicious fry pies." A bright smile crossed her oval-shaped face, where a smattering of freckles dotted her nose and upper cheeks. "We could choose any flavor, but I'm voting for lemon. It's a popular one with our customers—and me as well."

"I disagree," Hope interjected.

Charity's pale eyebrows drew together. "Are you saying that you don't like fry pies? Or is it the lemon flavor you don't care for?"

"I like fry pies just fine, and I have no objection to lemon either." Hope tapped her slender fingers against the tabletop. "I just don't think fry pies, no matter which flavor we'd choose, would win us the grand prize."

"Hope might be right." Charity bobbed her head. "With a fry pie, we might win second or third place, but if we want to walk away with the twenty-five-thousand-dollar grand prize, then we need to enter a baked good that will really impress the judges."

Faith folded her hands and placed them in her lap as she reflected on all the wonderful pastries she and her sisters created here in the bakery. Some folks came all the way from Akron just to visit their bakery, and the best-selling pastry was always the cinnamon rolls. She was on the verge of saying so when Hope spoke again.

"If we're going to expand our business, or build a new one, then we really need to win that prize money, which means we must offer something that will impress the judges."

"I agree with you, Sister," Charity concurred. "We need to knock their socks off."

Faith chuckled. "It's not their socks we need to worry about. It's their taste buds, and how our entry makes them feel right here." She lifted one hand from her lap and gave her belly a couple of pats.

Hope, who sat to the right, reached over and gave Faith's arm a few taps. "What do you suggest we make to enter in the contest that might give us an edge and win the grand prize?"

"It's as simple as the *naas* on your face." Faith tweaked her sister's slightly pointed nose. "What is the one pastry we sell the most of in this bakery?"

"Cinnamon rolls," her sisters said in unison.

"Exactly! And the reason for that is because our sweet, plump cinnamon rolls are *appeditlich.*"

"You are right, Faith. They are very delicious, which is why they sell out so quickly." Charity clapped her hands. "What do you say, Sisters? Should we vote on it now?"

All heads nodded, and then Faith spoke again. "Everyone in favor of entering our cinnamon rolls lift your left hand."

Faith held up her left hand, but Charity and Hope just sat there with placid expressions.

"What's wrong?" Faith questioned. "How come neither of you voted yes?"

"I don't think we should enter our cinnamon rolls," Hope stated.

Faith cupped one hand under her chin. "How come?"

"I think we ought to make a delicious devil's food cake."

"But, Hope—"

"Think about it, Faith," Hope interrupted. "It's a moist, delectable dessert, and I'm sure the judges would all love it."

"Hope might be right," Charity interjected. "Maybe we should consider that suggestion. All in favor hold up your left hand."

Charity held up hers and so did Hope. Faith just sat with her eyes downcast.

"Well, it doesn't matter which of our hands are lifted. I'm satisfied that it was a unanimous vote," Charity stated in a firm voice. "And I declare that the devil's food cake is what we should enter in the baking contest, and I'm almost certain that it will be a winner."

Hope sat up straight and pulled her shoulders back. "I can hardly wait for the contest to begin. I am quite sure that we'll have a better chance at winning than any of the other contestants."

"You may be right," Faith agreed. "After all, being experienced bakers, I'm confident we'll beat out any and all competition."

Berlin, Ohio

Melissa Taylor entered the family room, which her husband, Michael, liked to call his "man cave," and stood off to the side of his chair.

Michael, apparently unaware of her presence, leaned forward with both elbows resting on his knees as he stared at the baseball game being televised on his big-screen television.

She cleared her throat a few times, hoping to get his attention, but

Michael didn't say a word or even glance her way.

"I'd like to talk to you about something, Michael," she said.

No response. Not even a quick glance.

Melissa tried again, speaking a little louder this time, but she received no acknowledgment at all.

Her lips pressed together, and she clamped both hands against her slender hips. Did he honestly not hear what she'd said, or was Michael deliberately ignoring her presence? Surely, at twenty-eight, he couldn't be hard of hearing.

She stood for several more seconds before deciding to try another tactic. Walking with purpose across the room, Melissa stepped directly in front of the television.

"Hey!" Michael's voice raised a notch. "You're blocking my view of the game!"

She folded her arms and looked directly at him, ignoring the firm set of his chiseled jaw. "How else am I supposed to get your attention?"

"You could have simply said you wanted to talk to me."

"Yeah, right," she said with a huff. "I tried that, and where did it get me?"

His only response was a brief shrug, and without bothering to ask what Melissa wanted to talk to him about, Michael leaned to one side and shouted, "Hit that ball, buddy! Come on—we need a home run right now!"

Melissa tapped her foot as her irritation increased. There had to be some way to get her dark-haired, blue-eyed handsome husband's attention. With no thought of the outcome, she marched up to the footstool in front of Michael's chair, grabbed the remote from where it lay, and shut off the television.

Michael's face reddened, and he nearly jumped out of his chair. "Hey! What'd you do that for? You knew I was watchin' the game."

"I came in here to talk to you about something, and since I couldn't get your attention, I saw no other way but to turn off the TV."

She couldn't miss the way the muscles in her husband's arms tightened, and the tone with which Michael spoke had a sharp edge to it.

"All right, already—you have my attention. Say whatever you have to say so I can get back to my game." His thick, black bangs fell over his forehead as he leaned forward.

Melissa moved closer to his chair. "It's about the baking contest."

He rubbed his chin and pulled his fingers down the sides of his clean-shaven face. "What baking contest?"

"You know—the Tenth Annual Tuscarawas and Surrounding Counties Baking Contest. Weren't you listening when our marriage counselor mentioned it during our last session with him?"

Michael drew in a quick breath and released it before answering her question. "I. . .umm. . .guess he did make some mention of it." Michael eyed the remote in Melissa's hand. "Can I please have that back now?"

"In a minute. When we are done talking."

"Is there more you wanted to say?" He tilted his head back and looked upward, as though already bored with their conversation, and no doubt resentful of her for interrupting his "very important" game.

"Yes, Michael, there is more to be said." Melissa's stomach muscles tightened in readiness of his response, which she felt certain would be negative.

"All right then—spit it out."

"I was wondering if you have given it any thought as to what we should make."

His thick, dark eyebrows almost squished together. "You mean for supper?"

She gave a firm shake of her head. "No, for the baking contest. I was thinking about our options. We could make a cherry pie, an angel food cake, a loaf of banana bread, or maybe—"

Michael held up his left hand and waved it about. "Have you lost your mind, Melissa? You're the baker, not me. So if you're set on entering that silly contest then go right ahead. But you're gonna have to count me out."

"But Michael, remember, this was our counselor's idea. He said we should find something we can do together, and that it might help to strengthen our relationship." She paused a few seconds before continuing. "And I think it could be fun for us to do some baking together." Melissa stepped to the left and put her hand on his broad, muscular shoulder, but he shook it off.

"Hear me well, dear wife," Michael said in a coarse tone. "I am not signing up for any stupid baking contest. If you think it's such a great idea, then you'll have to do it yourself."

Tears welled in her eyes. Melissa wanted desperately to try harder to convince Michael what a good opportunity this was for both of them—especially if they won the grand prize. The spots of color that had erupted on his cheeks, however, let her know that now was not a good time to plead with him to take on this challenge with her.

Melissa handed the remote back to Michael, turned, and quietly left the room. She would bring this topic up again when the time was right. Maybe then he would be in a better mood.

CHAPTER 2

Sugarcreek

Foster Bates had just taken a seat at the kitchen table, to drink a cup of coffee and eat the last of the cinnamon rolls he'd purchased a few days ago at the Three Sisters Bakery, when he heard an odd scratching noise at the back door. He tipped his head and listened as the sound continued.

Now that's sure strange, Foster thought. *If I didn't know any better, I'd think Chief was outside, begging to come in. But that's ridiculous—my dog is right here with me.* He glanced down at the shaggy pal he'd named Chief lying barely a foot from his chair, apparently sleeping too deeply to be aware of the noise on the other side of the door.

Scratch. . .scratch. . .scratch. . .

As a retired cop, turned detective, Foster had a keen intuitive sense about most things, and right now, his intuition said there must be another dog scratching at his door. How he would have gotten into the yard, though, would be a mystery, since it was completely fenced in.

Foster rose from his chair, skirted around Chief, and being careful not to step on the dog's tail, hurried over to the door. Grasping the knob, he jerked the door open and nearly fell backward when a bushy-tailed squirrel ran right between his legs. Before Foster could gain his wits, the crazy critter made a beeline for Chief's dog dish, which Foster had filled when he'd entered the kitchen. Chief had eaten some of it before taking a nap near the table, and the squirrel was now chomping the food faster than Foster could blink.

Suddenly, Chief came awake, barking, snarling, and chasing after the squirrel. In response, the oversized rodent gave off a high-pitched chirp. Round and round the table they went, and then under the table, and back again. It was impossible to keep up with the two animals, and Foster certainly wasn't up to the task this morning.

He wasn't sure if Chief was after the squirrel because it had been eating his food, or just because dogs can't help their predatory drive. He figured Chief's compulsion to go after the squirrel was hard-wired and came as naturally to the dog as eating cinnamon rolls did to Foster.

Things were getting a bit crazier than Foster would like, and when Chief knocked over the garbage can, Foster was more than ready to call a halt to the whole ordeal. He'd read once that activated noisemakers could scare off a squirrel, so he grabbed a kettle from the cupboard, along with a metal spoon, and began banging the bottom of the pan. Chief stopped running, tipped his head back, and howled. Meanwhile, the squirrel made a quick escape out the open door, which Foster promptly slammed shut.

"Whew!" He collapsed into his chair and gulped down the rest of his coffee. Foster figured Chief might be tired after the chase and return to the place he'd been resting before the squirrel escapade. Chief had other ideas, though, as he crunched the remaining food in his dish.

Foster ate what was left of his cinnamon roll and debated pouring himself another cup of coffee. But when he glanced at the clock on the far wall and saw the time, he decided it was past the hour when he should be heading for his office here in town. Something important might lie ahead for the day. Or if he was lucky, all might be quiet, and he wouldn't have to see or talk to a single person today. He could browse through some magazines he'd recently bought, or maybe take a snooze on the cot he kept in the back room.

Or maybe, Foster thought as he placed his dishes in the sink, *I might leave the office for a while and head over to the Three Sisters Bakery to buy another batch of cinnamon rolls.*

He glanced down at Chief. The dog had eaten all his food and was now slurping water from his other dish like there was no tomorrow. No doubt the merry chase with the squirrel had left the dog thirsty.

"What am I gonna do with you today, buddy?" Foster bent down and gave the dog's head a few pats. "If I leave you in the backyard while I'm at the office, you might end up tangling with that crazy squirrel again."

Foster gave a slow shake of his head. "That wouldn't be good, would it, pal?"

Chief responded with a few wags of his tail.

Foster reached for his hat, lying on one end of the counter, and slapped it on his head. "Wanna come to work with me this morning?" he asked the dog.

Woof! Woof!

Foster grinned. "Okay, then let's go."

Chief didn't have to be asked twice. He followed Foster out the door leading to the garage and happily got in when Foster opened the vehicle's back door.

"Sure hope I don't live to regret this," Foster mumbled when he hit the button on the remote to open the garage door. The last time he'd taken Chief to the office, the dog had gotten excited when Miss Fannie Miller dropped by, and he'd had an unfortunate accident on the floor.

Certainly wouldn't want that to happen again, Foster thought. *It would be just as embarrassing as the last time, and I didn't enjoy cleaning up the mess.* He shrugged his shoulders. *I probably have nothing to worry about, though, because it's not likely that Fannie will come by today. Thankfully, the two of us aren't working together to solve any kind of mystery case right now. And she'll no doubt be at her quilt shop all day, so there's not much chance of her dropping by.* That thought pleased Foster, since the woman did seem to bring a sewing basket full of troubles every time she stopped in. And he just didn't have time for anything like that today.

———

Fannie's excitement about the baking contest ran so high she could hardly contain herself. It had been a week since she'd signed up for the event, and even though the details about it had been in the newspaper, and probably a few other places, she decided it would be a good idea to make some flyers up about the event and hang them around Sugarcreek and the surrounding area. So between customers dropping by her quilt shop,

Fannie got busy and made several dozen eye-catching flyers.

She smiled, looking down at the finished posters lying on an empty table near the back of her store. This was where she normally sat to draw designs for some of her smaller quilted items, like potholders, placemats, and table runners. But today she'd put the table to good use in another way, and she felt pretty pleased with how well the posters had turned out.

Not everyone who saw the flyers would enter the contest, but that was not her primary reason for taking the time to make them. Fannie's goal was to let not only her town but also some of the nearby towns know all about the event so they would make plans to attend. An annual event such as this was big news, and she wanted to do her part to advertise so there would be a good turnout.

She gathered each poster and placed it neatly in a cardboard box, being careful not to wrinkle or bend the heavy paper she'd used. Each one said the same thing—name of the event, date and time the preliminaries would be held, and what the grand prize would be for the winning entry that would be given out at the end of the finals.

Ah, the grand prize. . . Fannie drew in a breath and released it slowly. *I can only imagine how wonderful it would feel to win first place and have enough money to do whatever I want here at the quilt shop or do some fixing up at home.*

Pulling her thoughts back to the job at hand, she made her way up front and put the CLOSED sign in the window. No customers were in the shop currently, and Ann, the driver she'd called on a while ago, should be here soon. As soon as Ann arrived, they would head out and make stops at all the prime locations in town so Fannie could hang the flyers.

She smiled and reached up to make sure her head covering was on straight. These next several weeks would be so exciting.

———

"How many more posters do you have to hang up?" Ann asked when Fannie got back into the van.

"Just a few," Fannie replied. "Are you in a hurry to get home?"

Ann shook her head. "I won't be going home yet. There's an Amish family I need to pick up an hour from now. They need a ride to Millersburg to do some shopping."

"Okay, that shouldn't be a problem. You can drop me off at Foster Bates' office, and after I hang the last two posters, I'll walk back to my quilt shop from there."

"Are you sure you don't mind walking?"

"Not at all. The quilt shop isn't far from Foster's place of business, and after I close my shop for the day, I can go home on foot. The walk will do me good."

"Alrighty then." Ann pulled her vehicle out into traffic—what little there was in Sugarcreek today. Since tourist season wasn't in full swing yet, the vehicles were mostly driven by locals who either lived in town or were out doing business.

Fannie buckled her seatbelt, knowing that if she didn't, Ann would give her a firm reminder to buckle up. Even in town, with a lower speed limit, accidents could occur, and it was better to be safe than sorry.

In short order, they were pulling up to the small building that housed the Foster Bates Private Detective Agency office. Fannie paid her driver, picked up the last two posters, and got out of the van. "Thank you, Ann. I'll give you a call the next time I need a good driver," she said before closing the passenger door.

Through the window, Fannie saw Ann smile and wave. Fannie waved in response and hurried into the gift shop next to Foster's office. She was met with a cheerful greeting from the owner, and when Fannie explained what the flyers were about, she was told to "go right ahead and hang one in the window."

Fannie did as directed, told the owner "thank you," and scurried out the door. A ripple of excitement traveled through her body as she knocked on Foster's door.

———

With arms folded on his desk and head resting on his arms, Foster was almost asleep when Chief let out a couple of loud barks.

"Wh–what do you want, boy?" Foster's head came up. "You need me to take ya outside?"

Woof! Woof! The dog raced to the door.

"Okay, okay. . .just let me get your leash." There was no way Foster would ever turn Chief loose on the street to do his business. For one thing, he might run off. Or the dog could get hit by a car. It also wouldn't be good if he did his business on the sidewalk. No, Foster would need to take Chief around to the back of the building, where there was grass and dirt. Even then, he would have to take a shovel and a plastic bag to clean up after the dog.

Foster scratched his head. In his groggy state, he couldn't remember where he kept the shovel or the container of plastic bags. He was headed for the back room to see if he could locate the items, when a knock sounded on the door, followed by several more barks from his furry companion.

"Get back, Chief! Let me open the door!" Foster grabbed the dog by his collar and held him there as he slowly opened the door.

Fannie Miller poked her head in and smiled. "Are you busy, Foster?"

He cleared his throat. "Um. . .no, not really." Although Foster had come to consider this Amish woman a friend, she always managed to get him in the middle of messes. And he was not in the mood for any of that today.

Arf! Arf! Arf! Chief pawed at the hem of Fannie's dress.

"Stop that!" Foster scolded. "And you'd better hold your bladder." He looked at Fannie and sucked in his bottom lip. "You know what happens when Chief gets excited. And he's always excited when he sees you."

Just like you, Foster Bates, a little voice in his head taunted.

Foster pushed that nonsense away. He needed to keep Fannie at arm's length. "What brings you by here today, Fannie?" he questioned. "Is there a problem somewhere that I should know about?"

"Oh, no," she said with a shake of her head. "Everything's just as it should be in Sugarcreek." Fannie took a step forward. "Mind if I come in?"

"Uh, no. That is, I guess not." Foster felt like a bumbling idiot who couldn't form a sensible sentence. *Why does this Amish woman rattle me so? Just being in her presence makes me feel so discombobulated.*

Woof! Woof! Woof!

"A few more barks like that out of you, and I'm gonna stick you in the back room," Foster threatened, shaking his finger at Chief. Then he looked over at Fannie again, gestured with his head toward the chair on the opposite of his desk, and said, "Would you like to take a seat?"

"Well, I really can't stay," she said as she sat down. "I just came to. . ." Fannie paused and gave Chief's head a couple of pats when he followed her over to the chair. "What a nice *hund.* Your head is so silky."

"I'm guessin' *hund* means dog?" Foster asked.

She gave a brief nod. "As I said, I can't stay long, but I did come here with a favor to ask."

"And what would that be?" Foster lowered himself into the chair behind his desk. He couldn't help rolling his eyes when Chief laid his head in Fannie's lap. She obliged by stroking the dog's ears.

"That mutt really likes you, Fannie."

Her dimples deepened when she grinned at Foster. "The feeling is mutual."

Although Fannie wasn't strikingly beautiful, she had light brown hair peeking out from under her head covering, pretty blue eyes, and a nicely shaped nose. Fannie stood about five and a half feet tall, and couldn't have weighed more than 120 pounds. Her skin was mostly smooth, with just a few wrinkles around her eyes. Foster was surprised she'd never been married. Surely, some nice Amish man should have come along by now and swept Miss Fannie off her feet.

"So to what do I owe the pleasure of your company today?" Foster asked, pulling his thoughts back to the moment at hand.

Fannie smiled and handed him a rolled-up piece of paper. "I was wondering if I could hang this in your front window."

Foster opened it up and studied the words on the poster before looking back at Fannie. "There's going to be a baking contest in our area, huh?"

Her smile widened. "Oh yes. I enter it every year, and this year, I'm planning to enter with one of my favorite baked goods."

"Is that a fact?"

With her blue eyes shining like two iridescent marbles, Fannie's head bobbed up and down. "Would you like to know what I'm planning to bake?"

"Certainly." What else could he say? If Foster had stated that he wasn't interested in a baking contest or what Fannie planned to bake, it would hurt her feelings. And he wasn't about to do that. Not to a friend like Fannie Miller.

"Will you be making a pie, a cake, or some cookies?" he asked.

"None of those. I'm planning to make Aunt Selma's buttermilk biscuits." She licked her lips and gave Chief another pat. "They're absolutely *appeditlich*—or as you English would say, they are delicious."

"I'm a biscuits-and-gravy kind of guy, so I bet they'd be good for breakfast."

"No doubt, but they aren't just for breakfast. Aunt Selma's buttermilk biscuits go well with any meal." Fannie gestured to the poster Foster still held in his hand. "So is it okay if I hang that in your window?"

"I have no problem with it." He handed the item back to Fannie. "Did you make this poster yourself?"

"Yes, I sure did. I made several dozen and put them up all over town and some other nearby towns as well. An event like this is good for our community, and I think we should let as many people know about it as possible."

"I agree." Foster knew he'd better be in agreement with her, or she'd be sitting here all day trying to convince him of it. Besides, he had to admit that the baking contest was a good idea and so was advertising for it.

Foster took a roll of tape from his desk and handed it to Fannie. "Be my guest."

"Thank you." She jumped up and headed straight over to the window, with Chief on her heels.

Foster leaned back in his chair, with his hands behind his head. One thing about Fannie Miller—she didn't let any grass grow under her feet. If Fannie had a goal, she went for it. He admired her for that. *And maybe a few other things as well.* But that thought he would definitely keep to himself.

CHAPTER 3

"Do you have a lot of studying to do today?" Iva Troyer asked when she stepped up to the front of the desk where her husband, John, sat with his open Bible.

"*Jah*, as a matter of fact, I do," he replied, looking up just long enough to give her a brief nod. "I have a wedding to preach at next week, remember?"

"I understand, but I was hoping you could take a few minutes to talk with me now—it's about Jeb."

John reached up and rubbed the back of his neck. "It's always about Jeb, isn't it? What's our younger boy up to now? I hope he's not in some kind of trouble with his boss. We don't need him losing another job and then moping around here or hiding out in his room the way the boy did after he got fired from the feed store because he refused to answer anyone's questions."

Iva cringed. It was bad enough that their son suffered from social anxiety. Did Jeb's father have to criticize everything the boy did? Why wasn't John more understanding, like the way he was with the people in their church? What had happened to the once-patient man she had married thirty years ago? And why didn't he spend more time with Jeb, the way he had with their older boys before they got married?

Iva knew how busy her husband was, working a full-time job building gazebos and outdoor furniture, plus trying to keep up with all his responsibilities as their church district's bishop. Even so, she felt that her husband should be able to take some time away to spend with his family—especially Jeb, who needed his father's attention. She wondered if John's lack of interest in spending time with their son had something to do with the fact that Jeb was different from their other two boys, who were now out on their own. Abner and Mark were both outgoing and could carry on a meaningful conversation with most people—even strangers. Not Jeb, though. He lacked self-confidence and had trouble making friends. At the age of eighteen, Jeb had barely talked to any girls, much less had a girlfriend, and he rarely attended singings and other young people's functions.

Iva pinched the skin at her throat in an attempt to swallow the lump that always formed when she was on the verge of tears. *If our son had a good friend he could do things with, maybe he would become more social like other young men his age. And if Jeb's father took more interest in him, Jeb might gain more confidence.*

Iva worried that in addition to lacking certain social skills, her son might suffer from depression. It wasn't good for Jeb to stay in his room so much of the time when he wasn't working, or to be so quiet and sullen when he was around other people. Lately, Jeb had become somewhat of a recluse, even around his own parents. Iva was concerned and couldn't help worrying about their son's future. Unless something changed, he might not make it in the real world.

"Are we done talking now, so I can get back to my studies?" John asked, pulling Iva's troubling thoughts aside.

"But what about Jeb, and the way he—"

"He'll be fine, Iva. Someday Jeb will wake up and realize that he has to pull himself outta his shell and become a responsible man." John flapped a hand, as if to dismiss her—or at least the topic she'd tried so hard to talk with him about.

"All right then," she said, fighting tears of frustration behind her eyes. "I'll leave you to your studies." Iva turned to depart, but she paused to glance over her shoulder. She saw John reading his Bible again, which was no surprise. *Studying the scriptures is always a good thing,* she told herself.

But taking time out to spend with Jeb is important too. I just wish John could see that before it's too late.

Iva left the room her husband used for his studies and headed for the kitchen with her head down. *Maybe I'll bake a batch of peanut butter* kichlin. *Those are Jeb's favorite cookies, and I'm sure he'll be happy when he gets home from work today and sees the cookie jar filled with them.*

She entered the kitchen and got out her baking supplies. *I think while the kichlin are baking, I'll sit at the table and spend some time in prayer, while I take in the sweet aroma of those cookies my son likes so much.*

John sniffed deeply and looked up from the Bible references he'd been jotting on a piece of paper. He recognized the familiar odor of peanut butter kichlin drifting into his study through the slightly open door. No doubt Iva had been doing some baking. He figured she'd probably made Jeb's favorite cookies to offer him when he came from work.

I can't believe my fraa *interrupted my studies to talk about Jeb. Doesn't she realize how much I have on my plate, what with having to keep up with my business, plus studying for church services, weddings, and funerals—not to mention, counseling church members when needed? My dear wife worries too much about the boy,* John assured himself. *Jeb is not a child anymore, and he needs to grow up. Iva needs to quit pampering him all the time and let Jeb find his own way.* He squinted over the top of his reading glasses, while tapping his pen on the notepad. *If Jeb has social anxiety, as Iva put it, then he needs to get out more and mingle with other young people his age. He can't hang out here for the rest of his life, with no outside interests at all.*

John took a drink from his cup of coffee that had gone cold. *I don't know what Iva thinks I can do about it, anyway. Whenever I've tried talking to Jeb in the past, he clams up and runs off to the barn or his room. If my son wanted to talk to me, he'd stick around.*

Truth be told, at times John was embarrassed by his son's odd behavior. He'd hoped that by now Jeb would have grown out of it, but things didn't look good at this point.

John set his cup down and turned his attention to the notes on his desk again. Right now he had more pressing things on his mind than worrying about Jeb.

———

Foster stared at the backside of the poster Fannie had hung in his window yesterday. She'd sure been excited about the baking contest and spreading the news regarding the event. He hoped all the advertising that had been done, including Fannie's posters, would help draw a big crowd. He also felt sure that the biscuits she planned to make would be a hit with the judges.

He thumped his belly a few times. "They'd be a hit with me, that's for sure. I'm a sucker for most baked goods—biscuits, fry pies, cakes, cookies, and especially cinnamon rolls." Foster's mouth watered just thinking about all those delicious things, and it made him wish he'd brought something sweet to the office this morning. Unfortunately, he was all out of pastries and hadn't taken the time to renew his supply.

Foster grabbed a notepad and pen to start a list, but a knock sounded on his office door, interrupting his plan. He had put the CLOSED sign in the window ten minutes ago to give him some undisturbed time to get a few things done without interruption. Yet despite the sign, someone was out there, wanting to come inside.

I wonder if it could be Fannie. Foster rose from his chair. *Maybe she made a different poster and wants to put that in my window too. Or she might have brought some of her biscuits for me to try.* He grinned and licked his lips. *I sure wouldn't say no to that.*

Foster ambled across the room and opened the door.

"Oh, you are here, Mr. Bates. With your CLOSED sign in the window, I thought you might be in your back office closing up for the evening, but then I saw a light on and figured I should knock, in case you were still open for business and might be willing to serve one last customer." Charity Beiler stood looking at him with bright eyes and rosy cheeks.

Foster swallowed hard. "Uh. . .can I help you with something, Miss Blustery?" His face heated and he quickly rephrased his question. "Can I help you with something, Miss Beiler?"

She shook her head vigorously, making no mention of the fact that he'd said *Blustery* instead of *Beiler*. No doubt Charity had heard others refer to her and her siblings as "the Blustery Sisters." It was no secret here in Sugarcreek that the three women liked to talk about certain people and spread all kinds of "well-meaning" gossip. Hence—the Blustery nickname.

"I don't need any help, Mr. Bates," Charity said. "I came here because I've been concerned about you."

His eyebrows shot up. "Me? Why would you be concerned about me, Miss Beiler?"

"You didn't come into the bakery today for your usual order of cinnamon rolls. I thought perhaps you might be sick or something."

"No, I'm not sick. I've just been busy sorting through paperwork here and didn't go anywhere but my office today."

"Are you out of cinnamon rolls?"

"As a matter of fact, I am, but. . ."

Charity tilted her head slightly and batted her thick lashes as she looked up at Foster with a smile that stretched wide. "Not a problem, sir. I set some rolls aside for you, and I have them out in the car. I'll go get them right now." She whirled around quicker than a fly dodging a swatter and practically ran to her vehicle.

Foster remained in the open doorway and watched as she opened the passenger door and reached inside. He'd often wondered why Charity hadn't joined the Amish church, like her two sisters had done. Instead, she'd become a Mennonite. Was it so that she could drive a car? Or did it have more to do with the fact that the Mennonite church Charity attended had fewer rules than most Amish churches? Charity was kind of a free spirit and obviously didn't have a problem with owning a cell phone or a sporty-looking car, even if it was an older model.

Soon, Charity walked back to where Foster stood and handed him a plastic container. "There's a dozen cinnamon rolls in here," she announced.

He smiled. "How much do I owe you?"

She shook her head. "Not a thing. They're my gift to you."

Foster wasn't sure how to respond to that, so he simply said, "Thank you. I'll stop at the bakery sometime next week and bring your container back to you."

She flapped her hand in his direction. "Oh, don't you worry about that. It's disposable." There was a brief pause. "Or maybe I'll stop back sometime and pick it up."

Charity remained there, staring at Foster, until he broke out in a cold sweat. He wanted to bid this Mennonite woman good day and shut the door behind her, keeping the cinnamon rolls safely in his hands. But it was obvious that she wasn't done conversing. Did she expect him to invite her in or continue their conversation here in the doorway? As much as he appreciated the tasty treat, Foster would prefer to be left alone to finish going through his paperwork.

Charity took a step closer to him. So close that Foster could smell the scent of rose water on her neck. He moved back a bit and held his breath, afraid he might sneeze.

"I see you're advertising the baking contest." Charity motioned to the flyer in Foster's window.

"Uh, yes. A friend put it there."

"It's going to be a really big event," she said. "My sisters and I are going to enter, and we're hoping to win the grand prize."

"With your cinnamon rolls?" he asked.

"Oh, no. We are planning to make a devil's food cake for the contest."

"Oh, I see." Foster was surprised at their choice, but he kept his thoughts to himself, because it was really none of his business what the Beiler sisters chose to enter in the baking contest.

"I hope you'll be at the event to cheer us on." Charity moved even closer this time.

He took one more step back and cleared his throat a couple of times. "Yes, I do have plans to attend the contest. It should be interesting to see what all the contestants make and who'll end up with the grand prize." No point in telling Charity that he would be there to cheer her, Faith, and Hope on, as well as Fannie. She might get the wrong idea.

Charity stared at Foster with a peculiar expression, and then she opened her mouth like she might say something more, but he spoke first.

"Well, thank you again for the cinnamon rolls, Miss Charity. I'll see you at the bakery sometime next week."

Her shoulders drooped as she lowered her head. "Oh, okay. I'll let you get back to work then."

She was clearly disappointed, and Foster felt guilty. She probably thought he was being rude, since he hadn't invited her in. Even so, Foster wasn't about to do that. There was no point in encouraging this woman if she had any designs on him. He thanked her again and said that he hoped the rest of her day went well. Then Foster stepped back inside and quickly shut the door. As quietly as possible, he turned the deadbolt to its locked position. Foster hoped for his sake and hers that no one they knew had seen them talking to each other. It could be the beginning of some fresh gossip spread around town, and that was the last thing he needed.

Struggling with the feelings of disappointment that had set in, Charity got back in her car, started the engine, and pulled out onto the road. She had a hunch that showing up at Foster's place of business unexpectedly had not been as appreciated as she'd hoped it would be—even with the cinnamon rolls, which she knew the man liked. *Was Foster Bates embarrassed to be seen with me?* she asked herself. *Is he only nice to me because of my cinnamon rolls?*

She pursed her lips and gave the steering wheel a few raps with the knuckles on her left hand. *Maybe my actions and thoughtfulness make it seem too obvious that I'm looking for a husband. Foster might sense that, and I may have scared him off. I'll have to be more careful from now on and approach things differently with him.*

All the way home, Charity berated herself. She couldn't help wondering if there was something about her that Foster didn't like. Maybe it was the color of her eyes. Foster might be partial to brown instead of blue. Perhaps he didn't care for the sweet smell of her rose water cologne. Or could it be that Foster was a confirmed bachelor who had no plans of ever falling in love and settling down with a wife who would also be his best friend and confidante? Had he given thought to all the joy he was missing out of life?

Charity turned on some music, hoping to drown out her contemplations, but it was useless. Thoughts of Foster Bates remained stuck in her mind. She would either have to figure out some way to win his heart, or give up entirely and find another available man. Maybe someone who favored cinnamon rolls even more than Mr. Bates.

CHAPTER 4

When Fannie stepped out the front door of her house, a few drops of rain landed right on her nose. "Well, for goodness' sake," she exclaimed, wiping the water away with her hand. "I had no idea it was going to rain today."

She quickly stepped back inside and grabbed her black umbrella. It had been a lovely spring day when she'd looked out the kitchen window a short time ago. But the weather could change fast during the late spring months, and since there was no time to call a driver to take her to the quilt shop today, she would go there on foot, as she had originally planned.

As Fannie started her trek down the sidewalk, she couldn't help smiling at the bluebirds up ahead, taking a drink from a small puddle that had formed. Between drinks, they bathed, splashing water onto the sidewalk.

Those cute little birds don't let the rain dampen their spirits, Fannie mused. *In fact, I believe they appreciate the water God sent this morning. And who knows. . .maybe He allowed the rain to fall just for the birds' enjoyment or to provide them with water to drink and bathe in.*

Fannie always tried to look on the bright side of things. It put a person in a better frame of mind than focusing on all the negative things going on in the world—things she read about in the newspaper almost every day and heard customers talk about when they came to her store.

As she passed a neighbor's yard, Fannie caught sight of the lovely pink-and-yellow tulips blooming in the flowerbed, where there were no weeds in sight. Helen Jones, the English lady who lived there, had recently turned eighty. In spite of her age and a slight case of arthritis, the elderly woman kept herself busy in the yard and never complained about any aches and pains.

I hope I can be that cheerful when I'm Helen's age, Fannie thought. *It's good to be around happy, positive people.*

Fannie thought of the words in Proverbs 15:13: *"A merry heart makes a cheerful countenance, but by sorrow of the heart the spirit is broken."*

Like the birds splashing happily in the water, and the lovely flowers growing strong and healthy, she had every reason to have a merry heart today.

The baking contest preliminaries would be starting soon, and she was over the top with excitement. Of course, with that feeling of excitement came a sense of nervousness, for she had no idea if her biscuits would be good enough to please the judges and get her a score that would allow her to move on to the finals.

I can't worry about that right now, though. Win or lose—everything I do is in my Lord's hands, and I must not fret or dwell on the future too much. Fannie drew in some air between her lips and whistled a merry tune that she'd learned as a child, which made her feel even more joyous. Fannie smiled to herself. *I haven't forgotten how to whistle, and my baking skills are better now than ever.*

She pulled the umbrella aside, tilted her head back, and opened her mouth. A few raindrops landed on Fannie's tongue. *No brag. Just facts.*

When Fannie arrived at her quilt shop a short time later, she was surprised to see a blond woman sporting a stylish bob and wearing a pink raincoat while holding a matching umbrella over her head as she waited outside Fannie's front door.

The woman did not look familiar, and as far as Fannie recalled, she had never seen her here in the shop before.

"Hello, I'm Fannie Miller." Gripping her own umbrella with one hand, she extended her other hand to the young woman.

"You're the owner of this shop, aren't you?"

"Yes, I am."

The woman smiled and shook Fannie's hand. "My name is Melissa Taylor. My husband, Michael, and I live in Berlin, but I enjoy coming to Sugarcreek to shop sometimes. Today, I decided it would be fun to drop by your quilt shop and see what you have for sale."

Fannie unlocked the door and opened it. "Please, come inside and let's get out of the rain." She allowed Melissa to go first, stepped in behind her, and closed the door. "Were you looking for anything in particular?"

Melissa closed her umbrella and propped it against the wall near the door. "Not really. Just curious to see how much your quilts cost compared to the ones being sold at the quilt shop in Berlin."

"There probably isn't much of a price difference," Fannie responded as she set her umbrella aside too. "Are you looking for a full-sized quilt, a queen, or maybe a king?"

"Our bed is a king-size, but I probably can't afford one. The larger quilts I have seen in Berlin were quite expensive. Depending on the cost, though, I might be able get a table runner."

Fannie led Melissa over to the table where the runners had been displayed. "This is a nice one," she said, pointing to a runner with yellow and green hues.

Melissa picked it up, looked at the underside, where the price tag had been placed, and set it back down. "What is your least expensive quilted item in the store?"

"I have some potholders over there." Fannie gestured to the table in question. "They're priced at $10 apiece."

Melissa smiled and gave a brief nod. "If I find the right colors, I believe I'll take two of those." She moved over to the table and began browsing through the various potholders.

To give the young woman some time and space, Fannie went to the checkout counter and waited.

Several minutes later, Melissa brought up two potholders of different colors and patterns and placed them on the counter. "I've decided on these. They are different, but will both look nice in my kitchen."

Fannie rang up her purchase on the battery-operated register, placed the potholders in a plastic bag, and handed it to Melissa. "It was nice meeting you. I hope you'll drop by again sometime when you're in the area."

"Oh, my husband and I will both be in Sugarcreek in a few weeks. We're coming for the first round of the preliminaries of the baking contest."

"Are you planning to enter something or just go there as spectators?"

"We're contestants. It wasn't an easy task, but I finally managed to talk Michael into helping me make a very special Italian cookie recipe that was handed down in my family."

"How did you hear about the contest?" Fannie questioned.

"Read the details in the newspaper, and I was surprised to find out that the first prize was for twenty-five thousand dollars." Melissa looked down for a few seconds, and then back at Fannie as though she might want to say something more, but she remained silent.

Fannie nodded. "Yes, I'm sure everyone who's entered the contest has hopes of winning and may already have plans for the prize money if they should win—me included."

Melissa blinked rapidly as her lips formed an O. "You've entered the baking contest?"

Fannie bobbed her head. "It's exciting to have such a big event hosted right here in our community, and I'm looking forward to being a part of it."

"Will you be making cookies too?" Melissa asked, offering Fannie what looked to be a supportive-looking smile.

"No, but I will be using one of my favorite family recipes, passed on to me from one of my aunts."

Melissa glanced around the room a few seconds, and then she turned to face Fannie again. "It was nice meeting you, Fannie—is it Miss or Mrs.?"

"I'm not married." Fannie tried to keep a smile on her face and speak without faltering. At her age, it wasn't likely that she would ever get married. Her life as a quilter—and more recently, a baker—would have to be enough. Of course, those weren't the only things Fannie enjoyed. She liked spending some of her free time reading mystery novels and always put herself in the role of the heroine in the story. It was fun trying to guess who was guilty of whatever crime had been written about in each of the books she'd read.

"I'm sure I will see you at the preliminaries."

Melissa's statement pulled Fannie's thoughts aside. "Yes, indeed," Fannie said, and then she gave Melissa's hand a friendly handshake.

When Melissa turned and started for the door, Fannie watched until the woman had stepped outside and gotten into her vehicle.

"So there goes one of my competitors," Fannie murmured as she made her way across the room and over to her sewing machine. "I bet the competition will be stiff this year."

———

An hour later, Fannie heard the bell on her front door jingle, and she turned to see who had entered the quilt shop. Seeing that it was her bishop's wife, Iva, Fannie left what she was doing and went to greet the kindly woman.

"*Wie geht's?*" Fannie asked, giving Iva a brief hug.

"I'm fine. How are you?" Iva offered Fannie a pleasant smile.

"Doing okay and busy as ever. What brought you by my quilt shop today?"

"I'm in need of some thread—several spools in fact, as I have material for several new dresses to make for myself and family members. My husband is also in need of new trousers," Iva added.

"You shouldn't have any problem finding what you need," Fannie said. "I got in a new shipment of thread the other day, and there are plenty of colors to choose from."

"That's good. I'll go take a look-see." Iva picked up one of the shopping baskets Fannie had available for her customers to use, and wandered over to the other side of the room where the notions were kept.

Fannie was tempted to follow, but she knew if she did, they'd end up gabbing and Iva might get distracted and choose the wrong color threads. Or worse—not buy anything at all. *The best thing I can do,* Fannie told herself, *is to wait up by the register until Iva's ready to check out. Then, if I don't get busy with other customers who might come in and Iva doesn't have to leave right away, maybe we can visit awhile before she leaves the store.*

———

Iva was pleased with the selection of threads available, and she piled several into the wicker basket.

She pursed her lips. *Let's see now. . .maybe while I'm here I should get some more straight pins. I never seem to have enough of those.* In the process of sewing dresses, trousers, or other items, some of the pins always managed to disappear. *Until I find them. . .the hard way.* She winced, thinking about how much it hurt whenever she got stuck by a pin, used as a closure near the neck opening of her dress. Some Amish women in their area had begun using snaps or hooks and eyes instead of pins. Being that she was the bishop's wife, however, Iva felt that she should adhere to the tradition of using straight pins.

Moving on, Iva picked up three packages of pins and added them to the basket. Next, she looked at the sewing scissors on display and decided to get a new one of those too. By the time Iva made it up to the counter where Fannie stood, the basket was filled with sewing notions.

"Looks like you may have found everything you needed," Fannie stated.

Iva snickered. "Jah and then some." She set the basket on the counter.

Fannie took everything out, rang up Iva's purchases, and put all the items in a paper sack, making mention that since it wasn't raining anymore, Iva shouldn't worry about anything getting wet.

"Paper is fine," Iva said. "You know, I read in the newspaper recently that paper is better for the environment than plastic."

"I've read that too," Fannie responded.

Iva picked up the sack and was about to tell Miss Fannie to have a good day, when the quilter spoke again. "I assume you've probably heard about the baking contest and the big grand prize that's being offered this year."

"Yes, I have," Iva replied. "I saw the flyer in your front window about it, and the event's been advertised in many other places as well."

"It has definitely gotten some good coverage." Fannie gestured to Iva. "You're a good cook. Our church potlucks have proved that. Have you considered entering the contest?"

Iva shook her head vigorously. "No, I have not. With all the sewing there is for me to do, I don't have time for something like that." She shrugged her slim shoulders. "Besides, I'm not sure I would have something in my recipe box exciting enough to enter a contest like that. I am quite certain that it will be a challenge for the judges to pick a winner."

A sigh escaped Fannie's lips. "I suppose you're right, but I have to try."

"So you're planning to enter, then?"

"I am, with a recipe one of my aunts gave me when I was a young girl."

"I wish you well, Miss Fannie," Iva said, reaching across the counter and giving Fannie's hand a pat. "My husband and I will try to be there to cheer you on—if he's not working on a sermon that day." Iva was tempted to tell Fannie that she was concerned because John was so busy that he didn't have time for Jeb, but she thought better of it. If Fannie were to say something about it to someone in their church district, it could start a round of gossip. No, it was better not to mention it at all.

Fannie smiled. "*Danki*, I will appreciate your support. I'll admit, I am feeling a bit *naerfich* about having to bake something in front of the judges and whoever is in the audience watching the event. I mean, it's one thing to make some baked goods in my own kitchen, but it's entirely different doing it in a public place. . .and with a clock ticking, besides."

"I hear what you're saying. I would be nervous too." Iva gave her head a quick shake. "I certainly wouldn't want to cook, bake, or even sew a new dress in front of anyone outside of my own family. I'd probably make all kinds of mistakes."

Fannie's forehead wrinkled as her brows lifted. "I sure hope I don't make a bunch of mistakes. That would be most embarrassing, might end up in the newspaper, and it wouldn't win me any prizes."

"Try not to worry about it," Iva said, hoping her words were an encouragement to Fannie.

"Guess the best thing for me to do is just give my worries to the Lord."

Iva patted Fannie's hand one more time. "Now that's real good thinking, my friend. Jah, you're on the right track with that."

CHAPTER 5

"It's my turn to take Peggy," Charity announced as she and her sisters were preparing to close the bakery for the day. "I can come over to your house for supper and take Peggy home with me after we eat."

Hope's face reddened, and she flexed her fingers repeatedly. "It's not your turn to have Peggy, and you know it. You took her to your house just one day ago."

"That's right," Faith interjected. "I get her for one night, and then she's Hope's for the second night, and then it's your turn, Charity."

Charity gave a frustrated shake of her head. "It's not fair that you get to have her two nights in a row."

"Hope and I live in the same house, remember?" Faith tapped her foot while crossing her arms.

"And need I remind you, Sister, that when you decided not to join the Amish church with us, you felt it was best to move out and buy a place of your own?" Hope added. "It was not our choice. It was yours."

Charity's internal temperature increased, and she was about to comment when Faith spoke first.

"Furthermore," Faith stated in a firm tone of voice, "when you made that decision to get a place of your own, you agreed that you would take Peggy overnight every third day."

Charity didn't have to think twice to realize that her sisters were getting impatient with her and maybe a little annoyed. She decided that it was best to drop the subject before a full-fledged quarrel ensued. This evening, she would simply go to her sisters' for supper and stay as late as she wanted so she could enjoy Peggy as much as possible. Then she would go home to her empty house and have a little pity party, like she often did during lonely hours. *Guess that goes along with being unmarried,* she thought with regret. *But so far, I have not found a suitable mate.* Her lips pressed together in a tight grimace. *Or more to the point—no eligible man has ever taken a serious interest in me. Maybe someday the right fellow will come along, so I plan to keep looking.*

———

Charity entered her sisters' house, and when Hope headed for the kitchen, Charity went straight for Peggy's cage. "What do you say, girl? Can you say a few words for me this evening?"

Awk! Awk! The parrot screeched, remaining stubbornly on her perch.

Charity leaned closer to the cage and said in a loud, clear voice: "Peggy the Parrot. Peggy the Parrot. Can you say your name for me?"

Peggy cocked her green head and jumped down from the perch. Charity took that as a sign that the colorful bird wanted out of her cage. She reached for the latch and was about to open the door when Faith hollered from across the room, "Please, don't let her out right now."

Charity pulled her hand back as Faith joined her in front of the parrot's cage. *That sister of mine must be a mind-reader. Either that or she knows me too well.*

"Why not?" Charity asked, turning to face Faith. "Can't you tell that Peggy wants to be out of her cage so she can sit on my shoulder?"

Faith's only response was a brief shrug.

Charity wondered if her sister might be a bit jealous because Peggy liked her better than the two sisters who lived in this house. Of course, she wasn't about to say that to Faith. Instead, she responded with a question. "Why don't you want me to take her out of the cage?"

"Because, as you know, sometimes it's hard to get Peggy back in, and we don't want her flying around the house while we're eating supper. Right?" Faith stared straight into Charity's eyes.

"Well, no, I suppose not. . .but. . ."

"We can take Peggy out as soon as we're done eating, and then we can all enjoy her antics for a while."

Since this was Hope and Faith's home, Charity decided it was best not to argue the point. "Since it's not my turn to cook, then is it okay with you if I stay out here in the living room and talk to Peggy while you and Hope fix supper?"

Faith gave a nod. "Sure, whatever you like."

I'd like to take the parrot out of her cage right now. Charity kept that thought to herself. Although the sisters usually got along quite well, there were times when Faith, being the oldest, could be rather bossy. *Like now.* Charity had to bite her tongue to keep from stating what was on her mind, which she knew would not go over well with her sister.

She moved away from Peggy's cage and waited until Faith left the room, then Charity leaned close to the parrot's cage again and said, "Pretty Peggy. Pretty Peggy."

Awk! Awk! "Pretty Peggy. Pretty Peggy," the bird repeated.

Charity grinned. "That's right, pretty bird."

"Pretty bird. Pretty bird."

"You're a smart one, aren't you?"

Peggy tipped her head as though she was listening to every word Charity said. When they'd first bought the parrot two years ago, Charity had been captivated with the bird. She was also convinced that Peggy was extremely smart and understood every word that was said to her.

After reading a book she'd picked up about having a parrot as a pet, Charity had learned that, on average, parrots had the emotional complexity of a four-year-old child and could have their ups and downs. The birds could have temper tantrums or jump for joy, and Charity had seen Peggy do both when she didn't get her own way or became excited about something.

Charity had also worked at getting Peggy to talk and had read that the best way to encourage parrots to speak was to choose a few short words in the beginning, like "Hello," "Pretty Bird," and "Bye-bye." She was intrigued that parrots were able to mimic a wide variety of sounds because they had a flexible tongue, which could be used by the bird to shape the sound as it came out of their beak.

Pet parrots quite often became one-person birds, and Charity had convinced herself that she was that "one person" Peggy preferred.

Think I'll try another phrase for Peggy to speak again, using three words this time instead of two, Charity thought. She leaned down and looked closely at Peggy. "Open the door. Open the door."

Peggy sat quietly for several seconds, and then she screeched a couple of times and said, "Open the door. Open the door."

Charity clapped and then covered her lips to keep from laughing out loud, which would have no doubt brought one or both sisters out of the kitchen to see what was so funny.

"Open the door. Open the door," Peggy kept repeating.

"Shh..." Charity put a finger against her lips.

"Open the door." Peggy repeated the words yet again, and Charity didn't know what to do to make the parrot stop.

Maybe I should open the cage door just a little bit. Peggy might quiet right down if she thinks I'm going to let her out. If I stroke her soft feathers, she'll probably relax and won't be so desperate to get out.

Charity lifted the latch and opened the cage door a mere crack, and the next thing she knew, Peggy pushed her feathered head against the opening and flew right out, swooping over Charity's head.

Oh, no! Charity exclaimed mentally rather than shouting it out loud. *How am I going to get that bird back in her cage before my sisters come out of the kitchen?*

———

Hope set aside the paring knife she'd been using to cut a tomato and looked over at Faith, who'd been busy tearing lettuce leaves into a bowl. "Did you hear something?"

Faith shook her head. "Nothing out of the ordinary, at least. The only noise I've heard since we came into the kitchen is the steady splattering of rain on the window."

Hope set the knife down and wrinkled her nose. "Jah, I'm aware of it too, but this noise was something different."

"What'd it sound like?"

"I—I'm not sure." Hope cupped an elbow with one hand while tapping her lips with four fingers on the other hand. "It sounded like the flapping of wings."

Faith's thin lips slackened a bit. "Are you serious?"

"Well...um...I am serious, but maybe I was just hearing things. Jah, that's probably it."

"Maybe what you heard was just the wind outside."

Hope shook her head. "No, if I heard anything at all, it sounded like it was coming from the living room."

"You don't suppose..." Faith closed her eyes and emitted a sigh.

Hope pointed to the kitchen door. "Listen. There it is again."

They both tipped their heads and moved closer to the door.

Hope felt kind of foolish since the noise seemed to have stopped. *Faith's right—it probably was the wind.*

When Hope's parents were alive, her daddy used to say that her imagination worked overtime. Once he'd even said, "Hope Beiler, you need to get your head outta the clouds and come back down to earth."

Thunk! Thunk!

Faith clasped Hope's arm and said, "Did you hear that?

"Jah, and something is definitely wrong. That *thunk* sounded like it came from the living room."

"I wonder if our sister's okay." Hope stood there, frozen, her breathing shallow.

"Well, we can't do anything if all we do is stand here talking about it. Let's go see what happened." Faith grabbed the knob and practically pushed Hope through the kitchen door when it swung open.

——————

When Faith entered the living room a step behind Hope, she couldn't believe her eyes. Charity sat on the floor near the sofa, with one arm held straight up, shouting, "Here Peggy! Come to Mama, you bad bird!"

A straight-backed chair had been knocked over and lay on its side, and Peggy the parrot flapped her wings as she flew about the room, screeching and hollering, "Bad bird! Bad bird!"

"Are you all right?" Hope asked, dropping to her knees beside Charity.

"I—I'm fine." Charity tried to get up, but she lost her balance and fell backward against one of the throw pillows that was also on the floor.

"Hope, you grab one of our dear sister's hands, and I'll take the other," Faith instructed. "We'll get Charity on her feet, and then she can tell us what happened here." She looked up at Peggy, still flying about the room, and rolled her eyes. "I'm sure our red-faced sister has an interesting explanation."

Hope took one of Charity's hands, Faith grabbed the other, and they pulled at the same time.

Charity bounced up like a rubber ball, and when Peggy soared overhead, a few green feathers drifted down and landed on the floor.

"Bad bird! Bad bird!" Peggy made another pass across the room, and she landed on Charity's head.

Faith made every effort not to laugh, but the scene was too funny—especially seeing her sister's wide-eyed expression.

After joining Faith and Charity in a round of laughter, Hope stepped forward and lifted the bird off their sister's head. Then she swiftly put Peggy back in her cage and shut the door.

"Would you mind telling us how the parrot got out, and what you were doing on the floor?" Faith asked Charity after everyone's laughter subsided.

Charity's chin dipped almost to her chest, and she murmured, "I just opened the door on Peggy's cage a little ways, and when I reached in to stroke her beautiful feathers, the next thing I knew, she was out." Charity pinned her arms against her stomach as she looked at Faith. "I tried to get her, but she wouldn't land. In my pursuit, I tripped on the chair leg, and then both the chair and I ended up on the floor."

"You shouldn't have opened the cage at all," Faith scolded with a shake of her index finger. "But I'm glad you weren't hurt."

Hope eased close to Faith and whispered in her ear, "Maybe we should let Charity take Peggy home with her after supper tonight. She seems pretty desperate to spend time with the silly bird."

Faith mulled that suggestion over a few seconds and finally nodded. When she turned to tell Charity what Hope had said, a broad smile swept across their sister's face. "Thank you. You can bring Peggy back here tomorrow evening, after you two have had supper at my house."

Faith and Hope nodded and said together, "That will be fine."

The sisters formed a group hug, followed by more laughter, which Hope started this time. They laughed and laughed, until tears ran down their cheeks.

Several minutes passed, and then Faith dried her eyes with a hanky she had tucked in the band of her apron. "I think we should all go to the kitchen now and finish preparing our supper. We can take pretty Peggy out of her cage after the meal and give her a chance to sit on each of our shoulders."

"Okay, that sounds fair," Charity commented.

"I concur," Hope agreed.

Hope led the way to the kitchen, followed by Charity, and Faith brought up the rear.

"Pretty bird! Pretty bird," Peggy said from her cage.

CHAPTER 6

Foster Bates sprang up from his swivel desk chair with the nimbleness of a teenager, even though the retired cop, now private detective, was far past his youth. With no thought to the resistance from his knees, he quickly made his way over to the large bay window. Like a man on a mission, he reached up and grabbed the OPEN sign hanging there and turned it over so it would read CLOSED to anyone walking by.

Satisfied, he lowered the blinds over the sign, stood back, and waited. It was two o'clock in the afternoon, and the sun was blazing today. He felt thankful to have air-conditioning in his office.

Normal business hours for the Foster Bates Private Detective Agency were 10:00 a.m. to 5:00 p.m., but Foster had caught a glimpse of an Amish woman walking toward his office at a determined clip. He'd seen right away that it was Fannie Miller again. As sweet as she was, Fannie seemed to attract trouble like bees to Amish peanut butter. And everything about her body language today spelled t-r-o-u-b-l-e.

Rarely, if ever, was the trouble Fannie's fault. But she did seem to multiply the depth of any normal situation by her naivete, natural curiosity, and passion for being in the thick of things when it came to solving mysteries. Foster was all too aware that Fannie fancied herself a serious crime solver, and ever since he, a real-life detective, had come into her life, she had held on to their acquaintance with a stranglehold.

Foster, on the other hand, was a man with authentic experience in the world of crime. He had little time for amateur sleuths. His training hadn't come from the pages of whodunits or by eavesdropping on the neighbors. He was eons beyond any rocking-chair detective and, in his mind at least, was in a class unto himself. He certainly was overqualified for the quaint and peaceful Amish community of Sugarcreek, Ohio, where his phone rarely rang. And he liked it that way.

Foster had nothing particular against Fannie. At times he even enjoyed her company. But he didn't have time for her chitchat today. He had other things to work on. Nothing he could put his finger on at the moment, but Foster was certain there was something he needed to do. For the sake of whatever that was, he could not entertain any distractions. And Fannie always brought distractions. She was an ongoing parade of them.

Whatever was on her mind would simply have to wait. The best thing for all concerned would be for Fannie to keep right on walking and leave well enough alone. And Foster desperately hoped she would do just that once she'd laid eyes on his CLOSED sign.

Foster drummed his fingers along the top of his desk. Sugarcreek, Ohio, was unusually crowded during the summer, and this June was no exception. Several large community events—including a national car show in nearby Millersburg, a charity auction in Charm, and the annual Tuscarawas and Surrounding Counties Baking Contest being held at the Carlisle Inn in Dutch Valley—added to the normal flow of tourists. Most hotels in the area were booked to capacity. Even the Miller Manor in Walnut Creek had been booked for weeks at a time. Foster knew this because he drove on the road below the manor, which was perched on a hill opposite the Walnut Creek Cheese store, and always saw cars parked in front of the expansive home. No doubt, those who rented the house during their stay in the area would have an unmatched view of the Walnut Creek Valley. Although Foster had never been inside the stately manor, he'd picked up a brochure with information about it once and was amazed to learn that with three floors and several bedrooms, it could accommodate as many as twenty guests at one time. The beautiful home had once been the residence of the town doctor and his family, and it was now managed by the Carlisle Inn in Walnut Creek.

After reading about the place, Foster had thought it would be fun to take a tour of the home, but he didn't think that would be possible unless he was a paying guest. And since he had his own home here in Sugarcreek, there was no reason for him to rent a home or even a hotel in the area. Besides, in his opinion there was nothing like his own bed to sleep in. And there was the issue of what to do with Chief. Some hotels did have pet-friendly rooms, but Foster was happy to stay close enough to home that he didn't have to worry about finding other accommodations for himself or the dog.

For the last two months, the baking contest had seemed to be on everyone's mind. In its tenth year, Miss Fannie Miller, who had been a perennial entrant, had made it through the first round and was moving forward toward a chance at being in the finals. Foster knew that bit of interesting news from reading about it in the local newspaper. He also had seen the flyers that Fannie herself had posted around town, at no small expense and effort—including the one she'd hung in his window when she'd wanted to get the word out about the contest. He was sure that all the advertising had been successful.

Perhaps that is the reason for her visit today, Foster told himself. *Maybe she is coming to let me know the good news and wants me to wish her well.*

He blew off some of the dust accumulating on his desk and grimaced. *Yes indeed, that makes perfect sense.*

But there were no guarantees. And that determined look he'd seen on Fannie's pretty oval face as she sprinted toward his office gave him pause. He simply couldn't allow himself to get trapped in the labyrinth of whatever was propelling her toward his door.

Foster held his breath as he heard her footsteps come up the walkway. He continued to hold it as she tried the doorknob. And then she knocked. And knocked again.

"Foster!" Her normally pleasant voice pierced through the solid wood door like a straw in a tornado. "Foster Bates!"

Foster remained perfectly still, which only caused her to yell the next inquiry loud enough for the cuckoo bird in the giant cuckoo clock in downtown Sugarcreek to cover its ears.

He sat motionless. *If I don't respond, she will give up soon enough and be on her way.*

Foster noticed a black umbrella that an elderly woman had left behind when she'd stopped at his office earlier today, asking for directions to Millersburg where her daughter lived. He'd never met the woman before, and she hadn't given him her name. Just said she was visiting from another state and wasn't familiar with the area. Foster had wondered if the woman had been traveling alone or had a companion waiting for her in the car. He should have asked for more details, because he had no way to contact her. All Foster could do was hope she might realize that she'd left the umbrella here and come back for it. The item in question sat precariously on the small table by his door. Without intervention, it seemed doomed to fall with a crash, casting doubt on the vacancy of his office.

Foster had to do something to prevent that from happening, or his ruse would surely be exposed. Getting up and reaching over ever so carefully, he grabbed for the umbrella, but in the tenseness of the moment, his fingers fumbled, pushing the item into a nearby flower vase, which sent them both, and Foster too, crashing to the floor.

"Foster Bates! I know you're in there!" Fannie hollered in a desperate tone as she pounded on his door. "Open up! I need to talk to you right away!"

Even though it now seemed hopeless, Foster continued trying to wait her out and remained quiet. But to his surprise, Fannie also fell silent.

Believing she had finally given up, Foster got back up on his feet and braved a peek through the blinds. He hoped to see her walking away. But at that precise moment, Fannie peeked in the window, startling the seasoned detective and sending him backward into his wooden coat rack, with arms flailing.

"Foster, you might as well open the door. I know you're in there. I can hear you whimpering."

Indeed, Foster had let out a few whimpers as he slid down the Mount Everest of hats, a raincoat, an umbrella, several spring sweaters, and broken coatrack pieces. It was time to surrender. He really had no choice.

Defeated, he rose, unlocked the deadbolt, and opened the door. "Why, Fannie Miller, how nice to see you."

Pushing past him with pursed lips and folded arms, Fannie flopped into a seat in front of his desk. "Let's dispense with the formalities. I need your help, Foster. Again."

52

"So soon?" Foster squeaked. What kind of help did she need this time?

He tried to pick up a few sweaters from the floor, but soon gave up in frustration and took a seat behind his desk, across from Fannie.

"Well," he said, taking a long, strength-gathering breath, "what is it this time, Fannie?"

"It's the baking contest."

"Ah yes. I don't know what your competition is like, but I heard you've done splendid so far, and I wish you well."

"I appreciate that, but it's not the reason I came here, Foster."

"Oh?"

"I need your help."

Foster sensed the conversation possibly going in a direction he didn't like. "Now, Miss Fannie," he said, carefully choosing his next words. "I know how badly you have wanted to win this contest, and I realize twenty-five thosuand dollars is a worthy amount for a grand prize, especially with the economy being what it is. But in all my years of law enforcement and, more recently, in private investigation, I am quite proud that I have never once taken any kind of graft, bribe, or kickback of any kind."

Fannie leaned forward, looking at him through half-closed eyes as if he'd suddenly lost his mind. "Foster Bates, what in the world do you think I'm asking? I'm not trying to bribe you. If I do win this contest, it must be fair and square."

"I'm sorry, Fannie. It just sounded like—"

"Foster, Foster. . .my dear friend. I have come here today to solicit your assistance in solving a most disturbing mystery."

Her piercing, blue-eyed gaze held him captive for a moment, and he had to look away. "Wh–what kind of mystery?" A trickle of sweat rolled off Foster's forehead and onto his cheeks.

———

Fannie hesitated before responding to Foster's question. Should she drop the complete buffet of clues on him all at once, or serve them one at a time so he could digest each piece of evidence separately?

She decided to lay out the entire clue bar. "Foster," she said, "I believe something nefarious is going on within the baking contest."

"Nefarious? In a baking contest?" Foster lifted a single brow and cocked his head.

"Oh, yes! Why, you would be surprised at the things you can hear over the whirl of a mixer or the hum of a carving knife," she replied.

"What kinds of things?"

Fannie knew as soon as she started describing the mysterious goings on over at the Dutch Valley Restaurant and Carlisle Inn, where the baking contest was being held, Foster would wonder if she was merely working herself into a frenzy because of the importance she had placed on winning. He would probably think her desperation was playing tricks on her mind. But that wasn't the case at all. Fannie's concerns were absolutely legit. She knew what she had seen and overheard. The distress she felt over her safety and that of her fellow contestants was not unwarranted. Clearly, someone was trying to fix the contest by sabotaging or scaring away the competition, one by one, until only one baker would be left to win by default.

Fannie was not the "keep walking and leave well enough alone" type of person. Not when there was a mystery to be solved. If her suspicions were correct, she and other contestants could be in grave danger. She had to take a chance and bring Foster in on the case. Whether the sixty-something, seasoned detective wanted to come along or not.

CHAPTER 7

The Foster Bates Private Detective Agency was tucked away on the north side of the last street in downtown Sugarcreek. It wasn't the kind of office you just "happened by." That was the thing that had drawn Foster to the empty office space in the first place.

But it also had a distinguished-looking storefront with black-framed windows and a matching black gutter accenting the red brick front. The sign above the door read FOSTER BATES PRIVATE DETECTIVE AGENCY, giving credence to the experienced and skilled detective working inside its walls. The font of the letters on the sign was script, giving it an almost invitational quality. A sense of "If you need help, I'm here."

But why would this ex-Chicago policeman, now turned private detective, open up shop in this peaceful Amish community in the first place? What would draw him to such a different setting?

The word *peaceful* seemed to have a lot to do with it. Big city policing had left its mark on Sergeant Foster Bates, and the scars ran deep. That's how he'd ended up in Sugarcreek, Ohio. *Peaceful* sounded good to him. He'd had it with nightly carjackings, assaults, robberies, and gang violence. He longed for a place where he could live quietly, go fishing whenever he felt like it, and pass the day rocking on his front porch. He'd found it here in Sugarcreek.

His work schedule was the best part. He worked whenever he felt like it. His office hours were not prominently posted anywhere, even though he had set some for himself, which due to circumstances or the way he felt on any given day, he didn't always keep. Any initial or follow-up meetings were done by appointment only. Foster didn't like drop-ins, but they did happen on occasion. He didn't even like prearranged appointments. Truth be told, he did not really want to work at all, unless it was absolutely necessary and he knew for certain that his help was needed. He'd only opened the office space to get himself out of the house for a few hours a day. As for people, he could take them or leave them. According to Foster Bates, this whole crazy world could walk on by and leave him alone.

But it seldom did.

He did handle a case or two from time to time. Mostly minor issues— slip and falls, neighbor disputes over property lines, and parking lot fender benders. Nothing too serious. It was the perfect retirement job for an ex-cop who'd seen it all and handcuffed most of it.

But now, Fannie Miller was here in his office, threatening to disrupt his entire schedule.

"So, what makes you think you're in danger?" he asked, holding tight to the edge of his wooden desk to keep from getting swept into the vortex of another complicated Fannie Miller case against his will and better judgment.

Foster felt bad for hesitating and taking so long to respond to Fannie. She was a nice enough woman, and they did have history. Too much history, in fact. First, there was the kidnapping case of the baby brother of a friend of hers. Foster was the officer in charge on that case. But he didn't solve the crime at the time. In fact, it went cold when Foster took a position with the Chicago Police Department, and didn't get any warmer for twenty years. It was reopened on its twentieth anniversary, and Foster, who had recently moved back to the area after his retirement, was brought in to work the case, reluctantly at first. It all ended well when his efforts, and to a certain extent Fannie's, had successfully produced a perpetrator.

Two people could not go through all that probing and deducing and not develop a certain degree of respect for each other's investigative skills. Still, trouble did seem to follow this Amish woman—there was no getting around that. Even so, Foster didn't have the energy these days to get involved in another whodunit with Fannie Miller. Besides, his blood pressure had finally gotten to a manageable level since the last time he'd worked with the energetic, determined woman. Foster was certain that his doctor would have his back on this—he had to watch his steps very carefully when it came to Fannie and her incessant passion for mystery solving.

"Miss Fannie," he began.

Fannie jumped at the opening. She leaned farther forward and placed both hands on Foster's desk. "So you'll help me?"

"No," he said. "I was simply asking why you think you are in danger."

"I have advanced to the next phase in the preliminaries for the baking contest." A pink hue erupted on Fannie's cheeks. "I—I'm not being prideful, you understand. Just pleased as punch and hopeful."

"Of course you're not prideful, Fannie. I've never believed you were full of *hochmut*. Isn't that the word you Amish use for prideful?"

She nodded.

"I'm so happy for you, Fannie! Didn't you tell me that the baking contest is something you've been pursuing for quite some time?"

"I've entered it every year for over a decade."

"And this year you made it further than before?"

She bobbed her head.

"Good for you!"

"Oh, Foster, I was so surprised when the judges called my name to advance to the next level of the competition!"

"I'm sure you were. Yes, indeed. Well, you deserve it," Foster said, warmly. And he meant it.

"Thank you, Foster." Her smile stretched wide.

"And it was nice to see you again, Fannie." He gestured to his desk. "But as you can probably tell, I have quite a pile of files to go through."

Fannie pointed at the single file on Foster's desk. "Looks like only one file in the pile to me."

"Yes, yes. . .it's just one, but it's a very important case. I have lots and lots of notes to go through." He scooped up the file quickly, causing one lone blank sheet of paper to drop out of it. "Oops!"

Fannie reached down to pick it up for him. "Not much of a note taker, are you?"

Foster released a nervous laugh. "Ah, so you remember that about me, don't you, Fannie? I prefer to fly by the seat of my pants, go where the wind and the clues take me, trust my gut and my instincts. I don't need no stinkin' notes!" he said, mimicking the old *Treasure of Sierra Madre* scene.

Fannie's blank stare was enough to remind him that the Amish don't have televisions, hence she had no point of reference.

"I'm sorry," he stated. "But like I said, I do need to—"

"Foster, I'm desperate," Fannie pressed on. "You're the only one I can turn to. Please say you'll help me again."

A sudden dryness hung in his throat. He tried to clear it away by swallowing several times, but it wouldn't go.

"Foster. . ." Fannie's eyes narrowed. "I'm going to be frank with you. Something strange is happening to the contestants in our baking contest."

"What do you mean?" Foster asked.

"Lately they have been meeting with"—Fannie took a deep breath, then continued—"disconcerting occurrences."

"What kind of 'disconcerting occurrences'?"

"Physical ones."

"I see. Well, Miss Fannie, I wouldn't stress too much over it. I've eaten your cooking, and I have never met with any. . .disconcerting occurrences."

"The disconcerting occurrences, Mr. Foster, that seem to be happening are. . .well, the contestants seem to be showing a propensity to. . .disappear."

"Disappear?"

Fannie nodded.

"I see." Foster leaned forward with his hands tightly clasped. "Go on."

"A few have left notes explaining where they have gone, which is why I didn't go to the police," Fannie said. "They need more than my suspicions to go on. They've assured me of that requirement multiple times over the years. But frankly, my instincts are usually right. And the reasons provided on those notes were highly suspicious."

"Can you give me an example?"

"Well, one said they were dropping out of the contest because they needed to attend to a sick relative."

"Maybe that's true."

"Foster, no one who enters the Tuscarawas and Surrounding Counties Baking Contest would leave town while we are still competing, and surely not before a winner is announced."

Foster stared at Fannie, unsure of where she was going, but certain he didn't want to join her on the adventure. As though sensing his hesitation, Fannie continued.

"One note even said the contestant was having an appendicitis attack. Seriously? Right in the middle of the contest?" She pursed her lips. "I don't believe that for one minute."

"One doesn't usually plan those sorts of things," Foster stated flatly.

"Think what you want, Foster, but I believe there is something nefarious at play here, and if you could find it in your heart to team up once again, I know you and I could get to the bottom of this."

"Fannie, baking contests hardly draw the underbelly of society," he said calmly. "Now, I think you are way overthinking all of this. Perhaps you need to get out of the kitchen more. Maybe the yeast you've been working with has gone to your brain."

Fannie planted both hands against her middle-aged hips. "I know my way around yeast, Mr. Bates! I am also aware of what my gut instinct tells me."

She left her seat and walked over to stand next to his chair. "Please help me, Foster. The police need proof."

"Well, you have been a little quick on the draw in the past. Jumping to the wrong conclusions and accusing the wrong people. Can you really blame them for not wanting to take another chance on your 'instincts'?"

"Some people don't appreciate my gift."

"That may be, Fannie." Foster rose to his feet, and they were close enough that her shoulder touched his arm. "You know I would love to help you, but like I said, I have previous plans."

"With your recliner?" She gave him a hint of a smile.

"Guilty as charged. I try not to keep it waiting." Foster winked.

When Fannie lowered her gaze, Foster figured the strong-minded woman knew she'd pushed the matter as far as she could—for the time being anyway. She would return, of course. They both knew she would. But for now, Foster was free.

Fannie walked toward the door, then stopped and looked back, "But what if I really am in danger? You would care, wouldn't you, Foster?"

Foster weighed his words carefully. "Of course I would, Fannie. You are a dear friend. If I had any inkling that you were in real danger, I would most certainly come to your aid. But the key word here is *real*. I don't believe anything going on should cause you to lose one minute's sleep."

"You're certain?"

"Are you forgetting, Fannie, this is Amish Country? There's no crime in Amish Country."

Fannie rolled her eyes as if to say, *"Foster, you know good and well that's not true."*

Foster laughed. "Just testing you, Miss Fannie. We solved a big crime together once, didn't we?"

"We certainly did."

"But there hasn't been anything like that since, has there, Fannie?"

"No, I suppose not."

"Then, go on and have yourself the time of your life in the baking contest, and win that first-place ribbon. Everything's going to be fine."

Fannie looked up at him, and he saw a measure of hope on her face. "You're probably right, Foster. What am I worried about? I'm going to focus all my attention on winning this contest. I'm going to put all these suspicions behind me and carry on like I live in the most peaceful community in America. Because I do!"

"Now, that's the Fannie I know." Foster led her a little closer to the door.

"So, I'm free to go about my day?"

Foster swung the door wide open. "Not only are you free to go, but I am highly recommending it. Lovely to see you again. Do have a nice rest of your day."

Fannie stepped outside, and Foster closed the door behind her. Just in time before she could turn around and take up more of his day. Just in time before she played on his sympathies. And just in time to hear a bone-chilling scream! It was a woman's voice, and it sounded as if it had come from about a block away.

Fannie banged on Foster's door again.

"Oh no," Foster mumbled under his breath. "I might have known."

After a few more desperate-sounding knocks, Foster opened the door ever so slightly, trying to pretend he hadn't heard the scream. He didn't want to get involved. Didn't want to get Fannie involved. And he did not want to leave his recliner at home unattended any longer than he already had.

But it was a real scream. And Fannie was out there.

Foster sheepishly opened the door and peered around it.

When Fannie saw him, she pushed the door open and rushed right in, quickly closing it behind her. "Did you hear that?" she asked in a panicked voice.

"Hear what?" Foster said, almost crying inside. He had been so close to moving on with his day.

"That scream. We've got to go check it out!"

He patted Fannie's arm, hoping to calm her down. "It's probably just a sale over at Yoder's."

"Foster Bates, that was no sale scream!" She clutched his shirtsleeve. "You're coming with me to check it out, right now!"

"Fannie, I'm sure it's nothing."

"That wasn't a question, Foster. Now please, come on!" She pulled him toward the door, stopping long enough to let him grab his hat from what was left of the coat rack. And the not-so-dynamic duo were off, into the summer air, and so very far away from Foster's recliner.

———

By the time Foster and Fannie reached the screaming lady, it was clear that she had sucked most of the pain out of her injured thumb. After her detailed explanation of how she had somehow managed to smash her finger in her car door, Foster was fairly certain that everyone within a mile radius knew about it, although no one had come to the poor woman's aid until now.

Foster checked out the injury, but it was hardly worth the scream that had gotten him dragged out of his office. Still, he asked if she wanted him to call an ambulance. The woman took a moment, as if to consider his suggestion, but ultimately declined it, saying, "That's not funny, Mr. Bates!" Brave soul that she was.

Foster would have more easily understood a "Yoder's sale scream," but now that the crisis seemed to be over, the woman went on her way, and Foster and Fannie began walking back to his office. *All's well that ends well*, he thought. Or was it?

As Foster and Fannie walked by other stores and offices, he couldn't help but notice something strange going on. The shop owners and tenants had simply watched the entire scream incident from the safety of their windows. A few had even pulled down their shades. No one had come to the woman's aid. Perhaps they were acquainted with her and knew she had a flair for the dramatic. *Or maybe Fannie was right,* Foster reasoned. *Could it be that something nefarious really is going on in our quaint little community?*

He had to admit that everyone's nerves did seem to be on edge these days. Could an innocent baking contest have brought out a certain hidden underbelly of their safe Amish and English community, and now everyone was in hiding? Was it possible that a seemingly harmless biscuit cutter, as round as the harvest moon, could be used as a lethal weapon if aimed at the perfect angle, rendering its victim helpless with dozens of dough-deep circular cuts?

A shiver shot up Foster's spine. Maybe a baking contest wasn't as safe an environment as he'd previously thought. Maybe Fannie's instincts were right. Maybe she *was* in grave danger.

Just then, a female store owner slammed her window shut and quickly backed away from her curtain.

Fannie had obviously taken note of it too. "So you believe me now, Foster?" she asked.

"People are acting a bit strange," he admitted as they walked back to his office and entered it again. Once inside the warmth and safety of its walls, Foster grabbed a yellow legal pad and motioned for Fannie to take the seat across from him once again.

"Okay, start at the beginning and tell me everything," he said.

A satisfied-looking smile crossed Fannie's face. "I thought you'd never ask."

CHAPTER 8

Berlin

When Fannie entered the Boyd & Wurthmann Restaurant on East Main Street, the line ahead of her indicated that she would be waiting more than a few minutes to be seated. This was nothing unusual, as many people, locals and tourists, enjoyed eating here, and throughout the summer months, tourism increased in Berlin.

Gazing around the room, Fannie caught sight of Melissa and Michael Taylor sitting at a table on the far side of the restaurant. Although she had met Melissa at her quilt shop in the spring and seen them both during the preliminary bake contest, she didn't know either of them well. Even so, Fannie was aware that, like her, the couple was in line to be finalists in the baking contest if they continued to do well.

It seemed odd that an English man and woman would have entered the event as a couple. Fannie figured maybe they both liked to bake, but neither of them felt comfortable or confident enough to take part in the contest on their own. Perhaps one of them was an expert at mixing the ingredients for their cookies, while the other person had a knack for rolling out the dough.

Mentally, Fannie shook her head. *There's no way I'd want someone in my kitchen, helping me bake or even cook, for that matter. They'd just be in the way, and we would probably end up bumping into each other, which would likely create quite a mess, with a dusting of flour spread from one end of the room to the other.*

She wrinkled her nose as if some foul odor had found its way into the restaurant. *Nope, teaming up in the baking contest would definitely not be for me!*

As Fannie continued to wait for the hostess to seat her at a table, she kept her eye on Mr. and Mrs. Taylor. Both appeared to be in their late twenties or maybe early thirties. Melissa still wore her blond hair in a stylish bob that accentuated her cute, perky nose. The young woman looked trim and fair skinned, just as she had when she'd visited Fannie's quilt shop and purchased two potholders. Michael had thick dark hair, which had been combed straight back, with a deliberate waterfall section that fell over his forehead. His skin was quite tan, and his arms looked muscular and toned. Fannie figured he probably worked outside a lot or had a membership in one of the fitness clubs in the area.

Fannie exhaled a small intake of breath when she realized she'd been openly staring at the couple. *What's the matter with me? If I want to know the reason Melissa and Michael entered the baking contest, I should just go on over to their table and ask.* She wouldn't say anything to them about it, of course, but she'd also heard a rumor that Mr. and Mrs. Taylor were on the brink of divorce.

With only a few seconds' deliberation, Fannie stepped out of her place in line and made a beeline over to the table where the couple was seated. There was no time like the present, and if she waited until she'd been seated at a table, Michael and Melissa may have finished their meal and been out the door before she would have a chance to speak with them.

"Hello there." Fannie positioned herself at their table so she could see and talk to both of them. "I'm sorry to interrupt your lunch, but I recognized you from the baking contest and thought I'd pop over and say hello." She put on her best smile and held out her hand toward Melissa's husband. "I met your wife at my quilt shop a few months ago, but you and I have not been formally introduced. My name is Fannie Miller. I'm one of the top six contestants too. We're sure to be named finalists soon, and I thought it would be nice if we got acquainted."

Michael mumbled something Fannie didn't understand and then he reached out and shook her hand. "Nice to meet you."

Melissa stood up and gave Fannie a brief hug. "It's nice to see you again. Things are so busy when we're baking for the judges over at the conference center in Sugarcreek, I haven't had a chance to even say hello to you there."

"I understand. All the contestants have been real busy baking and trying to impress the judges." Fannie waited until Melissa sat down, and then she looked over at Michael and said, "Do you enjoy baking?"

Michael's only response was a brief shrug as he reached for his glass of iced tea. Fannie wondered if he might be the unsociable type, or perhaps just a man of few words. Either way, she would not allow herself to be intimidated by his apparent unfriendliness and would proceed with her interrogation. *No, that's not the right word,* she scolded herself. *I just need to know enough about Melissa and her husband to find out what their motive was for entering the contest.*

If there had been a third chair at the table, Fannie would have asked if she could join them. But no, that would be too bold, and they might not appreciate the interruption. If what Fannie had heard about the state of the Taylors' marriage was true, perhaps they'd come here to eat a meal together in an effort to work things out. She certainly would not want to intrude. On the other hand, this might be Fannie's only opportunity to talk to the couple one-on-one.

She shifted her weight from one leg to the other and cleared her throat. "So I was wondering, if you don't mind my asking, what made you two decide to enter your Italian wedding cookies in the baking contest?"

Melissa's cheeks reddened, and she blinked a couple of times before looking at her husband. When Michael picked up his sandwich and took a bite, Melissa looked back at Fannie and said, "They're our favorite cookies, and we thought entering the contest would be something fun that we could do together." Her gaze swung back to her husband. "Isn't that right, dear?"

"Yeah, lots of fun," he mumbled around a hunk of his sandwich.

Fannie felt an icy chill in the room, and it wasn't from the air-conditioning. She was gearing up to ask her next question, when Michael yanked a pickle slice out of the sandwich and tossed it on his plate. "I've never liked sweet pickles!" His gaze swung to Melissa, "Sure,

Melissa. . .whatever you say about anything." Then, much to Fannie's surprise, he looked at her directly and said, "In case you're interested, Fannie, I'm just goin' along for the ride. . .and the hope of the money."

At this point, Fannie was almost certain that the couple must be on the brink of divorce, because in addition to not being able to ignore the sneers being exchanged, Fannie could have cut the air of dissension with one of her kitchen knives. She wondered if it might be time to excuse herself and get back in line. Or maybe a better idea would be to leave Boyd & Wurthmann and find another place to eat lunch before heading back to Sugarcreek. She was about to do just that, when Melissa spoke up.

"Actually, the truth is my husband and I are childless, and we'd like to adopt a baby. If we should take first place with our cookies, that grand prize money would certainly be a big help to us."

Michael's eyes narrowed, and he plucked at his shirt collar as if it was too tight. "Why don't you just tell everyone our personal business? Or better yet, let's take out an ad in the newspaper." He glared at Melissa. "That would get the news out quickly to let everyone here and in all the surrounding counties know that the Taylors are so desperate for money, they would do anything—even enter a stupid baking contest!"

Tears sprang to Melissa's eyes, and her chin quivered like a leaf in the wind. Fannie's heart went out to her. She wanted to offer the young woman some comfort, but no words would form on her tongue. After all, what did she know about love, marriage, or wanting to adopt a baby? She'd never even had a serious boyfriend. One thing Fannie did know, however, was that Michael was irritated with his wife, Melissa's feelings had been hurt, and she was probably more than a little embarrassed. Fannie wished she had remained in line and hadn't come over to their table. The only thing she had accomplished with her question was to ruin this struggling couple's lunch.

With a quiet, "It was nice to see you folks, but I'd better be on my way," Fannie managed a brief smile and hurriedly took her leave. No way was she going to stand in that line again to wait for a table. She would go on out to the hitching rack where she'd left her horse and buggy and head straight back to Sugarcreek. As far as missing the noon meal today, she didn't care. Nothing, not even a bite of her favorite dessert, could take away the humiliation she felt for ruining the Taylors' lunch. The only good thing that had come from talking with the couple was that she now knew why they had entered the contest and that Michael and Melissa were desperate for that prize money.

———

Melissa had watched as Fannie rushed out the door, and after the woman was out of sight, she leaned closer to Michael and said, "You weren't very polite to that Amish woman. I hope she doesn't think you have a grudge against her because she's sure to be one of the finalists in the competition."

He crossed both arms in front of his broad chest and shook his head. "Don't start criticizing me, Melissa. I have nothing personal against Fannie—whatever her last name is. I did think it was rude of her to interrupt our meal and then start plying us with a bunch of questions."

Melissa squinted, her brows lowering. "The woman only asked one question that you didn't like. I think she wanted to get to know us and was trying to be friendly and polite."

"Yeah, right. She was being nosey, and you told her something you had no right to blab."

"Why not? It's true. We do want to win the baking contest, and we really could use the grand prize money." Melissa leaned forward with her arms on the table. "Why do you have to be so critical and negative?"

"I'm not. Just stating the facts is all. If you want my opinion, Fannie what's her name is a middle-aged busybody who has nothing better to do than stick her nose in other people's business." He picked up the other half of his sandwich. "Now do you mind if I finish my lunch?"

Melissa pinched her lips together, determined not to say another word to Michael while they sat at this table. What was the use in putting forth the effort to try talking to him about anything at all? And now she'd completely lost her appetite and had to sit here and wait for him to finish eating. It wasn't fair!

Melissa thought about the first response she'd given to Fannie, when asked the reason she and Michael had entered the baking contest. *I told her we wanted to do something fun together, but that was a lie.* Her throat clogged up, and she felt tears pushing the back of her eyes. The real reason she and Michael had signed up for the contest was to try and save their marriage. The idea had come from their marriage counselor, Dr. John

Jacobson. He was the founder of Jacobson Marriage Counseling Services in Berlin, Ohio, and it was his professional opinion that working together as a team in such a contest might move the thrice-estranged couple along on their healing journey.

Then there was that prize money. If they had enough money to adopt a baby, she felt sure that would cement their marriage. Melissa and Michael had gotten along pretty well during the first years of their marriage. But once they'd decided to start their family, she'd had a few miscarriages, and they'd been told that the likelihood of her conceiving again was slim, things had gone sour rather quickly. While Michael and Melissa agreed that adoption could be an option, a lack of money stood in their way.

Melissa thought the idea of entering the baking contest and hoping to win the grand prize seemed a bit risky. Putting a married couple with seemingly insurmountable grievances together in a kitchen with meat tenderizers, metal whisks, melon ballers, not to mention potato peelers— what could possibly go wrong?

But the Taylors had heard that Dr. Jacobson was well known for his unconventional methods that often, to the surprise of those he counseled, seemed to work. With that kind of track record, Michael and Melissa had agreed that they would at least give the experiment a try. After all, they did, in their own unique and barely recognizable way, still love each other. The twenty-five thousand dollars was a nice incentive that could bring them back together.

The relationship between Melissa and her husband was complicated. There were times when she would be staunchly defensive of Michael, not allowing anyone to talk about her husband the way she often did. And vice-versa. No matter how many times Dr. Jacobson had tried to get them to stop undermining their marriage, Melissa and Michael could not seem to get off the hamster wheel of emotionally wounding each other.

The two were also horribly inaccurate record keepers. Whenever one of them did something kind or especially helpful for the other one, any acknowledgment of that good always fell to the bottom of a long list of wrongs. And there it stayed, seldom to be mentioned again. As for the other items on that list, they got a regular airing out, like seasonal coats in the back of a closet. Because of this unhealthy routine, the healing process could never get very far. Still, they had given their word to Dr. Jacobson that they would at least give the contest a try, and they were committed to doing so. Melissa, a little more than Michael, she feared.

———

"You know, I'll be missing football for this contest," Michael said on their drive home from the restaurant that afternoon.

"Which is more important, Michael? Football or our marriage?"

Unfortunately, Michael waited a little too long to answer her question, which he was certain didn't sit too well with Melissa, because she didn't hold back from telling him so.

"Why did we even enter this baking competition if your heart's not in it?" she snapped.

"Exactly!" he said, yet again without thinking. It was one of his short-comings he had been working on with Dr. Jacobson.

Melissa turned her head away from him to stare out the window on her side of the car.

Still, Michael pressed on. "Does the hotel we'll be staying at for the final bakeoff even have a TV? The game always starts at six, you know." Michael cringed. He'd forgotten all the rules about digging holes and how to stop. By this time, Michael was so deep in his verbal cavern, his voice almost echoed.

"Yes," Melissa answered matter-of-factly. "They have TV *and* a pool."

"Yeah, well, they probably won't even air the game. And you know gas is going to be expensive in a tourist community."

"We can ride around in a horse and buggy. No gas needed." He couldn't miss her sarcastic tone.

"Oh, yeah...the perfect second car," Michael countered. The hint of a smile crossed his face when Melissa turned to look at him, and he noticed one on hers too. Temporarily, at least.

"Look, just forget about the game. And swimming," she said. "And horses and buggies. Not one of those things is what this contest is about. It's to benefit our marriage. And don't blame any of this on me, Michael. This was all Dr. Jacobson's idea. But I'm willing to try if you are."

He gave a halfhearted nod.

"Good enough. They'll be holding the next phase of the competition in one of the kitchens at the Dutch Valley Restaurant. They've roped off a section for the contestants and the press."

"Press?! Seriously?"

"That's what Dr. Jacobson said. Apparently, this contest is a really big event for the area, so there'll be reporters there. And with the novelty of it being held in Amish Country, it could even go national."

"And I'm in an *apron*? Do you have any idea what my football buddies are going to say if they see me on the news wearing an *apron*?"

"If they knew there was a twenty-five-thousand-dollar grand prize, they'd be entering the contest themselves."

———

When they arrived home, Melissa stopped engaging in the conversation that was obviously going nowhere. Instead, she went to their room to continue packing, trying to stay focused on everything they needed to bring—several changes of summer clothing, her makeup bag, a nightgown, a jacket, snacks for the journey, some magazines to catch up on, and the reservation number for their stay at the Carlisle Inn, which was adjacent to the Dutch Valley Restaurant.

The thought of packing a Bible for additional reading material had crossed Melissa's mind, considering the desperate state her marriage was in. But then she remembered that most hotels provided Gideon Bibles in their rooms. If things got desperate, she could always get it out of the nightstand.

Seeking God's Word in times of trouble had been something Melissa used to do when she was a teenager. But it had been a long time since those teen years, and like good acne medicine, she didn't see the need for it anymore once everything cleared up.

But Dr. Jacobson had encouraged both of them to read the Good Book.

"The Bible has a lot to say about relationships," he'd told them. "It might help your marriage. It sure wouldn't hurt it."

Michael had immediately nixed the idea. He'd looked right at the counselor and said, "Thanks, but I've never been much of a reader, much less read a book with all those archaic words like *thee* and *thou* and *verily*."

Apparently, sensing Michael's resistance, Dr. Jacobson had moved on with the session. But Melissa tucked the suggestion in the back of her mind. Just in case.

For a few months after their wedding, Melissa had tried to get Michael to have devotions with her, like she had seen her grandparents do. She'd even used the Bible Grandpa and Grandma had given them for a wedding gift—one of the newer, more modern translations. But the practice didn't last long, considering their work schedules and football season and all the household chores that had piled up on their respective "honey do" lists.

But in the current state of their marriage, she wondered if Dr. Jacobson was on to something. Maybe the Bible really could help.

And now that they had almost made it to the finals in the baking contest, Melissa wondered if maybe, just maybe, they had a shot at winning their marriage back too. They did seem to be opening up a little more to each other in a way they never had before. Like the night when the list of those who would be moving on in the contest was first announced. They'd celebrated afterward by going to dinner at the Dutch Valley Restaurant. Michael had been the first to dive a little deeper into their personal lives.

"So, be honest," he'd said, after finishing his first plate at the buffet. "Have you enjoyed *any* of it?"

"What wasn't there to enjoy? Fried chicken, mashed potatoes and gravy, stuffing. . ."

As soon as the words had left Melissa's mouth, she'd realized that wasn't what he was asking.

"Of course. There's lots about our marriage I enjoy," she had gone on to say.

"So, you believe it's worth saving?" Michael asked.

"Worth saving? Absolutely!" she'd said, hoping he agreed. "I just don't know if we're brave enough to do it."

"Hey, I've been wearing an apron for several weeks now. That's the uniform of the brave, isn't it?" Michael had apparently been trying to lighten things up a bit.

"It does look good on you," Melissa had responded with a grin.

"Oh, really? Well, I can wear it this way, or I can wear it like a cape." She smiled at the remembrance of how Michael had turned the apron around and struck a superhero pose. "For twenty-five thousand dollars, I'll call in *all* my superpowers."

An extra twenty-five thousand dollars would take the pressure off a lot of struggling married couples. Finances are the source of most arguments in a marriage, Melissa thought as she placed the next item in her suitcase. But she knew that their marriage was more complicated than that. And while neither one wanted to admit it, the baking contest was their last hope. If this didn't work, their counselor would surely suggest another temporary separation.

She heaved a lingering sigh. *Temporary separations can invite more problems because once marital issues are opened to friends and family and even complete strangers, everyone's true opinions start to come out. Inviting work friends and childhood friends and sometimes even some church friends to interject their destructive opinions into the situation can be taking the fast track to a divorce.*

Melissa wanted to say that she regretted how much of their lives had been wasted bickering over the smallest of infractions. She should really express to Michael how she wished they could both take back every harsh word they'd ever spoken between them in the heat of the moment. How she really did love him and wanted their marriage to work. But somehow the words failed to come out.

She wanted to say all that but spoke not a word of it. Michael didn't fill the silence either. Melissa wished they could go back to their early married years when they were so very much in love. Back to the years before the bills piled up, the miscarriages happened, and their dreams fell apart.

But neither one of them had the courage to say what needed to be said, even though their marriage hung in the balance. She feared if something didn't change soon, they might be seeking a divorce.

CHAPTER 9

Sugarcreek

When Fannie returned home after her shopping trip in Berlin, she considered going to the Three Sisters Bakery, hoping a few of the delicious pastries the Beiler sisters sold might make her feel a bit better and perhaps make up for the lunch she hadn't eaten. The business was a favorite among locals and tourists alike, and Fannie couldn't help but agree. However, she'd made up her mind to stay home for the rest of the day. She would treat herself to a glass of lemonade and a brownie or two that she'd made two days ago.

Fannie had heard that those who knew the Beiler sisters personally often wondered if they had been misnamed at birth. It seemed that Faith, the eldest, was often full of doubt and fear. Hope was a staunch pessimist who often looked at the negative side of things. If Hope was clinging to any hope at all, you sure couldn't see it. And as for Charity? One would be hard-pressed to find a more self-centered, self-serving person than the woman bearing such a loving name.

But those were the names the three of them had been given, and at this point in their lives, they apparently had little interest in changing their names or their personalities.

The baked goods at the Three Sisters Bakery certainly deserved the names they had been given, however. Delectable, Delicious, Scrumptious, and Mouthwatering. It would be impossible to walk into the bakery and come out with nothing at all.

The real draw, though, was the extra scoops of small-town gossip one could get by simply eavesdropping on the sisters' conversation. Catch them at the right time and their tongues would be moving faster than the rotary blades on their dough mixer.

Many a reputation in the county had been sliced, diced, chopped, and shredded by these three women with such innocent-sounding names. So much so that the locals with any good sense at all would have steered clear of the little bakeshop at the edge of town. Of course, most kept going to the bakery for the wonderful pastries. Fannie figured if a bishop or any of the Amish church ministers had caught one of their members repeating anything the three sisters said when they were in a gossiping, blustery mode, they would get a good talking-to, for sure.

It was out-of-town tourists who kept the bakery in business so well, though. Being in the dark concerning the sisters' troublemaking reputation, strangers would innocently wander into the establishment and be mesmerized in an instant by the delectable aroma of the place.

Cinnamon and vanilla can seem to cover a multitude of sins to the untrained nose, Fannie thought as she entered her living room and flopped onto the couch. She felt tired all of a sudden, and the brownies and lemonade could wait.

Since securing a position on the list of the top six contestants who would likely be finalists in the baking contest, the Three Sisters Bakery had somewhat redeemed and legitimized itself among some of the locals. Word had it that neighbors and church friends were starting to show up there more often—Fannie included. Just not today.

Fannie eagerly kicked her shoes off and pulled her feet up onto the couch as she contemplated things further. In the past, professional bakers had been prohibited from entering the baking contest. The judges figured it wouldn't be fair for average folk to compete with that kind of expertise. But it was the average folk that rebelled, citing that some of them, with families of ten or more, probably had more expertise than many of the pros.

Thus, the contest was opened to all, and the sisters were the first professional bakery owners to sign up.

———

"I am still so excited about the opportunity of being able to prove ourselves at being the very best bakers in Tuscarawas and the surrounding counties." Faith placed a tray of lemon-flavored fry pies in the display case and turned to face her sisters with a wide smile.

"Jah," Hope acknowledged. "And it has also provided free press for our Three Sisters Bakery." She cracked the knuckles on her left hand and then on her right. "We need all the free advertising we can get."

"That's right," Charity agreed. "Let's not forget that several local newspapers have already interviewed us, and I'm sure that helped the readers to have the unique chance to get to know each of us sisters on a deeper level."

"I sure wish we'd known beforehand that our faces would be included in the article." Faith tugged on her head-covering ties and grimaced. "But there it was in black and white for all our neighbors to see. And the worse part was, they didn't even ask—just snapped those photos before we knew it."

"Guess maybe the news media people aren't aware that we Amish don't pose for pictures." Hope looked at Charity. "But since you never joined the church and chose to become Mennonite, maybe they figured you'd be all right with posing for a picture."

"I didn't really pose, Sister. Like Faith said, the reporters just snapped the pictures." Charity shrugged. "Either way, Faith is right—they should have asked, and we should have said something. Guess we were so caught up in the excitement of it all, we got tongue-tied."

Faith moved away from the display case to allow her sister to reach in with a tray of freshly baked peanut butter cookies.

"I still can't believe that reporter asked our ages." After Hope set the tray in place, she clasped her hands so tightly together that her knuckles turned white. "I mean, does it really matter that you are forty-five, Faith? Or that I'm forty-three, and Charity's forty-one?"

Charity's chest puffed out a bit. "In my estimation, each of us could pass for much younger women and have tried to do so on many occasions—state-issued ID cards excluded." She shook her head vigorously. "No, we never would lie on a formal government document. That would not be good for our reputations."

"That's true," Faith agreed. "But then, after the newspaper article came out, our real ages were staring back at us from the front pages of the *Times Reporter* that covered Tuscarawas County, as well as *The Budget* out of Sugarcreek, serving all the Amish and Mennonite communities in Ohio. Why even the *Akron Beacon Herald* and the *Cincinnati Enquirer* ran human interest stories on the contest." She clicked her tongue against the roof of her mouth. "Every single one of those articles mentioned how old we are too."

"I suppose the giant cuckoo clock in downtown Sugarcreek will be hollering out our ages next!" Hope's dark eyebrows squeezed together.

"Well, you know what they say—fame comes at a price," Faith stated, trying to lighten up the moment.

It didn't work. Charity picked up a copy of the *Cleveland Plain Dealer*, which one of their customers had brought into the bakery earlier and left behind. She waved it in front of her sisters' faces. "Did you both see this one?"

"Jah," Hope and Faith said in unison.

"I still can't believe that the reporters felt it was necessary to tell how we sisters had a less than stellar reputation in the Shipshewana, Indiana, Amish community." Hope jabbed a slender finger at the newspaper. "They even mentioned that we had previously caused a ruckus at the Blue Gate Restaurant and Bakery, which later became known as the "Chicken Wing Brawl of 2010."

Faith bobbed her head. "But we survived that. And once we felt confident enough to start our own business, and after one too many divisive rumors that had been accurately traced back to us, we figured it was time to give Ohio a try."

"Well, since none of us has ever been married, at least there are no husbands or children to suffer the embarrassment we faced when those articles came out," Charity interjected.

Hope clasped her hands under her chin in a prayer-like gesture. "But it's not for lack of trying. I, for one, am certainly friendly enough, greeting most single men with a friendly, 'Hi, my name is Hope. Do you want to get married?'"

Faith rolled her eyes. "Unfortunately, that isn't exactly how most Amish bachelors would prefer to be greeted. As you well know, he typically initiates a courting period, and even that is preceded by a proper introduction."

Charity released an undignified grunt. "You are so right, but the pickings are getting slimmer with each tick of the clock. If we are ever going to find husbands, we cannot take the slow lane to matrimony."

Faith chose not to voice her thoughts on that comment, but there was another hindrance to their wedding-day hopes. Jealousy. Whenever one of them received any attention from a prospective suitor, the other two would become jealous and overly protective, and then they would do whatever they could to scare the poor fellow off. This included stories as to the curious demise of former suitors, rare and contagious diseases of which the sisters were carriers, and of course, their Amish mafia connections. Not one of those stories was true, of course. But they warded off any man coming between the three sisters. The suitors would run out of town, some more quickly than others, and the sisters' relationships remained safely intact.

But this time Faith's attention, and she felt certain her sisters' as well, wasn't on male suitors. It was on winning the annual baking contest. The fact that they had made it this far told her where their focus needed to be. If they could knock off their opponents, figuratively speaking of course, they might be able to open up a second bakery in Berlin, Walnut Creek, or Charm. That had been a dream of theirs, and they already had a few storefronts in mind.

"First things first." Faith leaned in with one hand on her knee and spoke in a steady, lower-pitched voice. "Our Three Sisters Bakery has to win!"

———

Fannie left the living room and meandered into the kitchen to see what she could fix for supper. The brownie she'd eventually eaten hadn't done enough to fill her stomach, so Fannie was more than ready to eat a real meal.

Yesterday, she had stopped at the Dutch Valley Market, which was located next to the Dutch Valley Restaurant and Carlisle Inn. It was fun to shop there, and she'd returned home with some trail bologna, as well as packages of provolone and mozzarella cheese. Layering the meat and cheeses inside two slices of wheat bread she'd made yesterday morning would make a tasty sandwich. Throw on plenty of mayonnaise, mustard, and a couple of dill pickle slices and she would have a hearty meal that would no doubt satisfy her stomach.

As Fannie took out a plate and assembled the sandwich, her thoughts turned to the Blustery Sisters once more. The other day, before the names of the contestants moving on were announced, Fannie had tried to talk to Faith, Hope, and Charity to see what they knew about the mysterious disappearances of a few of the contestants throughout the elimination process. But the sisters hadn't seemed too concerned. Like the contest organizers and most of the other contestants, they accepted the speculated excuses for the no-shows. "After all," Charity had said, "sometimes things come up in life that force people to change their plans." The sisters insisted that they didn't see anything suspicious about it. Well, except for Faith, who'd surprisingly said she had her doubts.

"That male contestant, the good-looking one," Faith had told Fannie, "I did overhear him telling one of the judges that he thought someone had been following him."

Fannie then asked Faith if she had overheard anything else.

"No," Faith said. "Our eyes locked, and I felt a wave of guilt come over me for being caught eavesdropping."

Fannie figured it was a first for any of those Blustery Sisters. And it was the first real hint that something nefarious might really be going on behind the scenes of the beloved baking contest.

She hurriedly finished making her sandwich and took it over to the table. Before bowing her head for silent prayer, one more thought popped into Fannie's head. *What if Foster Bates doesn't believe any of the things I said to him previously? What if his promise to help me get to the bottom of all this was said merely to placate me?*

Fannie put a hand over her face and closed her eyes. *Well, if that should be the case, Lord, then I'll need Your help in solving this mystery, because I won't let it go until I have some solid answers.*

CHAPTER 10

Foster Bates' stomach growled when he spotted the Three Sisters Bakery sign up ahead. It was Friday, almost noon, and he hoped they had some of his favorite cinnamon rolls left.

Foster pulled his vehicle into the parking lot, turned off the engine, and got out. His slacks and shirt looked a little disheveled, but right now, he didn't care what he or any part of his attire looked like. The only thing on Foster's mind was getting inside and out of the pelting rain that had started on his drive over here. "A summer rain," he muttered. "Those can be the worst, when thunder and lightning are involved." Hopefully, the weather would improve before the day was out.

Upon entering the bakery, Foster's nostrils twitched as the wonderful aroma of sweet spices, maple frosting, and buttery delicacies tantalized his senses. His gaze went to the glass case, filled with glazed, sugared, and powdered doughnuts. There were also several kinds of cookies, fry pies, and a selection of cakes, but no cinnamon rolls in sight.

Foster's shoulders drooped, and he pressed a hand to his stomach. *What a big disappointment. Guess I drove over here for nothing.*

"May I help you with something, Mr. Bates?" Faith asked from the other side of the pastry cabinet.

"I came here for some cinnamon rolls, but it looks like you're all out of my favorite dessert." Squinting, Foster gestured to the glass case. "I'm guessing you must have sold every one of them this morning."

Faith bobbed her head, where a few strands of sandy-blond hair stuck out from under her white, cone-shaped *kapp*. "But don't fret—my sisters are in the back, making more cinnamon rolls and some other pastries we're running low on. Today we're having a sale, so we were quite busy this morning and expect to be for the rest of the day as well." There was a sparkle in the woman's blue eyes when she smiled. "If you can wait a few minutes, I'm sure one of my sisters will be out with the cinnamon rolls soon."

"No problem. I have plenty of time." Truthfully, Foster was in no hurry to return to his office or go back out in the rain.

"Why don't you have a seat over there while you wait?" Faith pointed to a small area across the room where two modest tables with chairs had been placed for customers who wanted to sit and eat their baked goods or couldn't wait to sample the goodies until they got home.

"Sure." Foster ambled over and took a seat. He felt certain that the wait, however long it took, would be worth every bite of the cinnamon rolls forthcoming.

Faith stepped out from behind the counter and seated herself in the chair beside him. "Since there are no customers at the moment, I figured it would be nice to get off my feet and visit with you for a while."

"Oh. . .umm. . .sure." Foster figured Faith, especially known for her wagging tongue, must have some juicy gossip to share. He was in no mood to hear it, but he felt trapped. It was either sit here and listen to whatever Faith had to say, or leave without any cinnamon rolls, which was not an option for him today.

She leaned a bit closer to him and spoke in a low-pitched voice, just above a whisper. "I assume you know all about the baking contest going on in our area?"

"Of course," Foster replied. "It's been in all the papers, and early on, Fannie Miller even made a bunch of flyers to hang in places of business here in Sugarcreek, as well as some of the other nearby towns."

"In case you didn't know it, my sisters and I have entered the baking contest, and we hope to win the grand prize." She pushed her shoulders back. "We really need that prize money."

He opened his mouth to comment, but she cut him off before he could get a word out.

"Several people have dropped out already." Faith's voice lowered again, as she spoke her next words. "I think those folks must realize that they don't stand a chance against us."

Foster tried to express his thoughts once more, but this time he was interrupted when Hope and Charity came out, each holding a tray of pastries. Foster got up right away to see if one of the trays held the pastry he'd come here for and was pleased to see that the one Charity held was indeed full of plump, delicious-looking cinnamon rolls.

Foster made his way swiftly to the checkout counter. "I'd like a dozen of those cinnamon rolls," he announced before Charity had a chance to set the tray inside the glass pastry case.

"Are you sure that's enough?" she asked with a wink in his direction.

He scratched the side of his head. "Well on second thought—better make it thirteen, because I'll want to eat at least one on the drive back to my office."

Faith snickered and looked over at Charity. "See, Sister—I'm not the only person with a desire for plump, sweet, melt-in-your-mouth cinnamon rolls. Mr. Bates is a man after my own heart."

Foster's ears warmed, and he figured he'd better waste no time in paying for his treats so he could make a quick escape. Everyone in Sugarcreek knew these sisters were single, and it was no secret that the ladies were still looking for the right man they could trap. . .er attract.

———

As Foster drove back to his office on the other side of town, he munched on one of the mouthwatering cinnamon rolls and thought about the Blustery Sisters and their different personalities. Faith always seemed a bit anxious, and of course she had a habit of spreading gossip. Hope, also prone to gossip, was kindhearted enough, but she seemed a bit hopeless at times. Charity liked to be the center of attention, and like her sisters, she enjoyed gossiping a little too much. Was it any wonder they were all still single?

Foster could still hear the desperation in Faith's voice when she'd told him that she and her sisters needed to win the competition. The question was—how badly did they want to win? Could these three Plain women be so desperate that they would do about anything to take home the grand prize and walk away with all that money?

Foster's thoughts turned to other things, like Fannie's plea to help him solve a mystery that she had probably blown out of proportion. Or had she? Was it possible that Fannie's suspicions were accurate and there was actually something going on that was taking competitors out of the baking contest?

––––––

Half an hour later, Foster sat at his office desk, eating another cinnamon roll and washing it down with a cup of coffee. He sat across from the wall bearing numerous awards and citations from his career. Perspiration beaded unexpectedly on his forehead as he did some reminiscing about his past.

By the time Foster had retired from the Chicago Police Department, he was beyond frustrated with all the changes that had taken place during his tour of service. The yellow legal pads he'd been so accustomed to using had been replaced by high-tech computers. Instead of memorizing street names and learning all the shortcuts through town, the new rookies had the advantage of a GPS, which, Foster found, could be as testy as any field sergeant.

As for crime on the street, that had changed the most. Especially in places like Chicago. Instead of focusing on getting the really bad guys, a cop's day was filled with blatant shoplifting, senseless riots, and noisy demonstrations, followed by a lot of paperwork and arrests that never seemed to go anywhere.

Foster flexed his fingers repeatedly. *Who could blame me for turning in my badge?*

When the day came that enough was clearly enough, there was no second-guessing the situation. Foster had filled out his retirement papers and told himself that there would be no looking back. This middle-aged cop was more than ready to regain the peace, quiet, and sanity that was sure to come with semiretirement life.

Sitting in his recliner, watching police shows on television wasn't the same as actual police work, however, but it required so much less of him. His bones would no longer be abused in street scuffles or chasing criminals down the streets. Let the thirty-year-olds hop the fences now. And most importantly, there were no more code three calls, speeding down the highway to some address where unknown dangers awaited him.

Quiet—that's all he wanted. And maybe a little fishing. Was that too much to ask?

Since moving back to the Sugarcreek area, Foster had taken a few odd jobs just to see if he might enjoy something new. His first was at a local supermarket, bagging groceries. He enjoyed getting to meet some of the locals, especially the Amish families who shopped there. They'd come in, mother and father, followed by a string of youngins, all well-behaved and perfectly decked out in their Amish attire. Not a wrinkle or stain among them.

Embarrassed, Foster would often glance down at his own clothes, feeling the need to explain away his missing button, wrinkled shirt, and completely disheveled look. His police uniform may have always been properly pressed, but Foster's casual shirts hadn't seen an iron since Ronald Reagan was in office.

Despite his own feelings of inadequacy, not one of the Amish or Mennonites ever passed judgment on his appearance—at least not to his face. They simply did their weekly shopping, shared a bit of small talk, loaded up their buggies, and headed back home.

Foster had enjoyed the job at first, but after one too many fumbles with the giant bags of flour and cereal, requiring one too many "Cleanup on Aisle 5" announcements, the manager and Foster mutually agreed they would part ways.

Foster's next job was at the local Amish history exhibit Behalt. Always curious, Foster never tired of learning about Amish history and their beliefs, and that was the perfect place to do it. He could spend hours looking over the giant mural that had been painted on its walls and ceiling, depicting important events in their past and helping to educate visitors about Amish heritage and faith.

The only problem with that job was Foster would get so enthralled in studying the mural, that he'd forget he was supposed to be leading the tour. Unsure of what they were supposed to do, the group of people would eventually move on without him.

Once again, Foster was urged to find a job "more suitable for his talents."

But all Foster really knew was police work. That's when the idea struck him. He would open up his own private investigation office. That way he could set his hours "whenever to whenever," and he'd made a vow to himself that he would only accept the easiest of cases.

"Yeah, right," he muttered after finishing his coffee that had almost grown cold. "So much for keeping promises to myself."

For the most part, his plan worked, except whenever Fannie Miller was involved. Nothing was ever easy when that determined Amish woman was in the picture.

Now she had brought him the most complicated case yet. Fannie told him that, in her estimation, four contestants had either dropped out of the baking contest or had been eliminated one way or another, and had not been seen since. Foster wondered once again, Could it be that someone wanted to win so badly that they were knocking off their competition? No baking contest would be worth going to jail for murder. Or would it?

Foster knew that stranger things had happened in the world of crime, so he was keeping his mind open.

Reaching across his desk, he grabbed a missing person file. It was for Bessie Carson, a widow from Charm, Ohio. Bessie had entered her chocolate brownie cake, which most of the locals described as a chocolate cake to die for. But had she? Was it possible that Bessie had met with an unforeseen danger and actually died for her cake? Had the fact that her baking talents—so far ahead of her competition—pushed a competitor over the edge, and he. . .or she. . . had done the unthinkable?

The thought of such a thing happening in their quiet little community, much less in a baking contest, was more than Foster could fathom. But then again, where was Bessie? She'd disappeared just before the preliminaries were held.

According to Bessie's family, she always let someone know where she was at all times. If she had a doctor's appointment, they knew about it. If she was going on a trip, they were informed weeks in advance. She even called when she was going for a walk or working out in the garden.

But now the elderly widow had disappeared without a trace. There wasn't even a brownie cake crumb trail for Foster to follow, much to his bafflement and chagrin.

He tapped two fingers on his desktop. *Strange. Very strange indeed.*

Foster reached over and grabbed another file. Dorothy Dexter, an English woman from Akron. Dorothy had entered her lemon bars in the contest, Foster's personal favorite, which he had tasted at many a bake sale. *What kind of a monster would deprive the world of lemon bars?* Foster wondered.

Like Bessie, Dorothy and her lemon bars had not been seen since she'd made it through the preliminaries. That's how quickly someone wanted her out of the competition.

Friends, family, and the local police had searched for her, but not a single clue had turned up, other than a slight dusting of powdered sugar on the woman's kitchen counter. Foster had bravely taken a taste to be sure. It was Dorothy's famous recipe all right; there had been no mistaking that fact.

"Fannie's right," he said under his breath. "As always, her instincts are dead on. We must be dealing with an absolute monster." The mere thought of those lemon bars being in the hands of some maniac made his blood boil.

I did the right thing by agreeing to help Fannie solve this case, Foster reminded himself, as he prepared to spend the evening looking over the various files Fannie had dropped off earlier that day. This was one of the most important criminal cases to hit the Ohio area since John Dillinger was making bank withdrawals the hard way back in the 1930s.

"Dillinger may be long gone now," Foster nearly shouted, "but even though this is just a small-town baking contest, my country needs me every bit as much as they needed those FBI agents back then. Public enemy number one may have robbed banks in Ohio, but I have a feeling that today's public enemy has a desperate determination to take first place in the baking contest at any cost. And if I have anything to say about it, this monster is going down!"

CHAPTER 11

Foster leaned back in his office chair, with both hands resting behind his head. He'd only had one phone call so far today, and it had been a wrong number. That was fine and dandy with him.

Foster enjoyed slow days like this, when no one asked anything of him. It gave him plenty of time to think, and more often than not, he took the opportunity to doze off a bit. While it wasn't as relaxing as sitting in his rocker on the front porch at home with his trusty dog, Chief, lying by his feet, it was a close second. The mutt was a mixed-breed and smart as a whip. Chief never barked unless there was something amiss or he needed to go out. And he was good about staying in the yard when Foster was gone. Of course, it was fenced-in, but the dog had never tried to jump or climb over the fence, so Foster felt good about leaving Chief alone when he came to work. On rare occasions when Chief begged to go with him, Foster brought the dog to the office. Chief always found a comfortable spot to sleep and never bothered any of Foster's clientele.

Foster reached for his cup of coffee and took a drink. "Yuck! I sat here too long and let it get cold. Shoulda been paying closer attention," he muttered.

Foster had never liked coffee that wasn't at least mildly warm. He remembered how his deceased wife, Cheryl, had brewed such good coffee and always made sure he had a cup every morning before he left for work. Cheryl and their only child, Bobby, had been killed in an automobile accident fifteen years ago. Foster still missed them, and he'd remained single. He'd sometimes told himself that he might be open to the prospect of marriage again, but he wasn't really looking for a wife and didn't expect it to happen in the near future, if at all.

Being a bachelor wasn't so bad. At least he could do whatever, whenever he wanted.

Foster poked his tongue against the inside of his cheek. *Yeah, right. Who am I kidding? When have I ever been able to truly do whatever I want?* He remembered how, when he was a kid and wanted to do something that his parents had said no to, Foster's dad had looked at him and said, "When you're an adult, you can do whatever you want—go where you choose to and eat only the foods that you like."

Needing to take his mind in a different direction, Foster picked up one of the current "Baking Contest Mystery" files on his desk and studied it several minutes. *If Fannie is actually right about someone being responsible for the disappearance of certain people who had entered the baking contest, then I want to be the one who catches the criminal before further harm can be done.*

Fannie paced from one end of her quilt shop to the other. She'd recently put the CLOSED sign in the front window in case she decided to close early and go out on an errand. It might be futile, but Fannie had considered making a trip to check in with the judges to see what they might know about the mysterious contestant disappearances. She was, however, concerned that they might become suspicious of her and pass along her keen interest in the mystery to the police. Being too curious could cast a shadow of suspicion on the perfectly innocent, and Fannie certainly did not want to have anything counting against her in the contest. Being involved in a possible murder, or worst-case scenario, murders, would likely affect her chances at winning the grand prize.

She tilted her head from side to side, weighing the issue further, and finally decided that it might be better to let Foster check on the judges, while she interviewed another person connected to the baking contest—Hilo

Davis. Hilo was a local celebrity of sorts and the long-standing emcee of the Tuscarawas and Surrounding Counties Baking Contest. He was a local radio personality, and many believed the nickname Hilo referred to the ups and downs of his show business career.

Even though Fannie did not have a radio in her buggy and only a wind-up weather alert radio in her house, she had been to plenty of events where Hilo Davis had emceed around town, and she'd always enjoyed his banter with the audience. Hilo's biggest credit was that of hosting the "Oldie but Goodies" program on the radio and also doing the four o'clock news and traffic report. If you were stuck in traffic, Hilo made a person's discomfort a bit more bearable. He often told interesting stories and could be quite amusing at times. At least Fannie thought so.

This would be the tenth year in a row that Hilo had played host to the baking contest. It wasn't exactly like hosting the Oscars, but for Tuscarawas County and its surrounding areas, Hilo Davis was as close to a real star as they came.

Fannie stopped pacing and stood with her shoulders back and chin lifted high. "My instinct tells me that I need to speak with Hilo, and I'm going to do it today."

She hurried to the other end of the quilt shop, slipped on her outer garments, and went out the back door. Fannie's home wasn't far from her place of business, and she'd come here on foot today, since hiring a driver would have been a waste of money. Now she needed to get to the house quickly and hitch her horse to the buggy for a trip to the radio station on the other side of town.

When Fannie arrived at the station sometime later and had entered the building, the red warning light was on, letting visitors know the studio was on air and no one could enter. Fannie was mesmerized by all the equipment and staff. She had never actually been inside a radio station before, and she enjoyed reading all the notices and various posters on the walls, watching through the glass window as Hilo wrapped up the show, and sampling the ample refreshments that had been provided by craft services.

Fannie kept quiet and waited until the red light was off before attempting to get Hilo's attention. As soon as the "all clear" was given and Hilo stepped through the door, Fannie approached him.

"Mr. Hilo Davis." She extended her hand. "I'm Fannie Miller, one of the contest entrants in the Tuscarawas and Surrounding Counties Baking Contest."

"Ah, well then, congratulations are in order for taking part in the special event where I will be hosting on the night of the finals."

"Thank you." Fannie smiled. "I was wondering if I might have a word with you."

Hilo offered her a hearty handshake. "Of course. I believe I remember you from years past. You've been a contestant before, right?" His tone of voice was deep and full-throttled, the perfect emcee kind of voice.

"Yes, every year for the last ten years," Fannie said with a decisive nod. "But this time I am in the top six. I'm certain to make it to the finals." She couldn't hide the excitement she felt.

"Indeed. So what can I help you with?"

Fannie took a few steps away, gathering her thoughts, then she turned back and looked him square in the eye. "Mr. Davis, are you aware that there have been concerns as to the well-being of some of the contestants in this year's contest?"

He shook his head. "I have no knowledge of that. It's nothing serious, I hope."

"Some contestants have been. . .well, for lack of a better term, 'disappearing.'"

Hilo emitted a small chuckle. "That usually happens during the elimination process. They don't make it, so they return home or go away for a few days to mourn their loss. Sometimes they refuse to take any phone calls for a while. I wouldn't worry too much about it, Miss Fannie."

"I'm afraid it could be more serious than that, Mr. Davis."

"What do you think has happened to them?"

"That's what we are trying to find out."

"We?"

"Foster Bates and me."

"Foster Bates, the private investigator?"

"Yes. I've asked him to help me get to the bottom of whatever it is that's going on."

"And what exactly do you think is going on?"

"Mr. Davis, I don't know if you have had a chance to look over my contestant bio, but I am not your typical Amish baker. I have a keen interest in crime solving."

He raised a brow. "An Amish private investigator?"

"Not officially. But I do read a lot of Amish mystery novels. I always know whodunit."

"I see." Hilo took a few steps toward the exit door. "I wish I could help you out, but since you are a contestant in the contest, it might be seen as a conflict of interest if you and I spend too much time together. I would not want to get you disqualified, nor would I want to be replaced as the host. My advice to you is to go on home and lock your mind into winning this contest. Leave the crime solving to the professionals." He cleared his throat a couple of times. "If there even is a crime to be solved."

"But. . ." Fannie tried to continue, but he cut her off.

"It's been a long day, ma'am. Now, if you don't mind, I will bid you goodbye."

With that, Hilo left the studio, leaving Fannie standing there in the company of his assistant and the show's producer, whom she felt sure could not have helped overhearing the conversation she'd just had with Mr. Davis.

Fannie tried to laugh it off, hoping to leave the premises with at least some sense of dignity.

"I'm probably being overly concerned," she said to the men as she gathered her coat and a few more refreshments from a table nearby. "This is Amish Country. Missing contestants in a baking contest—just the sound of that rings hardly plausible."

They both nodded in agreement.

"Well, then," Fannie said, popping a barbequed Vienna sausage into her mouth. "I shall simply go on home and not worry another minute about such a ridiculous notion."

Fannie walked out of the radio station and headed straight for her buggy. She released her horse from the post where she'd secured him and got in, determined to either return to the quilt shop for a while or go home, cook herself a nice dinner, and maybe do some sewing on that quilt for the missionaries she had been working on in her free time.

But before reaching for the reins, she saw it. A red envelope lying on the seat next to her. It was addressed to "Fannie Miller."

She tore it open and pulled out the note that had been tucked inside. Fannie's heart caught in her chest as she lifted the top of the note, revealing the inscription inside. It simply said, YOU WILL REGRET THIS.

Fannie's lips trembled, and she felt her veins beating a visible pulse beneath her skin. Images of what could be flashed through her mind. *Foster. I am not going home or back to my quilt shop. I need to see Foster Bates right away!*

CHAPTER 12

"Regret *what*?" Foster asked Fannie, making a notation in his yellow pad.

"Beats me." She took off her dark-colored jacket and placed it on the now-duct-taped coatrack. Miss Fannie was obviously planning to stay awhile. "The only thing I know for sure is that the note came from one of the contestants."

"How do you know?"

"Because I'm a contestant. We were all given a stationery set in our swag package. That notecard and the red envelope was in those packages. Someone in the contest used theirs to try to frighten me." He saw her shoulders tighten. "And it worked."

"I see. And how do you know about swag?" Foster asked curiously.

"Sometimes I read the headlines in the tabloids that tourists leave behind. I know our little contest is a long way from Hollywood, but we do what we can. Anyway, I thought I needed to let you know right away."

"I'm glad you did," Foster said, adding the note and card to the file.

"So you think it could be something?"

"Perhaps. In the meantime, please don't mention this to anyone else. Criminals are often caught by details that only they and the investigators know."

"My lips are sealed." Fannie swiped a hand across her mouth. "So what's our next step, Sarge?"

"I'm thinking I might pay a visit to the judges. See what, if anything, they've heard about the missing contestants."

"I could go with you," Fannie offered.

"Thanks, but I think I'd better handle this one alone. You're a contestant who hopes to become a finalist. Fraternizing with the judges could get you disqualified."

"Is fraternizing with them the same as interrogating them?"

"They're not going to like either, Fannie. We've got to keep a low profile. I'm simply going to ask them a few questions. If something comes up, you'll be the first to know about it. In the meantime, you should go on home and do whatever you need to do to get ready to win your contest."

She planted her hands firmly against her hips. "What I need to do is rescue anyone in the contest who might be in danger."

"And what if that's you? The note you brought for me to see was placed in your buggy, remember?"

———

Up until that moment, Fannie had not allowed her brain to go there. She assumed everyone else in the contest were potential victims. Not her. But she realized now that she too was a threat to whomever was trying to thin out the competition. Foster was right—she knew that in her gut. Maybe she did need to lie low for a while and see what Foster could find out. If there indeed was anything to find out. And she had a pretty good hunch there was.

"All right, Foster," she said after deliberating a few moments, "I'll go on to my house and sit tight while you see what you can find out." She leaned a bit closer to his desk. "But please keep me informed. Okay?"

"Of course." Foster gave a brief nod. "If I learn anything new, as I said, you'll be the first to know."

"Thank you." She reached out, with the thought to touch him, then quickly pulled her hand back, thinking he might take it the wrong way. "Goodbye, Foster Bates. I'm counting on you, and I'll be praying too." With that said, she sashayed out of his office and onto the street, where her horse waited at the hitching rail Foster had provided for Amish clients. The plot had thickened; there was no doubt about it. She just hoped they could get to the bottom of this before another contestant went missing.

With Fannie heading for home, Foster was free to interview the three contest judges. Through a series of phone calls, he was able to determine that the trio was having dinner at the Berlin Bistro to go over some last-minute details for the next phase of judging this weekend. Not wanting to miss out on the opportunity to question them all together, he grabbed his hat and rushed over there as quickly as he could.

Berlin

It took Foster's eyes a few minutes to adjust to the darkness of the dining room, but then he spotted three people sitting at a booth in the back. Since they were the only party of three, Foster figured he had found who he was looking for.

Foster asked the hostess if he could be seated at the booth in front of the three diners, and she politely obliged.

In accordance with his training, Foster sat with his back to their booth and his face toward the door of the restaurant. *Never sit with your back to the entrance.* That was a hard-and-fast rule left over from the gangster days of Al Capone. Sensible cops followed the same wisdom, as did Foster.

Being seated with his back to their booth also afforded ample opportunity for him to eavesdrop on their conversation before introducing himself.

After placing his order of coffee, black, a cup of homemade potato-cheese soup, and two slices of toast, Foster took out his yellow legal pad and began taking notes. To his dismay, most of what the three judges were discussing had nothing to do with any missing contestants. They didn't even bring up the matter. Instead, they spent their time reviewing the criteria by which they would be judging the contestants, their point system for determining the eventual winner, and how said winner would be announced.

Tradition reigned supreme in the Tuscarawas and Surrounding Counties Baking Contest, and these three had been around long enough to know what was expected of them. Adhering to the long-standing protocol was what probably had kept getting them invited back year after year, and no doubt they were not about to jeopardize that prestigious opportunity.

Foster was disappointed that he wasn't getting any juicy details he could report back to Fannie. But if they knew anything about the missing contestants at all, the judges were remaining tight lipped.

When the three rose to leave, Foster left the remainder of his soup in the bowl and stood to his feet. He really wanted the rest of that soup, but he couldn't let the judges get away without questioning them.

Taking a few steps toward their booth, he gave a nod and smiled, then spoke. "Excuse me."

"Yes?" asked the only male in the group.

"Forgive me, but I couldn't help overhearing bits and pieces of your conversation. Are you three the judges in the baking contest?"

The man nodded. "Why, yes. I'm the head chef at the Main Street Grill in Millersburg. Name's Nick Landers."

"You're up on the hill?"

"Yep. We make the best steaks in town."

"You do indeed. It's my favorite steakhouse."

The blond lady spoke up next. "I'm Betty Campbell. I own the Morning Glory Bakery in Berlin."

"Ah, yes, I've eaten there many times," Foster said. "Best gravy in Ohio."

"It's not even a contest," she said with all the confidence of a successful businesswoman.

"And I'm Alice Trumble. I teach at the Ohio Culinary College in Akron," the other woman stated.

"It's very nice meeting all of you," Foster said.

"And you are?" The question came from Alice.

"Foster Bates, private investigator."

A curious look came over each of their faces.

"Private investigator?" Betty repeated.

Foster bobbed his head. "If you don't mind, I'd like to ask the three of you a few questions."

"Uh, not at all," said Nick, "but I only have a few minutes. I need to get back to my restaurant. Preparations for the dinner rush, you know."

"It shouldn't take long," Foster promised.

"Well, this is a first." Betty sat back down in their booth. "We've never had the baking contest investigated before."

Nick took his seat again too, followed by Alice.

"Mind if I sit here?" Foster indicated to the seat next to Alice.

"Please. . ." Alice scooted over a bit more as though to give him plenty of room.

"I just need to know if any of you have any information on the strange occurrences going on with the baking contest this year."

"What kind of strange occurrences?" Nick asked.

"Well, has everyone. . .you know, been showing up for the competitions?"

"I think so," Alice said. "Why? Is someone missing?"

"Perhaps."

"We did have a few contestants drop out during the earlier preliminaries. But they each had their own reasons," Betty said.

Alice's forehead furrowed. "I do know of an incident that happened, which seemed a little odd. I didn't think too much about it at the time, but now I'm wondering if it might be something."

"What was it?" Foster asked.

"A few days ago, one of the contestants dropped off a note to the judges' table. It was in a red envelope, and it was addressed, 'To the judges.' I figured it might be something we needed to know, so I opened it."

"And what did it say?" asked Foster.

"Just four words: 'You will regret this.'"

"Why didn't you tell us?" Nick looked at Alice with eyes wide and raised brows.

"I figured it was just some kind of a prank, so I threw it away," she responded. "With the finals this close, none of us has time to play silly games with people who have nothing better to do than write crazy notes."

Nick's voice deepened as he looked at Foster and tilted his head to one side. "Do you think it's something we should be concerned about?"

"It could be. Anything else?"

Foster waited while they all went through the last several weeks, considering everything that had happened.

Finally, Betty shook her head. "I can't think of anything out of the ordinary."

"Me either," Nick agreed.

"If anything comes to mind, anything at all, please call me at this number." Foster passed out his business cards and thanked them for their time.

The three judges assured him that they would pass along anything suspicious and went on their way.

Foster paid his bill and walked to his car. The night air was a lot colder than it had been when he started out, so he hurriedly unlocked his door, got in, and turned on the engine. It would warm up soon enough, he figured. But then, his eyes caught a glimpse of something on his windshield. A red envelope.

He rolled down his window and stretched his arm out to retrieve the envelope. It was addressed to "Mr. Foster Bates." When he opened it, he discovered the same note Fannie and Alice had received. Foster's breath caught in his throat as he read the message: YOU WILL REGRET THIS.

And at this moment, Foster was starting to do exactly that.

CHAPTER 13

Fannie stopped by her quilt shop to do some tidying up before she closed for the weekend's contest festivities. She had hoped that all her customers would be attending the event in person to cheer her on to victory or console her should she lose. The sign in her window said as much, giving directions to the event location and time and stating that parking was free.

Fannie had stayed alone at her shop well past dark on plenty of occasions, and it was never of much concern to her. She knew just about everyone in town, and having grown up with brothers, she figured she could get out of any predicament with movements that would rival any skilled black belt.

But tonight, with the multiple notes being delivered around town, the darkness she saw out the window, and the low light in her shop, it seemed a bit more ominous.

Whatever was sending a shiver up her spine—whether it was the note, the missing contestants, or simply the cool night air blowing in through a partially open window near the back of her shop—Fannie knew she didn't want to be alone here any longer than she had to be.

After she finished straightening her bins of quilt squares, rolls of batting, and baskets of notions, Fannie closed and double-checked the locks on the windows and moved toward the front door to make sure the deadbolt was in position. She was going to catch up on her book work next and knew she'd breathe a little easier if she was 100 percent certain of her security.

When she reached for the deadbolt, she felt the pressure of someone on the other side of the door pushing it toward her. She let out a startled scream.

"Sorry, Fannie," the familiar voice said. "I didn't mean to frighten you." Fannie's heart felt like it was about to beat right out of her chest, and her fingers trembled as she opened the door.

"Why, Foster Bates! What are you doing here?"

"I saw the light on and figured I'd stop by and fill you in on my day's investigations. Wanna go for some coffee?"

"Well, I was just getting ready to work on my books," Fannie said. "But I'd be happy to make you a cup of coffee here."

Fannie tucked away the knitting needles she was holding in her hand for protection. "I could use a break anyway."

"And you do make a mighty fine cup of coffee."

"Why, thank you, Foster," Fannie said, grateful that her heart rate seemed to be returning to normal. She was also looking forward to hearing whatever new details Foster had uncovered.

Fannie was independent, to be sure, but there was no harm in having someone around to make sure she was safe. It wouldn't have mattered if it was Foster, one of her part-time coworkers, her church bishop, one of the ministers, or even the deacon. Company had the power to take her mind off the rustling wind, the unexplained creaks in the walls and flooring, and any flickering lights. None of those things seemed as scary when someone else was around. And right now, Fannie was thankful for Foster's presence.

Fannie asked Foster to take a seat at the small table where some quilting magazines had been displayed. Once she'd made the coffee, she set a cup in front of Foster, took a seat across from him, and told him to go ahead and tell her everything he had found out.

Foster blew on his coffee and nodded. "And when I'm done sharing, I want to hear about any clues you've uncovered."

Fannie smiled a confident smile. She did have some news to share. But first, it was Foster's turn.

"I was able to get in touch with the contest judges," Foster said.

"All of them?"

"Yes. They were eating together over at the Berlin Bistro, so I went over to see what I could find out."

"And. . .?"

"Well, it wasn't so much what they said as it was what they didn't say."

"I see. And what didn't they say?"

"There was no mention of any missing contestants."

"But they have to know about the rumors."

"Exactly. But they didn't utter a word about it."

"Do you think they're hiding something?"

"They're all professionals. Highly skilled chefs who know the importance of keeping the contest above reproach. So yes, I found their avoidance rather suspicious. Do you concur?"

"I concur. Anything else?" she asked.

"There was one more rather odd thing that happened."

"What's that?"

"What was the color of the envelope you said you found in your buggy?"

"Red."

"And tell me again what the card inside said."

"'You will regret this.' You read the note, Foster, and I gave it to you," Fannie reminded him.

"Oh, uh. . . Right." Foster reached into his pocket and pulled out the card he had discovered waiting for him on his windshield. He slid it across the table toward Fannie.

Fannie took the card out of the envelope and read it aloud. "You will regret this." Her eyes opened wide, and she blinked in rapid succession.

"They're on to both of us." Foster took a drink of coffee and stood.

"So what does that mean?"

"It means that something nefarious is indeed going on in the Tuscarawas and Surrounding Counties Baking Contest."

A gust of wind blew the shutters against the window, and Fannie found herself jumping up from her chair and into Foster's arms. When she realized where she was, a warm flush swept across her cheeks. Fannie figured her face must have turned a brighter shade of red than the roses on the quilt she had been working on earlier today.

"Oh, I'm so sorry," she said, pulling quickly away from him.

"No apology needed, Fannie," he said in a gentle voice. "A lot of strange things are happening. Our nerves are on edge."

"I know, but. . .I'm usually a lot more collected than that."

"If it makes you feel any better, had you not run into my arms, I probably would have run into yours." Foster gave her a quick wink, and they both had a good laugh.

"Maybe we should call it a night," Fannie said. "I'll head on home now and work on the books tomorrow."

"That's probably a good idea. If we're a target, no sense in making it easier for them."

"Right," Fannie agreed.

"My car's parked right out front, and I'll drive you to your house. Unless you have a driver coming to pick you up."

"No, I don't have a driver, and it's thoughtful of you to offer."

"After I drop you off, I'll head on to my home."

"Now, Foster, you don't have to take me home," Fannie said, not wanting to be too much of a burden but appreciating his kindness. And truthfully, she didn't relish the idea of walking home this evening in the dark—especially believing she might very well be the next person in the baking contest to disappear.

"It's no bother. After all, I need my partner in crime solving to stay safe, right?"

Partner in crime solving? Those words felt good. Had she finally earned Foster's respect? It was sure starting to seem that way.

"Thank you, Foster." Fannie smiled up at him.

There was a slight pause as they both stood in the doorway. Then Fannie turned out the light and shut and locked the door behind them.

———

"Thanks for the ride, Foster." Fannie opened the car door and stepped out. She was surprised when Foster turned off the engine and got out too, and even more surprised when he started walking toward the house with her.

"Oh, you don't have to see me to the door," she was quick to say. "I'll just get my key out of my purse and let myself in, and then you can be on your way."

A few weeks ago, Fannie wouldn't have bothered to lock her house, but now, with all the strange occurrences and threatening notes, she wasn't about to go anywhere without locking both front and back doors, as well as making sure that every window in her home was closed and secured.

"No way," Foster said. "I'm going to make sure you get safely into the house." He glanced around as though scrutinizing Fannie's yard, lit only by the moon above. She figured Foster was probably making sure that no one was lurking in the shadows or behind any of the bushes. She appreciated that too.

Fannie fumbled around in her purse until she located her house key, and then she stepped onto the porch, put the key in the keyhole, and opened the door. Fannie hesitated a few seconds, wondering if she should invite Foster in, but that idea was quickly dismissed. What if one of her neighbors was watching? It could cause some tongues to wag if they saw Fannie enter her house with a man at her side.

Fannie turned to Foster and said in what she felt was a confident tone, "Good night, Foster, and thank you again for bringing me home."

"Want me to come inside and check around—just to be sure you are safe and sound?"

Avoiding direct eye contact with him, she gave a quick shake of her head. "I'll be fine." Fannie forced a smile. "You go on home now and have a pleasant night."

Foster hesitated but finally nodded. "I'll be in touch if I learn anything new." He stepped off the porch and headed straight for his car.

Fannie heaved a sigh and entered her house.

As she went from room to room, turning on all the battery-operated lights, as well as a few gas lamps, her nerves settled a bit. It was good to be home, where she felt safe and could relax for the rest of the evening. Now if she could just turn off her thoughts.

As Foster headed down the road in the direction of his house, he replayed the events of the day. He couldn't believe how something as simple as a baking contest could have turned into an opportunity for him to use his detective skills once again. And he'd certainly never expected to be solving another crime with Fannie Miller at his side.

"And this evening Fannie was more than just at my side," Foster mumbled, reliving the moment. "Why that poor frightened woman practically threw herself into my arms."

Foster hadn't been that close to a female since Cheryl died. The feel of Fannie's breath against his face, coupled with the warmth of her arms clasped firmly around his neck, had unnerved him.

He smacked the steering wheel with the palm of one hand. *Get a hold of yourself, Foster! You're just tired and not thinking straight. Some food in your belly, a little time spent with Chief, and a good night's rest is all that you need. Come morning, your mind will be clear as glass, and you won't be focused on Fannie anymore.*

CHAPTER 14

"You said you wanted to see me?"

Foster finished a notation on the yellow pad in front of him without looking up.

"Yes, yes. . . Glad you could make it on such short notice." Foster dropped his pen and greeted his visitor.

"Mike? Or do you prefer to be called Michael?"

"Most people call me Michael." He took a seat on the other side of Foster's desk. "I would have been here sooner, but the 'honey do' list interfered. Again."

"I understand."

"So you're married too?"

"Was. My wife and son passed away fifteen years ago in a car accident. I've had a thing for drunk drivers ever since. Taken a lot of them off the streets." Foster stared at the paperwork on his desk as he struggled not to let the memory of his wife and son's untimely death take over his thoughts.

"And I thought my wife and I had faced some challenges." Michael gave a slow shake of his head. "Losing your wife and kid. . .I can't imagine dealing with something like that. I'm real sorry, Mr. Bates."

Foster lifted his head to make eye contact. "What is it they say—we all have our crosses to bear."

"Unfortunately that's true." Michael gave a brief nod. "Um...I hope it's okay that my wife didn't come here with me today. I figured I could answer most of your questions."

"Well, I was hoping to speak with you both, but if necessary, guess I can meet with her later."

"After the contest might be easier. Melissa's really busy and stressed right now."

"Yes of course, but I might need to talk with her before." Foster flicked at a fly that had been bugging him most of the day. "Either way, I'll be in touch."

Foster knew from Michael's somber expression that he had taken note of his verbal tactics. Foster had set the boundaries of exactly who was in charge, and it wasn't Michael Taylor.

Positioning the yellow pad in front of him, Foster prepared to take notes. "Michael, the reason I wanted to speak with you today was to see what you might have heard about any contestants who may or may not have...well, for lack of a better term..."

"Disappeared?" Michael said in a matter-of-fact tone, as though filling in the blank for a game of Password.

"Well, yes," Foster said, surprised at Michael's lack of concern over the matter. Still, he pressed on. "It seems a few of the contestants in the baking contest have not been seen or heard from since early in the pre-liminaries. My assistant and I are just trying to determine if there has been any foul play."

"Foul play?" Michael looked away from Foster and seemed to be scrutinizing his office.

Does he think the place doesn't have a professional feel? In his eyes, am I just a middle-aged has-been cop? Sensing Michael's curiosity, Foster clarified. "My assistant works out of her home. But I assure you, she is quite thorough, and so am I."

Foster told himself that most likely neither Michael nor his wife was a suspect in the missing persons case. But he also couldn't help noticing that the young man was a rather nervous individual, thinking through each answer he gave with careful reflection. Almost too careful.

Perhaps that was because this was his first visit to a private investigator's office. First timers often acted guarded, knowing their words, their memories, and their body language were all being analyzed, if not recorded.

Or. . .did this young man know more than what he was saying?

Foster pressed a little more. "Tell me about your marriage."

Michael drew in a deep breath and released it slowly. "Well, as you already seem to know, my wife's name is Melissa."

"How long have you and Melissa been married?"

"We eloped right after our high school graduation."

"So obviously, you're both a bit impulsive?"

"To a fault."

"And what made the two of you decide to enter the baking contest?"

Michael took another deep breath before answering. "Truth?"

"That usually works best in an investigation," Foster advised.

"Well, the truth is our marriage counselor suggested it. He thought working together on a shared goal might help us work some things out in our marriage."

"So am I correct in assuming that the two of you have had a lot of disagreements?"

"We don't disagree on everything. We have, however, agreed to separate on three different occasions."

"But you keep giving yourselves another chance?"

"Yeah. For all the good it's done us." A tightness formed around Michael's blue eyes as he spoke.

Foster couldn't help but feel some degree of empathy for the young man who had perhaps taken on far more responsibilities in life than he was prepared to handle.

"So how has the contest been going for you so far?" Foster asked, hoping there was some good news in the story that was unfolding before him.

"Sticking to the truth, I'd have to say stressful," Michael replied. "But we're trying to get through it."

"Well, you've made it this far. Heard you're a finalist. That's something to be proud of."

"Yes, we sure are." Michael thrust out his chest a bit. "And we're actually feeling pretty good about the possibility of winning."

"You've got as good a chance as any of the other finalists," Foster said.

"Better," Michael said. "This is going to sound crazy, but we both believe it's our turn now. We've had a lot of disappointments in life. Maybe all that's about to change."

"I can understand that," Foster said, and he did. He'd been there himself on more occasions than he could count.

"If you do win, have you decided what you're going to do with the prize money?" Foster asked. "A vacation to Paris? A fishing boat? A house remodel?"

"We have plans. We both know exactly what we're going to do with the money. . .if it even happens."

Foster sensed Michael's hesitation to reveal more, so he didn't press the issue.

"Well, you've got a goal. That's the important thing," Foster said. "And if you don't win?"

"Then, it's back to square one, I guess." The smile left Michael's face as quickly as it had come.

"Back to life as it was before you entered the contest, huh?" Foster asked.

Michael took a few seconds before responding. "Back to life as it was before we met."

So many thoughts spiraled through Michael's head as he drove back to Berlin. His and Melissa's marriage was going to take more than a twenty-five thousand dollar grand prize to heal. Decades of hurt, disappointment, harsh words spoken and taken back and spoken again, dashed dreams, failed businesses, health concerns—it had all caused damage.

A string of marriage counselors had tried their best to help them, but the dysfunction ran deep.

Michael knew this baking contest was their last hope. For better or worse, this was the line in the sand. If this didn't work, another trial separation would be recommended, only this time there was little doubt that the separation would turn into a more permanent one.

Michael knew that, statistically, couples who had endured great loss tended to keep adding to it. They didn't intend to, but in trying to make sense of the incomprehensible, it could happen. The blame game would kick in, and instead of healing together, the couple would sometimes grow apart. Even though Melissa's pregnancies had never lasted very long—twelve weeks, eighteen weeks, sixteen weeks, five months—each one represented the death of a dream. To date, Michael and Melissa had suffered six failed pregnancies. How they had managed to pick themselves up after each one and find the strength to try again had been a testament to their faith and stamina. Both of those resources, however, were fast being depleted.

Each miscarriage wasn't simply a disappointment to add to their list of cancelled vacations, rejected home purchases, and lost jobs. Those kinds of disappointments came with a totally different pain.

When you're desperately wanting to become a parent, little else compares to that level of repeated disappointment, he thought. *No matter how short the pregnancy, the blame game usually shows up too.*

Michael remembered all too well the frequent accusations and questions that came up each time Melissa lost a baby.

Were you taking your vitamins?

You should have gotten more rest.

We should have gone to a different doctor.

A different hospital.

If we weren't in this community, this town, this state, things might have turned out differently.

Michael's heart filled with so many regrets—none of which he could change. *If only one of those pregnancies had gone to full term, I'm sure we would have had a different outlook on life.*

Over the years, Michael and Melissa had done plenty of blaming, soul-searching, and questioning God. And it was getting increasingly hard to reason their way out of the bitterness and hopelessness that hung around their house like angry storm clouds.

We are never going to be parents, he told himself. *So why even keep trying?*

Maybe at long last it was time to throw their hands in the air and go their separate ways. Maybe life held better outcomes for each of them separately. Away from each other and their lifetime of losses.

Yet each one of these losses was a shared battle. They had faced every disappointment together. Cried together. Held onto each other and sometimes even prayed together. In some ways, too easily overlooked, the losses made them both stronger. Sometimes Michael felt like a soldier coming back from the battlefield. They may be bearing both physical and emotional injuries, but they had made it through together. They were still here. Still able to dream and hope for a better future. If they won the baking contest, maybe they would find it after all. He had to cling to that hope. It was either that or give up and permanently go their separate ways.

Could we dare to let go of the pain of the past and learn to appreciate not only what was lost, but what we still have left? Michael's lips pressed together as he fought against the lump that had formed in his throat.

Only time will tell.

The interview with Michael hadn't gone as Foster had imagined. He had gone into it with the belief that there was no way this couple was involved in any of the mysterious disappearances. Even at the beginning of his conversation with Michael, Foster had been fairly certain that the couple was not involved.

But after learning how much they had riding on winning the baking contest and taking home its twenty-five-thousand-dollar prize, he was beginning to have second thoughts.

Foster reached around and scratched the back of his head. *Could that likeable young man have been so desperate to make it to the finals and save his marriage that he would have done the unthinkable? And what about Melissa? What was the real reason she didn't come to the interview with her husband? Was he covering for her? Or was Melissa so desperate to get out of her marriage that she was setting Michael up to take the fall, while she took the prize money and moved on with her life?*

No matter how trusting Foster wanted to be of the young couple, all sorts of possible scenarios swirled around in his head. To this seasoned cop, Michael seemed like a good man. And he had no real reason to doubt Melissa's intentions either. Still, there was something that Foster couldn't quite put his finger on. He had been doing this type of work long enough to know that when you lift the lid and the stew smells funny, you don't have to sniff the rest of the house to know where the rotten odor is coming from.

CHAPTER 15

Rumors had been swirling around town about the missing persons, about the fairness of the baking contest, and about Fannie and Foster's deepening friendship. Just how deep was beginning to concern Bishop John, so he decided he ought to pay Fannie a visit.

As far as he knew, nothing untoward had happened. He felt confident that both Fannie and Foster were respectful of each other's boundaries. Still, the bishop thought he should check in with her just to make sure everything was going well in her life. And if not, he would offer his help and sage advice.

"Everything's fine," Fannie assured him when he entered Fannie's Quilt Shop that afternoon and asked how things were going in her life. "The contest has brought a lot of out-of-towners in, and I couldn't be happier. Sales have really picked up for me too."

Unlike the Blustery Sisters, John thought, *who always look for a cloud in the silver lining.* If there was a silver lining to something, he figured that Fannie would usually find it. She was a go-getter, all right.

The bishop was happy to hear that things were going relatively well for Fannie, despite all the rumors that had been swirling around town and making their way into his ears. When his church members were doing well, it made his prayer list a lot shorter. He slept better at night too.

"And what of your friend Foster Bates?" John couldn't resist asking what was really on his mind—the real reason he'd come here to speak with Fannie.

"He's doing fine too."

"How's his investigation going?"

"Like a typical investigation. You keep ruling out suspects until the only one left is your culprit," Fannie responded.

He tipped his head to one side. "And how many are left now?"

———

Fannie had known the bishop for decades, and she had no reason whatsoever to be suspicious of his sudden interest in the contest and Foster Bates. But his questions were starting to make her feel a bit uneasy. An investigation needed to be kept as private as possible in order to maintain its integrity and unfettered access to witnesses. If Bishop John read Amish mysteries, he'd know that. All she knew at the moment was that she couldn't disclose any more information. Fannie hoped that the bishop would understand.

The bishop took a step closer and said, "The reason I ask is I'm a little concerned about some notes that I've heard about. Are you aware of them?"

She twisted one of the ties on her head covering around her index finger and blew out a series of short breaths. *So he knows. Bishop John knows about the cryptic messages going around.*

"Yes, I've heard," Fannie replied honestly. "Foster and I both received one of those notes."

"Red envelopes and the card says: YOU WILL REGRET THIS. Is that correct?" The bishop's eyes narrowed a bit as he stared at Fannie.

"Jah, that's right. We're looking into the matter, though," Fannie assured him.

The bishop's lips parted as though he wanted to say more, but Fannie smoothly changed the subject.

To her surprise, the bishop just as smoothly changed it back.

"Any idea who's behind them?" he questioned.

"Not yet, but we'll figure it out." She waved a hand dismissively. "All mysteries are puzzles to be solved. Piece by piece you put it together until the answer appears in front of you."

"I am impressed with your sleuthing ability, Fannie." Bishop John gave his lengthy beard a slight tug.

"Danki." Fannie smiled, and when he moved toward the door, she followed and bid him farewell, thankful that their conversation had ended.

———

Foster started his vehicle and yawned as he took his seat behind the wheel. He hadn't slept well last night, and two cups of coffee plus a cinnamon roll had done little to get him moving this morning. He'd been tempted to stay home in bed or lounge on the front porch with Chief, but there was work to be done at the office.

Foster had been busy putting his pieces of the mystery puzzle together and seeing if he had any matches, and the whole ordeal was taking a toll on him. For his entire police career, Foster Bates had been a man of hunches. He couldn't always explain the what, when, where, or why of a crime, but he usually had a good hunch about who was responsible. Not that a hunch would stand up in court. He knew that would never happen. But his long history of following his hunches to a satisfying outcome now guided his direction and decisions. Unlikely as his hunch may seem to others, however, he would doggedly hold on to it until the rest of the details revealed themselves.

Between Foster's hunches and Fannie's intuition, they made a good pair. But so far, this case had baffled them. Why would contestants in a small-town baking contest be disappearing? It made no sense at all.

Where was Bessie Carson? Or Dorothy Dexter? Or that sweet couple from Toledo, Rick and Karen Bledsoe? And the others who had seemingly vanished into thin air? The only thing those people had in common was having entered the baking contest. Other than that, their paths would probably never have crossed.

But no one had heard from any of them. Who would want them out of the picture? Only someone else in the contest. After all, there was that twenty-five-thousand-dollar grand prize, and according to Foster's interviews, each of the finalists could use the money. But enough to have killed for it? Perhaps. In this economy, with prices continuing to rise and some businesses on the verge of bankruptcy, it couldn't be totally ruled out. But kidnapping, or even murder, would be turning a financial problem into a whole other can of worms. Foster doubted that anyone in their right mind would do something so foolish.

And there was his answer: in their right mind. Foster had six finalists—the Blustery Sisters, Michael and Melissa Taylor, and Fannie Miller—but he had yet to discover whose personality had a side he hadn't seen. A dark side. A side that held no empathy for others and was determined to get what he or she wanted. And in this situation, it was twenty-five thousand dollars.

When Foster's car slowed, almost to a stop, he looked down at his gas gauge. To his chagrin, the arrow hovering over the E gave testament to an uncomfortable truth. He was out of gas.

"Again?" The pain of paying those high gas prices had begun piercing both his heart and his wallet.

Five-dollars-per-gallon gas had become the norm in most of the surrounding area, and the thought of paying that kind of money just to get around town made his stomach churn.

Fannie's got the right idea, he thought. *A horse and buggy. A little hay and water, and you're good to go.* But a horse and buggy would not work for Foster. Not only did he not have a place to keep a horse—or a buggy either—Foster also wasn't Amish and didn't know the first thing about sitting on the right side of the buggy with reins in his hands that he really didn't know what to do with. He closed his eyes briefly and tried to visualize how peculiar he would look dressed in Amish attire, trying to make a stubborn horse move when it didn't want to. And what about making the horse stop when it was supposed to?

"No thanks," Foster said, opening his eyes. "In addition to being a nervous wreck, if I could actually drive a horse and buggy, it would take me too long to get to all the places I'd need to be."

He shook his head. "Nope. I'll just deal with the high price of gas and hope it will eventually come down."

Foster had a few clients who still owed him money, and he knew it would help his bottom line if they'd ever pay up, but he couldn't bring himself to send out "past due" notices—the kind of "past due" notices he so frequently had received himself during his financially leaner years.

Everybody's hurting these days, he reasoned. *Why make it harder on my clients and friends to push for the money they owe me?*

Foster was content to patiently wait for the payments to come in, gas and grocery prices to go down, and for his hunches to at long last be proved correct.

━━━━━━

"What are your hunches telling you about this case?" Fannie had asked Foster when they'd met for coffee later that day.

Foster shrugged his shoulders. Now that he was back in his office and his mind was working overtime, he recalled some of the things he and Fannie had said while drinking their beverages. He'd wanted to share his thoughts about many things with Fannie. After all, she was his crime-solving partner. They had been through a lot together. But this hunch he'd been mulling over hadn't been thoroughly thought out yet. There were holes and detours and questions that had to be navigated around. He didn't want to cast any unfair aspersions on someone, nor did he want to overlook a suspect who might be right under his nose.

No, he was going to have to keep this hunch a little closer to his vest. He was going to have to work through this hunch on his own, because his latest hunch involved Fannie Miller herself. This hunch, as much as he didn't want to feel it, was pointing directly to his partner.

Foster knew it sounded crazy, and he had falsely accused Fannie once before. The memory of that fiasco still stung. Somehow their friendship had survived it, but he was in no hurry to go, down that path again.

But in this case, Fannie did have a motive. She had been wanting to win the baking contest for as long as he'd known her. She also had access. Fannie was actually competing in the contest. And she had the opportunity. As one of the contestants, moving closer to the finals, she had a front-row seat to everyone's private conversations, insight into their weaknesses, and Fannie knew their schedules.

Could Fannie Miller be the mastermind I've been looking for?

Foster brushed the thought aside. He wasn't about to make such an outrageous charge against Fannie, no matter how loud the hunch spoke to him. Fannie Miller was a sweet, kind, gentle woman who was always putting other people's needs ahead of her own. And she owned a quilt shop, for goodness' sake! There was no way his hunch was correct. No way, no how, no sir!

Fannie Miller was above reproach. Everyone in town knew that. And she was a friend.

Foster's fingers curled into the palm of his hands. *You don't repay a friend with a charge of "contest tampering, kidnapping, and possibly murder."* *Where's the Hallmark card for that?* Foster knew he'd never find such a card, no matter how many stores he went to.

No, he told himself. *This time my hunch has to be clearly wrong.* His police instincts were misfiring. His investigative skills had packed up and left. Fannie was looking for the culprit just like he was. She was the one who had brought the case to him. If she was the perpetrator, why would she have brought in her own PI?

Because to the criminal mind it's all part of the game they play, Foster reasoned. *Didn't Jack the Ripper toy with the cops while they were hot on his trail, leaving notes and clues behind? And what about Bonnie and Clyde—they certainly had a "catch me if you can" attitude with the FBI agents who gave them chase.*

But that was them, and this was Fannie Miller, and it wasn't the Fannie he knew. Besides, hadn't she received one of those "red envelope" notes herself?

True, he analyzed, *but it could have been a red herring, just to throw me off.*

Still, he couldn't see Fannie being that conniving, that manipulative, that desperate to rig a baking contest. Her biscuits were delicious. She didn't need to cheat. If she were to win, she would want it to be fair and square. Follow all the rules—that was the Fannie he knew.

Back and forth Foster's thoughts swung from "She could be guilty," to "No, not Fannie." It was driving him crazy!

"A lie detector test?" Fannie asked, indignantly. "You want me to take a lie detector test? Foster Bates, are you off your rocker?!"

Foster smiled. "Fannie, my dear friend, although I do have a rocker, I would never want to be off of it."

Fannie couldn't help smiling just a little, but she stayed on point.

"You were right, Foster, when you said we are good friends. And good friends don't lie to each other."

"True, as a general rule. But sometimes desperate circumstances cause people to do things they wouldn't ordinarily do."

"Well," Fannie said, "I do *not* lie."

"Then you shouldn't mind taking a test. If you're telling the truth, which we both know is in your nature, then you'll be validated. And if you're not, it'll tell me that too."

"And what if I'm just nervous and it gives you a false positive?"

"There are ways to determine that," Foster assured her.

It took a bit more convincing, but Fannie finally agreed to take the test. She had no doubt that she would pass it with flying colors and therefore establish her innocence to Foster once and for all. It would also go well for her if she ever needed to go to court over the matter. She'd already have the documents in hand proving that she was a truth teller.

As Foster hooked Fannie up to the lie detector, her eyes rolled in indignation. But Foster just ignored her display of dissatisfaction and did his job.

Once the machine was operational, he began asking Fannie questions. He started with general questions—questions she figured he already knew were truthful.

"What is your name?"

"Where do you live?"

"Where do you work?"

"What is your age?"

Fannie failed the last one three times, but then passed.

"Now, it's time to probe a bit deeper," he said. "Do you personally know any of the missing contestants?"

"Would you say that winning the contest is extremely important to you?"

Fannie answered that last question as honestly as she could, doing her best not to appear prideful.

"I've always dreamed of taking home that first-place ribbon and placing it someplace where the whole town could see it," she stated honestly.

"And the twenty-five thousand dollar grand prize. . .is that a motivating factor for you too?" asked Foster, as he monitored the graph on the lie detector.

"That would be nice, of course," Fannie confessed. "But when I lay my head on my pillow at night, it's that first-place ribbon I'm thinking about."

Fannie heaved a sigh of satisfaction at the thought, then continued. "For one whole year, I would be known as the best baker in all of Tuscarawas and the surrounding counties. That would mean the world to me."

Foster looked like he was squirming in his seat a bit, and then he said, "I apologize for this last question, but I do have to ask. . ."

"Go ahead," Fannie coaxed. *After an hour of questioning, what could be left?* she wondered.

Foster took a deep breath and released it slowly. She watched as his chest moved in and out. "What is your relationship with the investigator in this case—Mr. Foster Bates?"

Fannie took a peek at Foster's list of questions to make sure that was actually on there. It was.

"Well, answering truthfully for the official record, I consider him a friend."

"A good friend?"

"Until putting me on this lie detector machine today, yes."

"I see. A good friend." Foster repeated, as if for confirmation.

"Yes. Good friends. And crime partners. Nothing more, nothing less," Fannie said.

The machine disagreed and made its opinion known.

Foster took some notes but didn't comment. "So the two of you are both working this case?"

"Yes. I brought him in on it because we've worked together before, and he knows how much I love solving mysteries."

"So, you feel confident in his capabilities as a detective?"

"Quite confident," Fannie said. "He is thorough, experienced, and always looks out for my best interest and safety. Foster Bates is a good man."

"But he's still just a 'friend'?"

"Yes," Fannie answered, although she couldn't help wondering where he was going with this. *Does Foster think I care more for him than I'm admitting?* She closed her eyes briefly and emitted a sigh. *Do I?*

———

Foster looked down at the graph again. Its needle was well into overdrive. If that lie detector had been a seismograph, it would have been registering a magnitude 7 earthquake.

Fannie seemed to be squirming in her seat now. "The truth is," she said, blushing, "I am Amish and the investigator you speak of is not. So for me, I'm afraid the road stops there."

"And if he were to become Amish?" Foster's eyes locked with Fannie's.

"Umm. . .You would need to unplug this machine before I could answer that," she said.

"Don't you want to know the truth, Fannie?" Foster pressed.

"I don't want you to know that I know what we both know might possibly be the truth. Besides, it's just a machine. What does it know anyhow?"

"Yeah, right," Foster said as he began unplugging Fannie from the lie detector. Then, after quickly looking over the results, he announced, "Well, you passed the test, Fannie. The machine says you were giving honest answers."

"Good. Now, I think it'd be best if I go on home."

"Okay, that's probably a good idea," Foster agreed. "And that's probably your most honest answer yet."

———

Fannie was caught in a swirl of emotions. There was more that she wanted to say and felt sure there was more Foster wanted to say, but they both sat motionless.

Finally, Fannie broke the silence.

"Goodbye, Foster," she said, feeling almost as if she were in a trance.

"Goodbye, Miss Fannie."

Their words hung in the air, but neither one moved.

Fannie wondered if he felt the same thing she did, or was her mind simply playing a trick on her? She wondered if in reality she had already walked out the door minutes ago and none of this had really happened. Or. . .maybe it was as real as the giant Sugarcreek cuckoo clock announcing the eighth hour of the evening. *After all, cuckoo clocks don't lie,* Fannie assured herself. *And they don't even have to take a lie detector test to prove it.*

———

Foster watched as Fannie put on her jacket and gathered her things. "I'll look forward to our next. . .uh, meeting, Foster," she said.

He gave a nod. "As will I, Miss Fannie."

The sound of Fannie shutting the door behind her broke Foster's hopeful gaze, and a little piece of his heart went with her.

The following morning Foster stopped in at the Three Sisters Bakery. He was in the mood for another one of their delicious cinnamon rolls and whatever new clues he could pick up. As usual, the sisters were keeping the customers entertained with their latest gossip.

As their tongues wagged on and on, Foster thought to himself, *Loose lips sink ships.* Foster had used that phrase plenty of times throughout his investigative work, and it was certainly appropriate here. The Blustery Sisters' lips were so loose, they were barely hanging on.

Foster waited for the hustle and bustle of the breakfast crowd to die down before asking if he could have a word with one of them.

"Charity's available." Hope giggled, then she disappeared into the back to get her sister.

Meanwhile, Foster took advantage of the moment to review his notes. That was his plan, anyway. But before he could pull them out of his pocket and unfold them, Charity was standing tableside, breathless and looking at him with what he considered to be a hopeful expression. What was she hoping for anyway?

"Hope said you wanted to see me," Charity said, her words dripping with cinnamon sugar.

"Yes," Foster said. "I have a few more questions I would like to ask you."

"Well, if one of them is a marriage proposal, the answer is *yes!*" She spread her arms wide and leaned in toward him, a move to which Foster safely recoiled.

He ran his finger under his collar, giving himself more room to breathe. He could feel his ship sinking fast if he didn't get her back to reality.

"It's about your sisters, Hope and Faith," Foster said.

Charity's face fell, obviously disappointed. Raising an eyebrow, she changed her tone.

"My sisters? What is it you'd like to know?"

Foster could tell that Charity's guard was up. As a Mennonite, she was allowed to own a television set, and Foster figured she'd seen enough police dramas to know where he was heading. *Charity probably thinks that I'm trying to get the sisters to turn on each other. And she'd be right,* Foster reasoned. *But what if Charity, loyal sister that she seems to be, doesn't bite the bait?*

Foster needed to make some progress on the case. So he decided to continue doing everything he could to solve it.

I'm crossing Fannie Miller off my list of suspects, Foster thought with absolute clarity. *I am clearing her of all involvement. My hunches are good, but they're not infallible. And she did pass the lie detector test.*

Foster knew that whoever was behind the disappearances needed to be caught before someone got hurt. Wasting time interrogating Fannie Miller was not only unproductive, but dangerous. Someone's life could very well be in danger.

Maybe even Fannie's.

He proceeded to ask Charity some questions regarding her sisters, but she didn't divulge a single thing that brought Foster any closer to the answers he sought. Maybe he would try again some other time. Or perhaps he would question Hope and Faith. But not today. Right now, Foster needed to run a few errands, and then it was back to the office.

CHAPTER 16

Frustrated that so few clues were turning up, Fannie had gotten up early to take matters into her own hands. She'd stayed up past her normal bedtime last night and made some posters about the missing persons. At the crack of dawn, she'd begun hanging them around town, asking people to come forward with any information on the missing contestants.

Since several of those who'd gone missing were Amish, there were no photos of them to include on the posters, but Fannie had made good use of photos of some of the English folk.

In freehand, Fannie had also included that anyone who might know of the missing contestants' whereabouts should contact Foster Bates Private Detective Agency or the Tuscarawas County Sheriff's Department. Each of those phone numbers was also listed.

The whole ordeal reminded Fannie of the posters she had helped to mount all over town some twenty-five years prior, when a little boy had been kidnapped in the area. That case went unsolved for twenty years, but then the baby boy's sister contacted Foster to open the cold case. Fannie got involved in that situation too. And even though Foster had temporarily considered Fannie one of the suspects, everything eventually got straightened out. The twenty-year-old cold case had a happy ending, with the young man at long last being reunited with his family.

Hanging posters sure can't hurt, Fannie told herself as she approached another store on one of the streets in the middle of Sugarcreek. *I'll just hang a few more of these,* Fannie said to herself, *and then call it a day.*

She smacked her forehead with the palm of her hand. *Guess I can't really call it a day, since it's still early in the morning and I have plenty of work to do in my quilt shop. I'll just hang these last few posters and be on my way.*

———

Foster leaned against the back of his favorite recliner, enjoying the aroma and taste of his first cup of morning coffee. He wished he had a big fat cinnamon roll to go with the hot drink. Even a chocolate-covered doughnut or apple fry pie would do. Unfortunately, his pantry held no pastries at all right now. Foster had finished the remaining cinnamon roll last night for dessert.

Chief lay on the floor near Foster's chair. The dog always seemed content when Foster was home. Foster normally felt content too, but with this whole baking contest mystery hanging over him, it was difficult to relax and think about other things. These days, more than not, his mind seemed to be on the business of solving this case.

Foster's further research on the Blustery Sisters revealed that Faith, Hope, and Charity had decided on a devil's food cake for their entry in the finals. Considering all the trouble their gossip had caused around town over the years, the choice seemed appropriate. Beef tongue roast or roasted pig with an apple plugging up its mouth would have also worked.

Foster shook those thoughts out of his head. He had work to do, and a word game like that could go on for hours. If he was going to solve these missing persons cases before the end of the contest, he needed to get busy thinning out his suspect list. Besides, as far as he knew, the decision had been made. The sisters' entry would be the devil's food cake recipe that had been passed down in their family for generations.

Unlike Fannie, the Blustery Sisters had not been cleared in the missing persons cases. Not yet anyway. After all, they had motive—they needed the cash to save their business and possibly open another bakery. They also had access. They knew everyone in the area, including all the other contestants. And they had opportunity. They lived and worked in

THE RISE AND FALL OF MISS FANNIE'S BISCUITS

the town where the contest was being held. They set their own hours and could easily have divided their criminal involvement among the three of them.

Yet when Foster had questioned the three women one at a time, they acted like they didn't have an ounce of guilt among them. He'd come to the conclusion that they were either innocent or highly skilled criminals.

Foster drank the rest of his coffee and placed the mug on the small table at the left side of his chair. *Or what if it was one of the judges? Could they have been bribed to fix the contest for a percentage of the winnings?*

And what about Hilo? Had he finally snapped and worked out his own way to retire from the entertainment industry? Twenty-five thousand dollars could pay for a pretty nice retirement vacation. Or a down payment on a home in the Villages, where he could be on stage as often as he liked. As for access and opportunity, the man had a backstage pass to go wherever he needed to go.

Foster closed his eyes, while rubbing the middle of his forehead. *But would someone who was a respected member of the community ever do such a thing? Would he throw away years of a sterling reputation for a mere twenty-five thousand dollars?*

Foster had his doubts.

Reflecting on the inventory of suspects again, Foster knew he needed to move someone up on the list. But who?

The clock was ticking. If he ever wanted his peaceful and quiet community to return to its former self, he had to act now. This wasn't Chicago, New York, or even Los Angeles. It was Amish Country, for goodness' sake. The really bad stuff didn't happen here. That's what had drawn Foster to return to this area. He liked not having to be concerned about such things.

If he was going to save his tranquil little community, he had to hurry. The finals would soon be underway, a winner named, and the prize money distributed. There wasn't a moment to lose.

"Ladies, I'd like to have a word with you," Foster announced, when he entered the Three Sisters Bakery later that morning. He needed to settle a few more questions.

Faith, Hope, and Charity exchanged nervous glances as Foster made his way to one of the back tables in the bakery and took a seat.

"Can I bring you some coffee?" Hope asked. When she blinked rapidly, the skin around her eyes tightened.

"That would be nice," Foster said sincerely. His morning coffee had long since worn off.

"I don't suppose you'd have any cinnamon rolls left, would you?" he asked, desperate for some of that sugary fuel he'd grown so used to having.

"Coming right up. I'll even warm it for you." Faith and Hope scurried off.

The aroma of the cinnamon and other spices soon filled the air, and Foster almost forgot what he'd come there for. Almost.

"Ladies, I just need to ask you a few more questions, if you don't mind."

"We don't mind at all," said Charity with a smile in Foster's direction. "We know it's important."

Foster hoped she wasn't going to bring up a marriage proposal again.

They all took seats, with Charity and Hope directly across from Foster, and Faith seated to his right.

Foster appreciated their willingness to help him get to the bottom of the mystery. There was nothing he wanted more. His recliner and remote were missing him at home. And since he hadn't made much headway so far, this case had continued to frustrate him beyond measure.

With a cup of hot coffee and a warm cinnamon roll in hand, he watched the sisters, who sat in readiness to answer his questions.

"Now then, what do you need to know?" Hope asked.

Foster took his pen and notepad out of his pocket and prepared to write. "I had a long talk with the bishop this afternoon," he said.

The blood seemed to drain from all three of their faces. There was no doubt in Foster's mind—the Blustery Sisters were flustered.

"It seems that Bishop John's had to rein in the three of you on numerous occasions," Foster continued.

"He—he actually said that?" Faith sputtered, cupping the back of her neck with one hand. She was obviously surprised that the bishop had hung their dirty laundry on the clothesline, so to speak, and in front of Foster, no less.

"Well, the truth is, he has had to have a few talks with us," Hope admitted. "But that's been spread out over a lot of years."

With arms tucked in at their sides, both of Hope's sisters bobbed their heads.

"He says you have quite a reputation for causing problems in the community."

"He said that too?" Charity's voice cracked as she got up from her chair and took a step back.

"In so many words." Foster leaned his elbows on the table, hands clasped tightly together. "Well, all right, it *was* those exact words."

"Oh dear," said Faith. "But you know, it's not as bad as it sounds. You see, we're in charge of getting the word out regarding people's needs and prayer requests."

Foster tipped his head. "So you pray for them?"

"Eventually, Mr. Bates," she replied. "But what does this have to do with the missing persons?"

"I'm wondering if all this might just be another one of your rumors," Foster said. "Maybe nobody's missing at all. Perhaps the three of you have blown it all out of proportion." He tapped his pen against the notepad. *Of course if that were true, it would mean that Fannie's suspicions are not accurate either. So what am I thinking?*

Truthfully, Foster did believe there was foul play going on...and that it wasn't just idle gossip that several baking contestants were missing.

"Or maybe the genuine concern we feel for our community is being unfairly judged." Hope looked directly at Foster, jolting him out of his contemplations. It was ridiculous to keep riding the merry-go-round of different scenarios like this. It was enough to make him dizzy.

"Perhaps," Foster said, finishing off the last bite of his cinnamon roll. "That's what I intend to find out."

"Well, I'm sorry, but we really can't help you, Mr. Bates," Faith stated with a firm shake of her head. "None of us knows anything more than we've already told you."

Foster finished the coffee, thanked the sisters for their time and food, and left, tipping his hat before he stepped out the door.

———

The sisters looked at one another, sank into their chairs at the table, and sighed in unison.

"Well, shut my mouth!" Hope's hand trembled a bit as she scrubbed it over her face.

Faith and Charity nodded as though in complete agreement, apparently not realizing how appropriate those words happened to be at the moment.

Faith's brows lowered as she pursed her lips. "I hope Foster believed us. Because if he didn't, he may be back to question us further, and then what'll we say?"

"We shall say nothing at all," Hope stated in a tone of authority. "The truth is, dear sisters, we have already said way too much."

CHAPTER 17

It was the Blustery Sisters' careless gossip and lack of concern for the damage it caused that kept them near the top of Foster and Fannie's list of suspects. But being known as gossipmongers was one thing. Being possible murder suspects was quite another.

To even be talking about murder, however, seemed a bit premature without a body or any other physical evidence of foul play showing up. Talk about putting the buggy before the horse, as Foster had often said to make his point.

But. . .if the missing persons hadn't met with some tragic end, where were they? The fact that people were actually missing was a fact, not pure gossip. And what was the story behind those red envelopes and their cryptic notes? They were specifically addressed to certain people, all connected to the contest or the investigation of it in some way.

The puzzle pieces were all there, but few of them were falling into place.

Since this was all happening in an Amish community, and since many of the contestants were Amish or Mennonite, Foster left his office and decided to pay another visit to the bishop. Maybe this time he could learn something new.

———

Foster stopped his vehicle in front of Bishop John's house and got out. He ambled up the porch steps and resisted the urge to take a seat in one of the wicker chairs. *Boy, am I tired. I'll be so glad when this whole baking contest is over and I can go back to sitting on my own front porch and quit playing detective for a while.*

Moving past the chairs, Foster knocked on the door. When there was no response, he rapped on it again.

After several minutes and a few more knocks, each a little louder than the first, Foster gave up and decided that no one was home.

"Guess I came all the way out here for nothing," he mumbled, trudging back down the steps.

Foster paused and scratched his head. *Suppose I could have called first, but it's not likely anyone would have been in the phone shed to answer. And what would be the point in leaving a message if nobody was home to receive it?*

Foster was almost to his car when he spotted the bishop's son, Jeb, come out of the barn. Jeb must have seen Foster too, because he watched him for a while, then started walking slowly toward him.

"What brings ya out our way?" Jeb asked when he'd caught up to Foster.

"Came to see your *daed*."

"Dad's not here." Jeb looked down and kicked at a few pebbles on the ground. "He's down at the lake fishin'."

Foster had never asked Jeb's age, and if he had to guess, he figured the young man was about twenty years of age or maybe a little younger. He tried his best not to let that sink in, but a chilling thought pushed its way in anyway.

If my son, Bobby, were still alive, he'd be about that same age. Foster swallowed hard, hoping to push down the lump lodged in his throat. *If only. . .*

Foster willed his mind to go in a different direction. *I have far too much detective work to get done today, and sentiment only gets in the way.*

"Do you know when your dad will be back?"

Jeb shook his head, avoiding eye contact with Foster. "Could be anytime, if he's caught plenty of fish. Or he might not be home till suppertime."

"Where's your mother? Did she go fishing with him?"

Jeb slapped a hand against his thigh and snorted. "Not my *mamm*. No way! She's not the outdoors type, and holdin' a fishing pole with the hope of catching a big one ain't Mom's idea of having fun."

"I see." Foster was surprised that Jeb had said so much. Maybe the kid was the shy-type and it took a while for him to warm up. Foster thanked the young man and told him to have a nice day.

Jeb mumbled something that sounded like "Doesn't matter much what I do" and sauntered off toward the house.

The bishop's son is a little standoffish, but he seems nice enough, Foster contemplated as he got into his car and headed in the direction of the lake. It wasn't a long drive, but it did give Foster a few minutes to get his thoughts together. He hated to bother the bishop on such a beautiful fishing day. Blue skies, scattered clouds, a nice breeze. It looked like a storm might be brewing in the distance, but then fishing just before a storm always made for good results. At least that's what Foster's grandpa used to say.

Foster also knew he needed to gather more information. "You don't solve a crime without evidence, without witness interviews, and without finding that single clue that breaks the case wide open," he said aloud.

He hoped the bishop held that clue. Or at least could lead him to it.

———

When Foster reached the lake, he saw a man wearing a straw hat, fishing off the dock.

That's gotta be him over there.

Foster drove his car over to the dock, got out, and waved. It was the bishop all right. Foster was pleased that the man gave a friendly wave back. Some fishermen hated to be interrupted. Obviously, the bishop didn't mind. Perhaps he even appreciated the company.

"Any bites?" Foster shouted as he walked away from his car.

"Not a one," Bishop John called in return. "But I am having fun."

"So it's not a total loss?" Foster said, making his way over to the dock.

"Fishing is never a total loss," the bishop said, revealing his devotion to the sport. "How 'bout you? Any bites in the investigation?"

"Getting closer, I suppose. But nothing yet. And I am not having fun. Maybe I need to change the bait on my line."

"Could be. And maybe I do too." John chuckled, and Foster did as well.

The bishop reached over to his tackle box. When he lifted the lid, Foster couldn't help but notice the bright red envelope tucked inside.

"What's that?" Foster pointed to the object in question.

"Just some practical joke. As bishop to a fun-loving community, I get a lot of these kinds of things. Especially around April Fool's Day, but we're a bit past that. Last year, when I came home, some jokester had painted a racing stripe on the side of my buggy." The man slapped his thigh. "Can you imagine that?"

Foster grinned and shook his head. "Guess it takes all kinds."

"You got that right, and since I wasn't going to sign up for the Indianapolis 500, I painted over it." The bishop burst forth in a boisterous laugh. "I do have some real characters here in my community."

"I'll bet you do." Foster looked over at the tackle box again. "Mind if I take a look?"

"Not at all." The bishop handed the note to Foster. "I had moved away from the dock for a bit, and when I came back, the envelope was leaning up against my tackle box."

Foster brought the note out of the envelope and read it. Yep. It was the same message he and Fannie had gotten.

"You will regret this," the bishop quoted. "That's all it says. No signature, of course. But there never is. Pranks lose their punch if the person signs it. But don't worry. I'll find out who did it."

"So you're a sleuth too?"

Bishop John shook his head. "Just been at this a lot of years. If I wasn't Amish, I might have become a priest. Then I'd get everyone's confessions every week. Sure would make my job easier." The comment must have tickled the bishop, because he held his sides and laughed even harder.

"Who else knew you would be fishing today?" Foster asked once the man's laughter subsided.

"Everyone. The whole community knows that Tuesday is my fishing day. And they know this is my fishing spot. I try to work that bit of information into my sermons whenever I can, so the people can plan their emergencies accordingly."

That comment got a slight laugh out of Foster.

"I'm only kidding, of course," the bishop said. "If you've never hung around Amish preachers, you might not know this, but we do like to laugh and tell humorous stories."

Suddenly, Bishop John's mood took a more serious tone. "Mr. Bates, do you think that note has something to do with the baking contest?"

"It might," Foster said. "Some others who are connected with the contest or investigation have received notes like this too."

"So does this mean I'm a target as well?"

"I don't know what it means yet. But if I were you, I'd be careful."

The bishop's brows drew together as he gave a solemn nod.

"Please tell me right away if you get another one. Okay?" Foster asked.

"Of course. After me, you'll be the first to know."

Foster said goodbye and got back into his car. He had one more stop to make before returning home.

———

Fannie had been busy all day in her quilt shop with her own quilting project, plus waiting on customers who had come in to buy fabric and notions. As the time neared for her to close up her shop and she hadn't finished the project she'd been working on, Fannie decided to stay until she got it done.

Although she enjoyed quilting and managing her store, there were times when Fannie wished she was a married woman and had the option to quit working and be a stay-at-home wife with a household to run. One thing for sure—she would get a whole lot more baking done if she could be home all day and didn't have a job in town.

"It is what it is," Fannie murmured. "I don't have a husband, so I need to support myself, whether I like it or not."

There were times when Fannie felt sorry for herself because she didn't at least have a suitor. Other times, though, she felt content in the knowledge that she was an independent woman and could pretty much do whatever she wanted, without the added responsibility that came with matrimony.

Fannie's musings came to a halt when her shop door opened and Foster came in. She hadn't expected to see him today, but then admittedly, there were times when she popped in on him unannounced.

"It's nice to see you, Foster," she said cheerfully. "Have you had a good day?"

He took off his hat and clutched it against his chest. "It has certainly not been my best."

Fannie forgot the priority of her quilting project and rushed to his side. "What's wrong? Has something *baremlich* happened today?"

He quirked an eyebrow. "Baremlich? Is that another Pennsylvania Dutch word?"

"Yes, it is. The word means 'terrible.'"

Foster gave a huff and let his hands drop to his sides. "I saw Bishop John at the lake near his house today, and what he showed me was baremlich." He looked at Fannie. "Did I say that right?"

She gave a brief nod before posing her next question. "What exactly did my bishop show you, Foster?"

"A red envelope with a note inside. The words written on the card said the same thing as the ones we received, Fannie."

"Oh dear. How long is this going to go on, and who is responsible for those frightening messages?"

"I don't know."

A scary thought popped into Fannie's head. "Has my dream of winning this contest put our beloved bishop's life in jeopardy too?" she asked, hardly able to bear the thought.

Foster touched her arm. "Try not to worry, Miss Fannie. We're just gathering clues. We don't know what any of this means yet."

"Maybe I should drop out of the contest. Maybe all of this is connected and we're all in danger."

"If you drop out, you'll be giving the perpetrator what he or she wants."

Fannie knew he had a point, but she also knew that neither one of them was any closer to solving the mystery, and that was the most frightening part of all.

"Stay in the contest, Fannie. Interrupt their plans. Let's go forward and win."

Foster's words were true. Fannie knew that. But doing right required courage, and Fannie was starting to feel like her courage valve had sprung a serious leak. Then she remembered the words of Deuteronomy 31:6: "Be strong and of good courage, do not fear nor be afraid of them; for the LORD your God, He is the One who goes with you. He will not leave you nor forsake you."

Fannie bowed her head in reverence. *I'm sorry, God,* she prayed silently. *I will stay in the contest. I'll make the very best biscuits I know how to make. Whatever happens after that, win or lose, it's all in Your hands.*

She raised her head slowly, then quickly bowed it again. *But I'd sure like to win. . .and stay alive.*

CHAPTER 18

"So, what do you think, Chief?" Foster asked his furry friend as he opened a package of fresh dog food and poured the aromatic chunks into his dish.

"You eat better than I do," Foster said, feeling both pleased and a little jealous. "How does it feel to have someone take such good care of you?"

Foster felt sure Chief knew he was talking to him, but the dog probably had better things to do now than help his best friend solve yet another mystery.

But Foster was getting desperate to find the missing contestants, hopefully safe and sound. So desperate that he would have even taken suggestions from some of the stray cats who hung around his trash cans outside, if he thought it would help.

"Now, the last place that Dorothy Dixon was seen was at the preliminaries. After the names of those moving on to the next level were announced and her name wasn't among them, she said she was going home. But her family said Dorothy never showed up. The lady hasn't been seen or heard from since."

Chief sighed and shook his head so hard his ears slapped him in the face.

"I know, I know," Foster said. "This is a tough one. And what about

Bessie Carlson? The manager at the general store, Herb Walker, said she stopped by there on the morning of the preliminaries and bought herself a new pair of shoes and a roll of Necco candies. She said she was heading over to the competition but never showed up.

Foster pointed at his dog. "Who buys new shoes and candy and then vanishes into thin air? It makes no sense. It's especially weird that the Necco candy was found in the parking lot unopened."

Chief licked his empty bowl, moved closer to Foster, turned in a circle, and sat down with a grunt. Foster figured it was Chief's way of processing the information he'd been given.

"And what about a few others who disappeared right after signing up to compete? The registration fee was forty dollars. Who'd pay that and then never show up? Something very strange is going on," Foster continued.

Chief looked up at Foster and blinked his eyes a few times.

"Either these people have legitimate reasons for going dark and not communicating with anyone, or I fear they have met with foul play. I think you and I are both leaning toward the latter, don't you agree with that, boy?"

The only thing Chief was leaning toward was the fire in the fireplace, but he continued to look at Foster, as though he was truly listening.

"Thanks, Chief," Foster said sincerely. "You always help me in these situations."

As though picking up on the appreciative tone of Foster's voice, Chief's tail struck a beat on the hardwood floor. Foster knew exactly what his dog was trying to say.

Something was rotten in the Tuscarawas and Surrounding Counties Baking Contest, and it was up to Foster, Fannie, and maybe even his trusty dog to find out what that was.

With renewed energy, Foster stood and made his way over to the refrigerator to see what he could eat for dinner. Unfortunately, the pickings were sparse. There wasn't even an extra pouch of Chief's food.

"Yep," Foster said, "no doubt about it. You eat better than ole Foster."

Chief didn't seem to hear him. His eyes were closed, and Foster was pretty sure the dog had fallen asleep on a full stomach.

"Maybe I'll Uber something," Foster said.

He had no sooner uttered those words, than the doorbell rang, leaving him to wonder if AI was taking orders telepathically now.

But it wasn't Uber. It was Fannie Miller standing there with a bowl of her homemade beef stew. The savory aroma wafted to Foster's nose.

"I hope you haven't eaten yet," she said, barreling on into Foster's home and waking Chief up. Foster was sure that the delicious aroma was what had gotten his dog's tail to wag.

"No, not yet," Foster replied to Fannie's question. Truth was, he was thrilled at the nice surprise.

"I made a big pot of stew and figured you and Chief might like some."

Foster grabbed the bowl from her hand. "I'll take it. The dog's already eaten."

———

After Fannie left, Foster checked in with Chief again, bringing him up-to-date on the latest clues he and Fannie had discussed over their stew supper.

Fannie had informed Foster that someone had reported seeing Dorothy Dexter at a Wendy's in Millersburg, but upon closer scrutiny of the security cameras, the lead didn't pan out. To Foster's disappointment, Dorothy remained on the missing persons list. It had been a week since anyone had seen her.

Chief gave a sympathetic sigh, most likely for other issues, but Foster convinced himself that Chief was paying rapt attention to the update.

"And I got a little more information on a missing couple from Toledo too," Foster said, leaning close to his dog's face. "The speculation now is that they might have snuck off for a second honeymoon to Paris and didn't want their kids to know. If that story checks out, we can cross them off the list."

Chief lowered his head in what looked like preparation for another nap. Foster longed to do the same, but there was a lot more sleuthing to do on the case, and he didn't dare close his eyes.

Despite the best of intentions, Foster's eyes grew heavy. If he wasn't careful, both he and Chief would be sound asleep and snoring in concert within twenty minutes.

If this case was ever going to get solved, both he and Fannie would have to work overtime on it. But between Fannie overseeing everything at her quilt shop, competing in the baking contest, and keeping up with her household chores, Foster wondered when she would have the time to gather more evidence.

Foster yawned and leaned back in his recliner. *But leaving the case open isn't an option either.*

———

Akron, Ohio

Melissa's heart raced when Michael pulled into the driveway of the Homeward Bound Adoption Agency in Akron, Ohio. The agency was holding an informational meeting for prospective adoptive families this evening. Michael had told her that he'd seen the flyer posted on the wall of a hardware store in Berlin and had taken down the date and address.

Now here they were, taking the first step in a new direction in their quest to becoming parents, and something about it just felt right.

Still, Melissa tried not to get her hopes up like she had done so many times before. But it was always difficult not to hope, not to dream, not to plan for a new addition to their family. Even if every time they had hoped, dreamed, and planned, it had ended in disappointment.

She grabbed her purse and got out of the car. With a sliver of hope welling up in her soul, she followed her husband inside.

The director of the agency welcomed everyone to the meeting, then gave a brief overview of their operation, which he noted, was in its fortieth year.

He had a few families speak about their personal experiences with the agency, proudly introducing the audience to the child or children who were now an official part of their family. Then, he spoke about the current state of adoption, explaining how the waiting list worked and how that wait could be much shorter through international adoptions. Currently, there was a desperate need for families to adopt children who had lost their parents through war or disease, as well as those who had simply been abandoned due to lack of resources to care for the child.

Melissa took it all in, her heart swelling with compassion for these children, and from the serious expression she saw on her husband's face, she was certain that Michael felt the same way.

The speaker talked about the requirements for adoptive families, and Melissa was confident that she and Michael met each one. Then, he covered the expense. An adoption with this agency would run in the thirty-thousand-dollar range, for medical, legal, and other expenses—a figure that almost made Melissa choke on the refreshments they'd been served. Where would Michael and she ever get that kind of money? She was sure Michael was feeling the same angst. *Why do dreams always have to run into roadblocks?*

When the meeting dismissed, Melissa was in a hurry to leave. Even as Michael took a packet of information to peruse at home, she knew they had no way to make this happen. And once they got back into their car, she brought him back to reality.

"Michael, there's absolutely no way we can ever come up with that kind of money," she said, fighting back the tears clogging her throat.

"There is if we win the baking contest," he reminded her.

"Don't. . .don't even go there."

"But it's twenty-five thousand dollars. And we've got three thousand dollars in our savings, and maybe our folks could help with the rest."

"Look, the only reason we're in this baking contest is because of our marriage counselor. He just wanted us to have to work together on something. He never suggested that we might win. We're not expert cooks, Michael! All we ever do in the kitchen is argue over which frozen food item we're going to plop in the microwave. How are we going to win a baking contest?"

"I don't know, but we've made it to the finals, so there's still hope."

"And now we're being judged by professional chefs." She shook her head. "We don't stand a chance."

"We've got as good a chance as any of the other finalists."

"Against three sisters who own a bakery? And Fannie Miller who everyone knows makes the best biscuits around?"

"Every cook can have a bad day. Maybe they'll all have theirs during the finals competition, and we'll win by default."

"Please, Michael, quit trying to get my hopes up. I can't take much more disappointment," Melissa pleaded.

"Maybe there's a way to improve our chances of winning the prize."

"What are you talking about?"

"Maybe there's something I can do to help give us an edge."

Suddenly, a look came over Michael that Melissa couldn't quite interpret. It was clear he was thinking about something. She just wasn't sure what it was.

Berlin

That night, as Melissa prepared for bed, she pushed all thoughts about adoption out of her head. She knew they weren't going to win the contest. And their three-thousand-dollar savings wasn't thirty thousand dollars, so there was no point stressing over what could never happen. No matter what Michael was contemplating to give them an edge, it simply was not going to happen.

After he was certain that Melissa had fallen asleep, Michael got up and walked into the other room. He picked up the telephone and placed a call.

"Dad?" he said, when his father answered.

"Michael? Is everything okay?" He heard the tone of concern in his dad's voice.

"Everything's fine, Dad. But there is something I'd like to discuss with you and Mom."

"What is it, Son? You sound upset."

Michael went on to explain the situation of how they had gone to the adoption agency today and gotten the information, and how they might need some help on the adoption expenses, if it were to even happen.

"How much do you need?" his father said.

"If all goes according to plan, about two thousand dollars. But I'm thinking maybe Melissa's parents might be able to give us some money too."

"Well, let us know what you're short of and we'll sure help," Dad promised.

Michael felt better after the phone call and headed for bed. As he laid there watching Melissa sleep, he couldn't help but promise himself that he was going to do everything in his power to make sure they won that baking contest. And everything meant doing something he never thought he would do.

CHAPTER 19

It was already an exhausting day when Foster came across a tidbit of information that he found rather interesting. It was a newspaper article about a "Jane Doe" who had been injured in a hit-and-run while crossing a street in Cincinnati. The victim, who suffered a severe head injury, had been taken by ambulance to Christ Hospital, unconscious, alone, and without any identification on her. Doctors listed her as a "Jane Doe."

Wait a minute, Foster said to himself, moving the paper so close to his eyes that he could smell the ink. There was no time to look for his readers (one of twelve pairs he had bought at the dollar store). Could one of the answers to Sugar Creek's biggest mystery be waiting for him in Cincinnati? he wondered.

It certainly seemed worthy of a little deeper investigation. After all, a depressed contestant, who had failed to move on to the finals, could have gone on a trip to Cincinnati to forget about their loss.

Foster processed all the similarities between Cincinnati's Jane Doe and his Missing Contestant profiles. One missing contestant's similarities couldn't be ignored. She had family in the Cincinnati area and certainly could have traveled there to find consolation from them. The timing of the hit-and-run accident seemed about right to Foster. It happened two days after the baking contest preliminaries. That would have given the contestant plenty of time to get to Cincinnati. And the estimated age of the injured woman seemed to fit too.

"That could be her!" Foster said aloud, quickly starting to pack a few things for the trip.

On a light traffic day, Cincinnati is only about an hour's drive from the Sugar Creek area. Foster figured if he left soon, he could check into a hotel, go to the hospital to meet with the doctors overseeing Jane Doe's medical care, meet with the detectives in charge of the case, have a nice dinner, enjoy the hotel pool and spa for a few hours, then turn in for the night, and be back home to Sugar Creek by midmorning, after the free hotel breakfast.

He informed Fannie of his plans and hit the road.

Cincinnati, Ohio

Throughout his years of being a cop, going to hospitals to interview injured victims and perpetrators alike, emergency rooms were Foster's least favorite place to be. He never knew what he was going to find behind those ER doors and flimsy divider curtains. And he'd seen plenty—life-threatening injuries sustained in shootings, muggings, car jackings, car accidents, suicide attempts, drug overdoses, and more.

No matter how hard he tried to maintain that "tough street cop" image, he never could get used to the sight of blood. On more than one occasion, doctors had to roll in another gurney to keep Foster from hitting the floor. Sometimes he would be right in the middle of interviewing the patient when his knees would buckle, the room would start spinning, and the next thing he knew he was gone.

His partners took great delight in teasing Foster about it all, even to the point of nicknaming him Fainting Foster. He distained the name, of course, but he tolerated it, knowing that any amount of protesting would garner that much more teasing from a bunch of seasoned and hardened cops.

But this was Cincinnati, not Chicago, he told himself. How bad could an ER be here?

Plenty bad.

As Foster waited in the hallway for a chance to talk to the doctors, and hopefully even Jane Doe when and if she regained consciousness, he saw more trauma than he ever expected to see.

Not only did Cincinnati have its typical city crime, medical staff also had to handle all sorts of horrific farm accidents that happened in the neighboring rural areas. From silo explosions to appendages being severed by farm equipment, Cincinnati ER doctors saw it all. And now Foster was seeing it too.

All day long, EMTs brought in stretcher after stretcher with patients, young and old, suffering from all sorts of maladies. Like the lady who arrived by ambulance having had her long hair caught in a hay bailer blade. She was bleeding profusely from her scalp, or what was left of it, and Foster got way too close of a look as the poor woman was wheeled past him.

The worst that day was a boy who looked to be only nine or ten years old. He had been "corn walking" in his family's silo to level out the mountain of corn kernels. But an air pocket under the corn gave way and the child fell through the pile and was quickly buried. Since his family was nearby at the time, rescue efforts were successful. But he had nearly suffocated, inhaling corn and corn dust into his nose, throat, and lungs in the process.

Foster whispered a prayer for both victims and also for Jane Doe. I wonder where God receives more desperate prayers from—places of worship or emergency rooms? Foster figured it might be the latter.

"Foster Bates?" Dr. Carter asked as he approached Foster.

"Yes," Foster said, rising to his feet.

"Doctor Alan Carter. I understand you'd like to talk to me about our Jane Doe. Do you think you might know her?"

"I'm not sure, but I'm investigating multiple Missing Persons cases over in the Sugar Creek area, and your patient might be connected."

"Let's go over to my office where we can talk," the doctor said.

It wasn't really an office. More like a small room with two chairs and a desk. Nothing else.

"Now," the doctor said, taking a seat and inviting Foster to take one too. "What makes you believe that this patient might have a connection to your investigation?"

"Well, the day and time that she was brought in matches the day and time of some of our disappearances. And she seems to be approximately the same age as one of our missing contestants."

"Okay, you've got my attention," the doctor said. "But I'll need more details."

"Doctor, I don't know if you're familiar with the annual Best Baker Contest in Tuscarawas County. . ."

"Amish country?"

Foster nodded. "It's going on right now. And it may not mean much to folks in Cincinnati, but it's a pretty big deal down in our neck of the woods."

"And you think our Jane Doe could be one of the contestants?"

"I figured it was worth checking out," Foster said. "Could you provide me a photo that I could take back with me? Perhaps someone will recognize the young lady."

"Mr. Bates, I am sure you are aware of privacy laws concerning patients," the doctor reminded Foster.

"I will sign any paperwork necessary. I will also be meeting with the detectives handling your Jane Doe case."

"Good then. Get me their approval and we'll get you the photograph. Now, if you will excuse me. . ."

The doctor returned to his duties, and Foster made a few notes in his Missing Persons file.

Next stop: Cincinnati Police Department—Detectives.

The hallway was filled with criminals awaiting their interrogation meetings, innocents waiting to give their statements and alibis, and a variety of other characters right off the streets of Cincinnati.

Making his way through the crowd was Detective Stan Willoughby. Holding his hand out, Detective Willoughby took a chance.

"Foster Bates?"

"The one and only," Foster said, giving a friendly handshake. "Thank you for meeting with me."

"Well, I've got to tell you, your phone call intrigued me. So, you've really got a string of missing persons in Amish Country, huh?"

"I'm afraid so," Foster said. "And to think I retired there for the peace and quiet."

"Well, it's still a beautiful place. My wife and I go out there every chance we get. Love the food."

"You won't find any better in all of America," Foster said. "And believe me, I've looked. But getting back to your Jane Doe... Detective, I have reason to believe that she could very well be one of our missing persons. I can't say for sure, but she seems to have turned up here around the same time that our girl went missing. And Jane Doe's estimated age seems about right too."

"Any other matching features?"

"As you know, the Amish don't take photographs. All I've got is the description her family gave me. But I believe it's worth checking out."

"So, your missing contestant was Amish?" the detective asked.

Foster nodded.

"But Jane Doe wasn't wearing Amish clothing."

Foster's brow furrowed. Why would an Amish girl be wearing English clothes, and all the way out in Cincinnati?

Sensing Foster's disappointment over the clothing issue, the detective offered, "Maybe she snuck out of the house? Was she the type of girl to have done something like that?"

"From what I've learned from the family, no. But then again, if you've just been cut from the preliminaries of a baking contest that carries a twenty-five-thousand-dollar grand prize, perhaps?"

That there was even a possibility that the Jane Doe lying unconscious over at Christ Hospital was the missing Amish girl, Detective Willoughby offered his assistance. "Sounds to me like I need to take a trip over to Amish Country."

"Or better yet, why don't I arrange for one or more of her family members to come here? If she's not their loved one, they can spend a nice day in Cincinnati. But if it is, we'll reunite her with her family, and your fine hospital will have helped solve one of Tuscarawas County's biggest mysteries."

"Then, I shall wait to hear from you."

Foster nodded his head, thanked the detective, and headed back home. It was times like this that he really hated that Fannie didn't have a cell phone. He couldn't wait to get back home and fill her in on his day!

"You found her?!" Fannie exclaimed when Foster told her about Cincinnati's Jane Doe.

"Well, I don't want us to get our hopes up too high, but in my gut, I believe it could be Mary Ann Lengacher," Foster said.

"So, what's next?" she asked.

"I'm going to talk to Mary Ann's family and tell them what I know. Then, hopefully, we'll take a trip back to Cincinnati and let them either make a positive identification or let us know it's a dead end."

"Can I go?" Fannie asked, hoping he'd say yes.

Foster smiled. "I was hoping you'd want to. I need my partner there in case I miss something."

"You, Foster Bates?" Fannie smiled. "Never in a million years."

The family of the missing contestant couldn't hold back their excitement at the mere possibility that the Jane Doe in Cincinnati might be Mary Anne. Finally, they had a ray of hope of seeing their beloved family member again.

"How soon can we leave?" the girl's mother asked.

"First thing in the morning is fine with me," Foster said. "I'll check with Fannie, and if she's on, we'll leave at, say, eight o'clock."

That next morning Foster Bates picked up Fannie and then drove to the home of the missing contestant. He wasn't surprised to see them standing on their front porch, ready to go. *If I thought my son was lying in a hospital, unidentified and hanging on to life, I couldn't wait to get there too.* He didn't allow himself to dwell too long on that thought, though. It could easily have led him back to a night he had spent years trying to push out of his mind.

The hour-long return trip to Cincinnati seemed to fly by. Detective Willoughby met them at the hospital with all the necessary permissions in hand, and he and the missing girl's parents went in first to see the unnamed patient.

Foster and Fannie waited in the ER lobby, but it wasn't long before they heard screams of joy coming from beyond the ER doors.

That could have meant only one thing, Foster thought to himself. Fannie obviously agreed because she threw her arms around Foster. "It's her!" she said through tearful eyes.

Foster nodded. "It's her."

Dr. Carter filled the girl's parents in on the prognosis of their daughter, who had taken a turn for the better during the night. In his professional opinion, the young lady had a very good chance of a full recovery. She remained unconscious, but that was temporary. Her vitals had stabilized, her color was improving, and now she had a name.

"Mary Ann Lengacher," her father said proudly.

"Lengacher?" the doctor repeated, hoping he'd pronounced it correctly.

"It means *celebration*," the girl's mother said proudly.

Foster and Fannie couldn't have been happier. One less name on their Missing Persons list. It was a day for celebration indeed.

CHAPTER 20

It was the news Fannie had been waiting for, and she couldn't wait to bring Foster in on it. This had nothing to do with the baking contest, but everything to do with the Blustery Sisters. Fannie had heard that Bishop John was planning to give the three women a good talking-to over all the trouble their gossiping tongues had caused over the years. The good bishop had clearly had enough and finally reached the bottom of his patience barrel.

It was Fannie's understanding that if they couldn't control it on their own, Bishop John would have to resort to other measures to ensure the peace and tranquility of their Amish community. Charity, being Mennonite, wasn't really under his leadership, but he knew her pastor quite well and Fannie was certain that he wouldn't hesitate to enlist another minister's help with the matter.

Fannie wouldn't have wanted to be in the sisters' shoes for one moment. Whenever the bishop had to be called in to settle a matter, especially on the third or fourth time he had been told about it, a person could be sure they would get a good chastising. Not physically, but certainly admonishment that would be ringing in their ears for weeks.

It would be loud, much louder than his sermons, but delivered with the best of intentions. Since the Bible clearly stated that gossip is a sin, one of the deadliest, Bishop John would be in essence "snatching them out of the fire," as they say.

"Don't they realize the Bible says in Proverbs 6:16–19 that there are six things God hates—and also a seventh one?" Fannie knew each one and ticked them off in her head:

1. *A proud look*

2. *A lying tongue*

3. *Hands that shed innocent blood*

4. *A heart that devises wicked plans*

5. *Feet that are swift in running to evil*

6. *A false witness who speaks lies*

7. *One who sows discord among brethren*

As far as Fannie could estimate, the sisters were scoring six out of seven on a regular basis. And if they had anything to do with the missing contestants, they could be earning a perfect score.

The news that they were finally going to have to face the music was enough to get Fannie to leave the comfort of her home, hitch her horse to the buggy, and brave the five o'clock after-work traffic, the stifling summer air, and her own hunger pangs to personally deliver the news to Foster.

Foster's office wasn't too far from her house, so Fannie knew it wouldn't take long to get there. If only the cars in front of her would quit crowding and scooting her too close to the ditch, or cutting in front of her, or shining those flashing blue and white lights from the top of their. . .

Uh-oh! Fannie swallowed a large gulp of air, and shame caused her cheeks to burn.

Is that policeman pulling me over?

Fannie tried to give herself the benefit of a doubt. *Surely, he's not pulling me over. I did nothing wrong. I've just been driving my horse at a steady pace, while minding my own business.*

But his flailing arms, wide-open eyes and mouth appeared to indicate otherwise.

Fannie obliged the officer and pulled back on the horse's reins, bringing the animal and buggy to a halt.

As she went on a pocket excavation into both her right and left sweater pockets, looking for her travel identification, the officer got out of his vehicle and proceeded to walk to the driver's side of Fannie's buggy.

Meanwhile, one of her Mennonite neighbors drove by and waved at Fannie, no doubt offering her emotional support. Then, one of her part-time helpers at the quilt store drove her buggy past Fannie and waved, giving her the "I'm praying for you" signal of two hands brought together in prayer.

Fannie's embarrassment deepened when she saw Bishop John pass by, shaking his head, as though in frustration. Fannie figured he probably wondered what kind of mess Fannie was in this time.

When the rush of cars cleared out, it was only Fannie and the officer left in the road. One Amish buggy and one police cruiser. One law enforcer and one law... *Well,* Fannie thought, *law-breaker doesn't really apply, because I never intentionally broke whatever law the police officer believes I have.*

"Identification, please," the young officer said when he approached her buggy.

"I have this." She handed him the government ID she had been issued.

"You were a little late on that red light back there," the officer said, beginning to write in his ticket book.

"Oh? Was there a light?" Fannie asked, which didn't seem to sit well, by Fannie's estimation, with the dubious expression the officer had on his face as he looked at her. Questioning a policeman's question never did play well in a situation like this. Fannie knew good and well that there was a light in that intersection. She either rode home on her bike or walked that way every evening and also went that way every morning on her way to the quilt shop. *I should have told him the truth.*

As the officer continued to write out what could very well have been a ticket, Fannie said she was sorry, and then decided to name drop.

"Do you happen to know Foster Bates?"

"Foster Bates?"

"Yes. Detective Foster Bates. He has an office in downtown Sugarcreek. He's a retired police sergeant, who has gone into private detective work. He's a personal friend of mine."

"Is that so?"

"Yes, and we solve crimes together."

"You don't say?"

"He says I have a natural instinct for that type of work."

"Foster says that, huh?"

"Yes. So do you know him?"

"I might have pulled him over a few times."

"Foster?" Her mouth dropped open.

"If it's the fellow I'm thinking of, then yes, I know him."

"Trench coat?" Fannie asked.

"In his sixties?"

"Complains a lot?"

"A 'Get off my lawn!' bumper sticker?"

"Yeah, that'd be him," Fannie said.

"All right, look, here's what I'm going to do. I'll let you off with a warning this time. But the next time you come to a red light, the word is 'Whoa!' Understand, Miss Miller?"

"Whoa!" Fannie repeated, playing along to keep the moment light. "I think I've got it now."

"By the way, where were you heading in such a hurry?"

"Over to Foster's to tell him how some women we both know were finally getting into trouble for committing six out of the seven sins that God hates the most."

"And how does God feel about red lights?"

Fannie squirmed a bit on her seat. Then she sheepishly told the officer that she got his point, loud and clear. And she thanked God that the officer didn't know Foster personally. Fannie wasn't sure, but she figured Foster might never let her live this down.

By the time Fannie arrived at Foster's, she wasn't all that interested in passing along the news she'd heard about Bishop John's reprimand of the Blustery Sisters. When she considered the freshness of her own infraction, she thought it might be better to leave well enough alone.

But what would she say was the reason she had hurried to his office on such short notice, in rush-hour traffic, and when it had started to rain? She sat in her buggy and thought about that before ever getting out of it. She thought about it all the way up his walkway, and while she stood on his porch waiting for him to answer. And she thought about it as he opened the door and said, "Why, Fannie, what brought you over here on a night like this?"

"What brought me over here?" Fannie asked, buying herself a little extra time. "Why, to apologize for any time I've ever judged you too harshly."

"Okay, what'd you do?" Foster asked with a curious expression.

"What do you mean?"

"Well," he replied, "whenever someone gets caught doing the same or a similar offense as another person has done, who was shown no mercy, they often will seek out their forgiveness. So is that the case?"

"Maybe." Fannie lowered her gaze. "Sounds like you've been going to church."

"Not recently. Just TV preachers. . .and Dr. Phil."

"Who?"

"Never mind."

"Hey, if it's the truth, we should welcome it. And that certainly sounds like the truth. We don't want to see our own shortcomings, but we love having a front-row seat when we're looking for it in others."

"Can I have an 'Amen'?" Foster asked.

"Amen!" Fannie said. Then, she looked at the clock on the wall and told Foster that she needed to leave because she had a planning meeting with the bishop's wife, Iva. He told her to drive carefully and shut the door behind her.

Fannie walked back to her buggy, but before getting in, she reached into her pocket and took out the warning notice she had recieved from the officer. *I think maybe I should hang onto this whenever I need to be reminded about my own shortcomings. We all have our faults and strengths, and most importantly, we all have burdens to bear. Why should we make each other's lives harder than they need to be when we can choose to offer grace instead of judgment?*

"I was offered grace tonight by that kind policeman," Fannie said out loud. "And I should be willing to offer it to others, even if it is the Blustery Sisters."

———

Fannie may not have wanted to tell Foster about the encounter with the "Po Po," an endearing term she always enjoyed saying. But she did decide to confide in the bishop's wife.

"Well," Iva said when the two of them met to discuss the upcoming

Dinner in a Cornfield, which they were planning for the community, "I wouldn't worry too much about it, Fannie dear. It's not like you get pulled over all the time or go racing through red lights on a regular basis. Besides, you've had a lot on your mind lately—with the contest, the investigations, and trying to stay one step away from those Blustery Sisters."

Fannie thanked Iva for her understanding.

"And I assure you that John and I will be praying for you," Iva said.

"For me?"

"Yes, Fannie. We shall pray that you will remember to follow the rules of the road, which includes always stopping for red lights."

———

By the time Fannie and Iva parted ways, the day seemed a little more manageable.

One day at a time, that's how we're supposed to live, Fannie thought as she led her horse and buggy up to the hitching rack near her buggy shed. That's what her aunt Selma had always told her. *And even when several days attack you all at once, you've just got to slow down at the caution lights, stop at the red ones, and go full speed ahead at the green when it comes on,* Fannie mused. *That's how you win at life, and baking contests.* And Fannie was bound and determined to win at both!

And she would hang that warning notice the officer had given her in a place where she would see it, as a daily reminder of how important it was to remember that it's not just the destination that's important, but how you travel there.

CHAPTER 21

Berlin

Foster had already put in a full day's work when a call came in to see if he might be available to help out a friend of his who worked security at the three-story shopping complex in the heart of Berlin, Ohio. It was the graveyard shift, and Foster agreed to help since his friend would sometimes invite him out on his fishing boat.

Without jeopardizing the safety of the building, Foster figured he could use a night of quiet time to process the investigation involving those persons who'd entered the baking contest and had gone missing. Maybe with some quiet time and thought, he'd have a better chance at seeing if he could get any closer to solving the case.

Police officers were known for their bravery, and Foster was no exception. A man like Foster hadn't spent twenty years protecting the streets of Chicago without having a healthy dose of courage running through his veins.

But this particular case he'd been working on with Fannie had presented him with some very unique circumstances. People were vanishing into thin air. Then there were all of those cryptic notes in the red envelopes being mysteriously delivered to people, including him and Fannie.

Throw in working the graveyard shift in a big empty building, an ex-cop who didn't move as quickly as he used to, and most people would understand why Foster would be a little jumpy, like he was tonight.

The elevator suddenly arriving at his floor at precisely 3:12 a.m., doors opening, and no one walking out, only made matters worse.

Foster tried to steady his nerves by taking several deep breaths.

Cautiously, he drew his gun and began moving toward the elevator.

The bell on the elevator rang, causing Foster to jump. He quickly glanced inside the elevator.

"Stop right there!" Foster yelled, pointing his gun directly at the man who was pointing his gun directly at Foster.

"I said don't move!" Foster repeated.

Foster took a step toward him, and the man moved forward too—almost daring him to shoot. Foster obliged, shattering the glass into a thousand shards. It was at that moment—the moment of the gunshot—that the man disappeared and Foster realized he had just shot his own reflection.

Foster slapped a shaky hand against the back of his head. "Oh, boy...I must be losing it! How could I be so stupid not to realize the back wall of the elevator was mirrored?"

Thankful that he had been working alone so there were no witnesses to see what he'd done, Foster returned his firearm to its holster. He'd have to fill out an incident report on the gunshot, but Foster figured he could somehow explain it away. Keeping the entire event on the down-low would be best for all concerned.

"The elevator seems to be working just fine now," the building manager said the next morning when he showed up to make the repairs. "Sometimes there's a glitch in the system and its brain starts doing its own thing, showing up on floors to pick up or drop off people who aren't there." He gave Foster's back a couple of thumps. "Don't be embarrassed. That'd creep me out too."

"And the glass?"

"Already got it ordered.

Foster told the man he appreciated the speed with which he was taking care of everything.

"No problem at all, sir," the man said. "The important thing is you got a good look at the perp."

Foster kept his head down as he signed the work order. He couldn't bring himself to admit what had actually happened.

"You did get a good look at him, didn't you?" the man repeated.

"As good as I could in the moment," Foster said, clearing his throat several times to get the words out.

"About how tall would you say he was?"

"About my height, I guess." *At least that much was honest,* Foster told himself.

"Big and burly, or tall and thin?"

"Neither really."

"So about your build?"

"It was hard to see. Elevators can be pretty dark. And the man just disappeared before my eyes could focus."

The man gave Foster a copy of the work order and left.

"This is one caper I will not be telling Fannie about," Foster muttered, as shame took over. "Or my dog either."

But in his own defense, just before the incident, Foster had woken up from a short nap, and it had been two years since he'd gotten his last pair of prescription glasses.

Not to mention that working with Fannie always seems to keep me a little on edge, Foster told himself as he gathered up his things and headed out the door. It would be good to get home and try to catch a few winks before it was time to head for his office.

———

Sugarcreek

No matter how much Foster begged Chief to wait until after the crack of noon to take him for his walk, come six o'clock every morning, Chief would be at the front door, jumping at the knob and barking loud enough to get Foster's attention. So that morning when Foster was finally trying to get some much-needed sleep after returning home from his scary night at the shopping complex in Berlin, his dog did not disappoint.

Foster had enrolled Chief in obedience classes on numerous occasions only to be the dog parent to a perpetual dropout. Foster couldn't count the number of dog parent/teacher meetings he had to stay after class for, and he was in no hurry to repeat the experience. Foster was sure that he and Chief understood each other. It was a matter of rank. Chief outranked a retired sergeant, simple as that. Even at six o'clock in the morning.

So out of bed Foster rolled, and quickly put on his street clothes. Meanwhile, Chief continued to jump and bark.

"All right, all right, I'm coming!" And soon Foster and his dog were out the door.

Foster had seen enough sunrises on the beat in Chicago to last him a lifetime. He didn't need another one. Besides, sometimes during the early morning hours, a person could end up seeing things he wished he hadn't. Things that couldn't be unseen. Things he might be forced to take action against, and that was definitely not what Foster had in mind to do today— especially not before coffee.

That's when he saw a shadowy figure leaving the front porch of a yellow house after dropping off a package.

Foster and Chief were only a few blocks away from their home. Close enough to run to the safety within its walls, if necessary. But he could tell that Chief wasn't about to run away from danger. He was raring to run directly toward it if he had to, in order to save his home and family. That's how a trustworthy, well-trained dog behaved.

"Well behaved most of the time," Foster muttered.

Sensing Chief's natural instincts, Foster held on to his leash with everything he had in him. Whatever was going down at the yellow house in the darkness of these early morning hours, Foster wanted no part of it. But it was suspicious.

Foster thought about chasing after the figure, but his joints and lack of sleep thought otherwise. Chief, however, was obviously more than ready to give chase. But Foster held on tight, leading him instead to the front door to see what it was that had been delivered at such a suspicious hour.

When Foster leaned down to reach for the bag that was stapled shut, the owner of the house suddenly opened the door.

Foster jumped back, clamping his lips tightly shut so he wouldn't scream.

"Why, Foster Bates, are you doing Door Dash now?"

When Foster's vision focused, he saw that he was talking to Betty

Campbell, one of the esteemed judges in the baking contest.

Foster, with bag now in hand, couldn't think of anything clever to say in return. So he handed it to her and said, "Here's your order, Betty." And then he turned and high-tailed it right back to his house, with Chief at his side.

The dog gave one final bark, which Foster supposed meant, "I don't know him," and then quickly ran into the house.

Once again, Foster had been outsmarted by life. He had no idea that Betty lived so close to him or that the shadowy figure in the wee hours of the morning would be a delivery man. But most importantly, he didn't even know that he could get food delivered that early in the morning.

When Foster entered his home, he went straight to the kitchen and wrote himself a note, which he hung on his refrigerator door with a magnet. *Good to know*, he said to himself. That was the one worthwhile thing about progress—convenience. Other than that, he liked little else.

For years, life had been moving too fast for Foster. The whole reason he'd moved back to Amish Country was for the slower pace. But even in the short time he'd been here, he could see technology was moving in— even among some of the Amish who carried cell phones. Some even had computers in their place of business. Of course, they were not allowed to have them in their homes. Nor were Amish church members allowed to own their own cars or televisions. They were, however, allowed to ride in vehicles driven by their non-Amish drivers.

Foster was unabashedly old school and often wished he could go back to the old way of doing things. His friends had bought him a smartwatch for his retirement from the Chicago police force. The item was still sitting in its gift box. Foster was all about simple and basic Timex watches, landline phone service, and typewriters. And he liked it that way.

"Well, Chief," Foster said, to which Chief jumped up on his lap, as though awaiting his owner's attention. "What can we do? Time's not going to stop for you or me, huh? Does that sound about right to you?"

Chief wagged his tail and let out a bit of a whimper.

"Guess we've got to get up to speed on some of these things though. Eh, boy?"

Chief didn't comment with a bark or whine, as if doing so might encourage Foster to make some changes for him too. No, Foster had no inclination to do any major overhauls just yet. But it didn't matter. With eyes closed, Foster was almost asleep in his recliner, ready to chase more car thieves, catch more gangsters, and outsmart more white-collar criminals. All in his dreams, of course. All in his dreams.

———

Berlin

For a brief moment, and over his morning cup of coffee, Michael allowed his mind to wander—to consider all the "what ifs" that lay before him and Melissa. What if they did win the baking contest? What if they withdrew the three-thosuand dollars from their savings account, and their parents were able to give them the rest? What if they passed all the evaluations and met every requirement of the adoption agency? What if they were really given a child to raise and love as their very own flesh and blood?

He wondered if the child would be an infant, or a toddler or elementary-school-aged boy or girl. Or middle school? At this point, he might even consider taking in a high schooler. *It's never too late to give a child a family, is it?* he told himself. *Parenting is sometimes a lifelong endeavor. Parenthood always is.*

Michael could feel his heart warm even thinking about the prospect. After all, the agency seemed to indicate that it wouldn't take very long for them to receive an approval, once all the necessary paperwork was completed. He and Melissa would both easily pass the background check and medical requirements. And while they weren't rich by any stretch of the imagination, they could afford the expenses of raising a child.

By now, though, Melissa was fully awake. He didn't want to bring the matter up again, not knowing what her night had been like. Was she letting her mind go there too—getting her hopes up for something that was out of her control? Something that could potentially break his wife's heart all over again?

Or had she already tossed out the idea altogether? He wouldn't have blamed her if she had. But he prayed that wasn't the case. They needed something to go their way this time. Something that might help strengthen their marriage and give them a real incentive to truly start working together.

CHAPTER 22

Sugarcreek

"I'm thinking about going over to the Main Street Grill for a steak," Foster told Fannie as he straightened the growing files on his desk. "One of the judges is the chef there, and I'd like to ask him a few questions away from the other two. Care to join me?"

"Well, I'm not sure. . ." Fannie had stopped in at Foster's office to catch up on where the case was, but she hadn't figured on him inviting her to supper. Although, she supposed they could just as easily have a discussion over their meal.

"Best steaks in town." Foster rubbed his hands together.

"So I've heard." Fannie had always wanted to go to the Main Street Grill, but she'd never given herself permission to spend that much on a steak, not when she had a quarter of beef in her freezer, grazed on a relative's farm.

But she wanted to say yes. Then another thought hit her.

"What if someone sees us having a meal together?" Fannie questioned. She knew as soon as the words left her lips that they weren't the right ones. "They could think. . ."

"That we're two friends having a nice supper together?"

Fannie quickly backed out of the verbal dead-end she had driven into.

"Yes, yes of course," she said.

"Two friends eating together. What's wrong with that?"

"We do have to eat," Fannie stated with a nod.

"True. And we both like steak."

"Love it!"

"I'll even ask the waiter for an extra candle, so it won't be so dark."

"Hard to read the menu in the dark," Fannie agreed.

"Eyes aren't what they used to be." Foster touched the rim of his reading glasses.

"A lot of things aren't."

"So, it's a date... I—I mean, we can meet there." Foster sputtered, as though trying to find the right words. "Six o'clock. Unless you want me to pick you up."

"No, no. I'll take my horse and buggy," Fannie was quick to say. "I might stop by the general store on my way."

Fannie knew good and well that she didn't need anything at the general store. She was also quite sure that Foster knew that she knew the general store closed at five o'clock.

With a sharp intake of breath, Fannie rose from her chair. "I shall see you soon, Foster."

Foster smiled. "I look forward to it, Miss Fannie."

As Fannie walked out of his office, she scolded herself for even being nervous about their dinner. It wasn't a rendezvous. Fannie Miller had never used that word in her life and didn't really even know what it meant. But for some reason, it had popped into her head.

And it's certainly not a date, she reminded herself. *Foster said nothing about it being a date. So even if we do run into the bishop or one of the ministers, there is absolutely nothing to hide.* Fannie tapped a finger against her lips. *I'm Amish and Foster isn't, and we both are fully aware of that fact. Neither one of us are even thinking of being anything other than friends and fellow crime solvers. That's it. Friends and fellow crime solvers.*

Fannie gave a decisive nod. *Now then, what am I going to wear?*

Fannie hurried home to prepare for the evening. She put on a freshly pressed dress and apron. One of her light blue ones because it brought out the color of her eyes.

And even though her hair was tucked into her kapp, she looked in the mirror and checked it again. And then she. . . *Dear Lord, forgive me* (and she figured He would). . . rubbed a dab of cherry juice on her lips.

Fannie wasn't trying to flirt with Foster, she assured herself. She just wanted to look her best. And cherry juice had the knack of making her look a little younger and more vibrant than usual.

I've worn it to our church services before, and so far the bishop hasn't said anything about it.

Fannie looked at the battery-operated clock on her side table. Five thirty. Time to start heading over to the restaurant. She figured Foster would already have their table and the extra candle. All she had to do was join him there.

One more dab of cherry juice, and Fannie Miller was on her way.

———

When Fannie entered the restaurant, just as she imagined, Foster was sitting at their table. Fannie joined him, and upon his recommendation, she ordered the ribeye too. Then Foster handed the waiter his card and asked him to give it to the chef.

The waiter nodded, and Foster sat back in his seat.

"You look especially nice tonight, Fannie," Foster said. "Have you been out in the sun today?"

Fannie figured it was the cherry juice doing its job.

"Thank you, Foster. Yes, I did do a little gardening earlier today."

Fannie didn't bring up the cherry juice. *Men aren't interested in our beauty secrets.*

Just then, Chef Nick appeared at their table, looking dapper in his chef whites.

"Foster Bates," he said, sounding genuinely pleased. "Welcome. And please introduce me to your lady friend."

"Oh, of course. This is my dear friend and partner in crime solving. Miss Fannie Miller," he said.

"Well, Miss Fannie. It is a pleasure to meet you."

Nick gestured to the booth Foster and Fannie were sitting in. "This is my wife's and my favorite booth," he said, with the raise of an eyebrow.

"Nestled here in the back. Romantic, no?"

"Oh no," Fannie said, jumping in before it went any further. "Foster and I are working."

"Working, yes, of course," Nick said, this time throwing in a knowing wink.

"Fannie helps me with some of my cases," Foster said, as though trying to help.

"Of course she does," Nick said with a second wink. "But speaking of your cases, how are things going with the baking contest?"

"Still putting the pieces together," Foster responded. "But we'll get our man."

"Or woman," Fannie added.

With a knowing expression, Nick gave Fannie yet another wink. "Well, enjoy your meal," he said, then thanked them again for coming.

Once Nick had disappeared into the back, Fannie assessed what had just happened.

"Well, that was sure awkward," she said.

Foster agreed. "We're lucky it wasn't the Blustery Sisters."

"Yeah, the whole town would know about it before we even got past the appetizers."

"Stay focused on the case, Fannie," Foster said. "Now, I came here to find out what Nick knows, and when it's time for his break, I'm planning to ask him straight out."

"Right," Fannie agreed. "And I might have a question or two myself."

Foster got up from his seat for a few minutes, and when he came back, he informed Fannie that he'd found out Nick would be taking a break at seven o'clock, but it was only for fifteen minutes.

"That's more than enough time," Foster stated. And at 7:03, Nick walked through the kitchen doors, greeted a few tables, then looked in Foster and Fannie's direction.

Foster waved him over. "If you've got a minute, I'd like to ask you a few more questions."

"That's about all I've got," Nick said.

"I'll make it quick."

Chef Nick took a seat.

"How well do you know the finalists?" Foster questioned.

"I don't. Except for Fannie here, whom I just met tonight. As judges we don't always get to meet all the contestants. They only bring us in for the finals."

"Have you personally witnessed any unusual animosity between any of the finalists?"

"Well, you know, there's competitiveness in any contest."

"Yes, but I'm talking a deeper need to win. A jealousy or envy so strong that it would lead them to do something they normally wouldn't do."

"You mean. . .like get rid of the competition?"

"Perhaps."

"I didn't notice anything. Except. . .except for the Blustery Sisters. As you know, they are highly competitive."

"Did they say or do anything in particular that raised your suspicions?"

"Yes, but I've got to get back to the kitchen. Can you meet me here again in the morning? Say around ten? We don't open until eleven, so we can talk privately."

"I'll be here," Foster said.

Once Nick disappeared into the kitchen, Foster looked at Fannie and said, "Maybe we're going to get a break in the case. Huh, Fannie?"

"It's not the Blustery Sisters," Fannie said emphatically, with her head tilted back.

"How do you know? We haven't even heard what he has to say yet."

Fannie's heart beat faster than usual, and she clenched her jaw. "I've heard what my gut has to say. And it's not them!"

———

Foster decided to drop the topic for now and enjoy the rest of his meal. He took pleasure in every morsel of his steak, but between bites, he couldn't help glancing at Fannie. She seemed kind of jittery and nervous this evening—fiddling with her napkin and her gaze darting about the room. Was she upset because he had accused the Blustery Sisters? As far as Foster knew, none of them were Fannie's best friends. Of course, two of them were Amish. No doubt an Amish person would stand up for their kind, whether they were close friends or not.

Maybe Fannie is apprehensive about being seen eating supper here in this restaurant with me. She might be worried that if someone she knows sees us together, they will get the wrong idea and think we are out on a date.

He pushed his glasses to the bridge of his nose. *Well, we're certainly not on a date. This is a business meeting—nothing else.*

Foster set his knife and fork down and took a drink of water. *Nick knows a lot of people in Sugarcreek. Fannie may be concerned that he might spread the word about me and Fannie coming here together and then asking him questions regarding any animosity going on between the contestants in the baking contest.*

Foster drew in several quick breaths as he contemplated things further. *I wonder if there's something I can say or do to put Miss Fannie's mind at ease and help her relax so she can enjoy the rest of her supper. I sure don't want her to go home after our meal, wound up tighter than an eight-day clock.*

He debated a few more minutes, then throwing caution to the wind, Foster reached across the table and clasped Fannie's hand, just after she'd set her glass of water down.

Her eyes widened like a frightened deer in the headlights of an oncoming vehicle, and she released a squeal that sounded like one of the piglets he'd heard recently while visiting an Amish farm in the area where he often purchased fresh eggs.

With no hesitation, Foster pulled his hand back. "I–I'm sorry, Miss Fannie. I didn't mean to startle you. I thought you looked kind of tense, and I wanted to offer some reassurance, hoping to help you relax."

"I am anything but relaxed," she admitted. "Ever since the dough in this baking contest turned sour, if you know what I mean, I've been a ball of nerves. I really wish we could figure out why so many of the contestants have either unexpectedly quit or disappeared." The hand Foster had held only moments ago, trembled as she touched her flushed cheeks. "It's hard to fall asleep at night, thinking about all this and wondering who will be next."

Foster wanted to promise Fannie that she would be safe and nothing bad was going to happen, but the truth was, at this point, he couldn't be sure of anything except that he was going to keep the investigation going until the truth was finally revealed. And that he'd keep his hand off Fannie's hand, no matter how much he wanted to help her. Maybe tomorrow, when he met up with Nick, he would have more to go on—and perhaps a new suspect to pursue.

CHAPTER 23

"So, tell me about Foster Bates," Charity asked Fannie when she stopped in at the Three Sisters Bakery for a custard-filled doughnut the following morning.

"What would you like to know?" Fannie asked, curious about Charity's sudden interest in the private investigator. It made sense, she supposed. After all, Charity was single, she was Mennonite, and word had it that she hadn't been on a date in several years.

"Is he spoken for?" Charity pressed, moving into Fannie's personal space.

"He's a widower," Fannie replied, taking a step back. "As far as I know, he's not in any serious relationships."

"I'm not asking for me," Charity clarified, her words nearly drowned out by the giggle of her sisters, who stood behind the pastry counter.

"Okay, I *am* asking for me," the red-faced woman confessed. A slight flush appeared on her neck as well. "Mr. Bates is quite good looking, don't you think?"

"I...um...haven't really noticed," Fannie responded, knowing she was going to have to repent for the lie as soon as it left her lips.

Oh, and those dreamy blue eyes. Fannie's repentance list was getting longer with each word she'd spoken or thought to herself. But what else could she do? Act like a schoolgirl getting faint over her first crush? In other words, act like Charity was acting?

Fannie told herself she would never do such a thing. She and Foster were friends, that was all. Just friends. If Charity wanted to try gaining his attention, then Fannie wasn't going to stand in her way. Foster wasn't Amish, so courting him was not an option. If they ever did develop a serious relationship, she would either have to leave the Amish faith, or Foster would need to join the Amish church.

A shot of adrenaline shot through her body. *Jah, right—like that would ever happen.* Fannie couldn't begin to envision Foster Bates dressed in Amish clothes or trading his car in for a horse and buggy. She felt sure there was no way he would ever give up all of his modern conveniences to become part of the Plain life.

Fannie's ribs tightened at the thought of leaving the Amish faith to marry an Englisher. Trading her dependable horse and buggy in for a car held no appeal. Neither did owning modern conveniences, like a dishwasher, fancy electric appliances, or a television. *No thanks! None of those things would make me happy. In fact, I wouldn't know what to do with any of them.*

Fannie pulled her thoughts back to the conversation at hand and directed her next comment to Charity. "All I know is Foster's a very nice man. Any woman would be blessed to have him in her life."

Safe answer, Fannie mused. *Now let's move on to other topics.* She directed her gaze to the case full of pastries. After all, she had come here for a custard-filled doughnut, not to discuss Foster's good qualities. She was about to place her order, when Charity spoke again.

Practically bouncing on her toes, Charity clutched her hands together and spoke in a bubbly tone. "Foster Bates is a ruggedly handsome, dreamy-eyed man, who is unattached."

"That is true," Fannie admitted. "I—I mean, he's a single man with no attachments." Fannie felt a prickling along the back of her neck. She desperately wanted to change the course of their conversation.

"Oh and Sister, don't forget that in addition to Foster being unattached, he is quite *schmaert,*" Hope interjected. "And he's also still breathing." She giggled behind her hand.

"Being smart is important, and so is the fact that he's single," Charity stated. "But more important is the ability for a woman, like me, to find a single man who is still breathing. Those are the three main qualities of an eligible bachelor, right?" Charity let loose with a boisterous laugh that ended in an undignified snort.

This brought a round of laughter from her sisters.

Fannie didn't think any of this was humorous. She felt her heart sink all the way to her stomach. That ruggedly handsome, dreamy-eyed, unattached and breathing male was her best friend. And in her dreams, maybe more. She had patiently waited her whole life for someone like Foster Bates, who shared her love of crime solving, who had gone through enough pain in life to have a heart and empathy for others, and someone who was fun to be with. True, he wasn't Amish, but where were the Amish men asking for her hand in marriage? The only thing any of them had ever asked for was to have her biscuit recipe or to repair their grandmother's quilt.

Was she doomed to stay single for the rest of her life, or at least most of it, like her English aunt had done? That poor woman didn't go on a single date until she turned eighty. Then Aunt Edna finally met the man of her dreams in an exercise class at the YMCA. A few days after their wedding, Aunt Edna and her husband, Charlie, booked a cruise that ended up taking them around the world. She died off the Caribbean coast, sporting a sarong, a beautiful tan, and a great big smile on her face.

Actually, that end didn't sound half bad to Fannie. Especially if the man could be Foster Bates.

At that moment, a deep, resounding sigh could be heard throughout the entire bakery. Fannie, as well as the other customers, turned to see where it had come from. The three sisters blushed. Had these lovesick women sighed in concert at the very thought of having their dreams come true?

Fannie noticed the gleam in their eyes. *Oh, yes, they most assuredly had.*

————

After Fannie left the bakery, Charity went to the back room, while Hope and Faith waited on the remaining customers. Her face, neck, and ears felt impossibly hot. Surely it couldn't be that warm inside their store today.

What in the world possessed me to say all those things to Fannie about Foster Bates, and what must she have thought? Charity flopped into a chair at the table. *No doubt Miss Fannie believes I am desperate to find a husband, and she's not wrong.*

Charity's chin dipped down, and her hands curled around her stomach. *I'm so embarrassed. Fannie probably thinks I acted like a schoolgirl with a big crush on the man I've set my kapp for.*

Truthfully, Charity was envious of Fannie Miller. She was a smart, independent woman with many talents. And she was a good friend of Foster Bates. How good, Charity couldn't be certain. But from the look of adoration she'd seen on Fannie's face when Foster's name was mentioned, it was more than a good guess that the quilt lady cared more for Mr. Bates than she was willing to admit. Charity knew for a fact that Miss Fannie and the town's only detective had been seen together many times over the last few weeks, sometimes sitting with their heads together.

Charity rapped her knuckles on the tabletop. *She's got a thing for him, all right, and I wouldn't be surprised if the feeling is mutual. I wonder if the two have talked about marriage. Of course, that would mean Foster would have to give up his English ways and join the Amish church, or Fannie would have to jump the fence, so to speak, and replace her cone-shaped white head covering with a lacy bridal veil.*

A trickle of sweat dripped off Charity's forehead and onto the table. Or was that a tear that had fallen?

She sniffed deeply and wiped her eyes and then her face. *There must be some way I can get Foster's attention—make him see that I would make him a better wife than Fannie ever could. And he wouldn't have to give up his English ways if he married me, since I've chosen to be part of the Mennonite faith, which allows for more modern things and doesn't have so many rules.*

Charity's mind raced with the possibilities. *Instead of fretting about this, what I need to do is come up with a plan that will get Foster's mind off Fannie and onto me.*

She snapped her fingers and sat up straight. *The old saying is, The way to a man's heart is through his stomach. So maybe I'll start by taking some of Foster's favorite cinnamon rolls over to his office. Or if he's not there, I might stop by his house.*

Charity smiled and rose from her seat. *I will even sweeten the deal by taking a special treat for Foster's dog, and I'll go over there as soon as possible, before I lose my nerve.*

Foster was about to call it a day and head straight for home, when his office door opened and Charity Beiler (aka Blustery) stepped inside.

With quick strides she made her way across the room and placed a pastry box on his desk. "I know how much you like the cinnamon rolls from our Three Sisters Bakery, so I made these just for you." Charity's lips parted slightly, then her full mouth graced him with a wide smile.

Caught off guard, Foster hardly knew what to say.

"What a pleasant and unexpected surprise," he finally said. "How much do I owe you, Charity?"

She shook her head vigorously. "Nothing at all, Mr. Bates. These are a gift from me to you." Charity reached inside the tote bag, draped over one shoulder, and withdrew a plastic bag that had been zipped shut. "I also made some special doggie treats for Chief." She handed it to him.

Once again, Foster was speechless. "H–how did you know about Chief?" he stammered.

"Well, for goodness' sake—that's easy." Her eyes lit up with an inner glow. "Almost every time you've visited the bakery, you have made some mention about your dog, Chief."

Foster blinked rapidly and broke eye contact with her. After thinking it through, he had to admit that he did often brag about his dog to whomever would listen. Until now, he hadn't realized that Charity had actually listened to his ramblings or that she would make a treat just for Chief.

"On behalf of my dog, I thank you for this too." Foster pointed his left index finger at the small bag he held in his right hand.

"You are most welcome." She leaned forward with both hands on his desk. "Anytime you want more doggie treats, just say the word. I'd be most happy to accommodate."

Foster offered Charity a nervous smile. If he hadn't known better, he'd think this outgoing Mennonite woman might be flirting with him. She had before, even though it seemed ridiculous. Foster thought he'd given her enough clues that he wasn't interested, so why now?

Then another thought popped into Foster's head. *Could Charity, or one of her sisters, be guilty of leaving those threatening red-envelope notes? Might Charity have come here today with goodies for me and Chief to throw me off track or make me think she's too nice of a woman to be guilty of anything more than spreading rumors with her gossiping tongue?*

Foster cleared his throat a few times and made sure to look directly at Charity with a smile on his face. "I thank you very much for your thoughtfulness, and now, if you'll excuse me, I need to put the CLOSED sign on my front door and be on my way home."

Charity hesitated a few seconds before nodding. "You're more than welcome." She moved slowly toward the door, but after a few steps, she halted and turned back to face him. "Stop by the bakery anytime you like. I'll look forward to hearing if your dog liked the treats. And maybe," she added with a dimpled grin, "I'll have some extra cinnamon rolls to give you, Foster Bates."

Foster thanked her one more time and watched as she sashayed out the door.

He sank back into the chair from which he'd risen. Foster had a sinking feeling Charity had an ulterior motive for her visit. If she ever dropped by unannounced again, Foster hoped he would have the presence of mind to shoot some serious questions at her.

He thumped the top of the pastry box. *And next time I won't be swayed by the desire to eat one of my favorite treats.*

CHAPTER 24

When she was thinking clearly and "of sound mind," as the saying goes, Fannie wondered if Charity might actually be a good match for Foster. After all, Charity was a Mennonite, so she and Foster could date with the community's blessing. And he did love the Three Sisters cinnamon rolls. If he married Charity, he could have a lifetime of cinnamon roll bliss, which would make Charity's shortcomings pale in comparison.

And she was pretty, there was no denying that. In fact, to everyone's curiosity, Charity seemed to be looking younger and younger with each passing year. *Ah, one more unsolvable mystery in the Tuscarawas County area,* Fannie told herself as she tidied things up in the quilt shop, while chuckling a bit at the thought.

Fannie was surprised when Charity's sister Hope showed up at the quilt shop, saying she was in need of a new seam ripper, and since there weren't any other customers in the shop at the time, it afforded them a moment to talk.

"My sister's been using a wrinkle eraser," Hope brazenly revealed, without the slightest bit of guilt in her tone. "I bought it, thinking it'd help keep the wrinkles out of my apron, but apparently, it's for the face." Leaning in a little closer to Fannie, she whispered, "I've heard tell that it can lift sagging skin under the eyes and chin with the strength of a hay lifter!"

"So, *that's* her secret?"

Hope nodded. "She paid me for it, so I didn't have to take it back to the store. But yep, that's her secret!"

Fannie couldn't resist asking another question. "And what about all the weight she's lost? How's she doing that while working at a bakery?"

Fannie couldn't deny the twinge of jealousy she felt. She knew she couldn't date Foster herself, but she liked to think that if circumstances were different, he would be interested in her. But now, with Charity, newly slimmed down and much younger looking, vying for the lead position, she wanted to make sure Foster wasn't being bamboozled by less than honest means.

"The weight?" Hope repeated.

Fannie nodded.

"Oh, it's still there. She just repositions it. It's something called a body shaper."

Fannie's eyes widened. "You mean, like a girdle?"

"Times fifty!" Hope said.

"How does she breathe?"

"She doesn't. She says she's given up that luxury till after she's married."

Fannie couldn't believe her ears, and apparently she could no longer believe her eyes either.

"But isn't a groom going to be disappointed on the honeymoon when he realizes he's married much more of a woman than he'd imagined?" she questioned.

"I don't think my sister has thought that far ahead," Hope said with a shake of her head.

Fannie put both hands against her hips. "Well, I have no desire to squeeze this body into anything other than the bench at our Amish church services! If a man takes an interest in me, it's going to be because he likes my personality and character and because he likes and accepts my looks just the way God made me." She clicked her tongue against the roof of her mouth. "No way am I going to bind myself up like a mummy just to get a man to notice me!"

"I agree," said Hope, as the two women high-fived each other. "Even if she is my sister, I think she's going about this in the wrong way. After all, a lot of men like women with some meat on their bones."

"Or biscuits," Fannie added, and they both broke into a fit of laughter that was cut short only by the arrival of Fannie's quilting circle. The ladies, six of them including Iva, the bishop's wife, met at the quilt shop every Tuesday at five o'clock to work on their quilts, which would later be donated to the Amish and Mennonite auction that supported causes for elderly Plain folk and missionaries. It was a worthy mission, and Fannie had been involved with it for years.

As the group of ladies took their seats around the quilting table, Hope commented on how beautiful the quilt on the table before them was.

The ladies all nodded with smiles on their faces, and then Hope said to Fannie, "I'd better get on home so I can get supper ready. Charity will be joining Faith and me this evening. We take turns cooking the meal every evening, and sometimes Faith and I go to Charity's house for supper." Hope shrugged her shoulders. "But not tonight. This time it's my turn to cook, and I'm planning to fix a delicious stir-fry with rice casserole."

"So you stir-fry it in a pan first, and then put it in a casserole dish?"

"Jah. It doesn't take long to eat it, but the additional cooking makes all the veggies and meat very tender."

"I guess it would." Fannie thanked Hope for stopping by, and after she left the quilt shop, Fannie paused a few minutes to think things through before she joined the ladies to finish their charitable project. *It was Hope's unexpected visit that helped me feel a little better about the situation with Charity and her interest in Foster*, she told herself. *And now I don't have to wonder anymore why Hope's sister has been looking younger and thinner these days.*

Fannie pulled her thoughts aside and took her seat to join the other women who had begun working on the quilt. With each stitch she took, however, Fannie had trouble keeping her mind from wandering back to Foster and the missing persons cases. She thought about all the quilts that surrounded her, including the new quilt they were currently working on. She thought about the hundreds of quilts she had personally sewn over the years and how she had always been able to get each one of those squares of fabric to fit together perfectly. So why couldn't she do the same for a simple baking-contest mystery?

Fannie also thought about Hope, who would be arriving home soon, and wondered if she might possibly find her sister Charity there, writhing on the floor, trying to get out of her body shaper. It was difficult not to laugh out loud, imagining the scene, but she clamped her lips together to keep the giggle rising in her throat from pouring out.

What would these dear ladies think if I started laughing for no apparent reason? Someone would ask me what was so funny, and then I'd either have to make something up or tell them what Hope had told me about Charity. Fannie rubbed the thimble on her index finger against her thumb. *No way could I tell them that—it would be gossiping, and it wouldn't be very Christian.*

Fannie thought about the seam ripper that Hope had just purchased. Wasn't that the fourth one she'd bought within a week? What did Hope Blustery suddenly need with so many seam rippers?

What, indeed?

———

When the quilting circle was over, Fannie said goodbye to the ladies and began to close up her shop. The sun had already set for the evening, and it was time for her to be heading home.

Fannie didn't mind her ride home most evenings. It gave her a chance to greet those she passed on the road and to be alone with her thoughts.

Sometimes, though—like on a night like this when the moon wasn't doing a very good job of lighting up the road and the trees took on an eerie profile, appearing more like mysterious figures stretching out to grab anyone who happened by—the scene frightened her.

Maybe it needed to in order to keep her alert. Because on this particular night, something in the air didn't smell right, and it wasn't the large pile of autumn leaves that she had burned that morning. It was the unmistakable feeling that someone or something was following her.

But when she pedaled her bicycle up the driveway and looked around, she could see nothing out of the ordinary.

When she got off the bike in front of the barn and looked behind her, nothing unusual was there either.

After Fannie pushed the bike into the barn, the wind blew the barn door shut behind her, causing her to scream and jump simultaneously. She looked around but saw nothing there to worry about.

When she walked into her house and lit a lantern, she looked in every room, but nothing was out of the ordinary.

And yet. . .the feeling remained.

Fannie had always enjoyed her independence and, for the most part, liked not having to answer to anyone about how she spent her time. But tonight she wondered if she shouldn't have placed an ad in *The Budget* for a female roommate. Or maybe she should have gotten married long before now. Or perhaps she should have bought that 12-gauge shotgun she had seen at the sporting goods store in downtown Berlin—not that she would have used it.

But wondering about all the things she could have done differently wasn't going to protect her in the least. Tiptoeing to the kitchen area, she grabbed a metal pot from the lower cabinet, along with one of her large metal mixing spoons and banged them together as loud as she could, while making her way through the house, checking behind doors and in closets for whoever might be lurking there.

She found no one, of course. But then, just as she decided to calm down and cook herself a little something to eat with that pot and mixing spoon, there was a knock at the door.

Fannie froze. Wondering who it could be at that time of night, she made her way to the window to look out.

She recognized her elderly neighbor, Helen, standing on her porch, and breathed a sigh of relief.

When Fannie opened the door, the woman quickly poked her head inside and looked around. "You okay, Fannie?" she asked.

"Yes, yes, I'm fine," Fannie said, happy for the familiar company.

"Well, I was out walking my dog and heard a bunch of racket going on over here, so I thought I'd better come over and check on you. You sure you're fine?" she repeated.

Fannie told her she was sure and thanked Helen for coming over in the dark of night to check on her. The sweet lady, who was decades her senior and arthritic, had seemed ready to take on anything that would put Fannie in danger.

Fannie felt a little embarrassed for allowing her own fears to get carried away. After all, Helen lived alone too, and Fannie had never heard her banging on pots and pans in the middle of the night.

But Helen didn't know all the things she knew. Helen didn't know about the missing persons, or the growing list of possible suspects, or the suspicions surrounding her fellow baking contestants.

Sometimes you're better off not being an insider, Fannie told herself. *Anyone could be courageous in oblivion. Even a toothless eighty-year-old widow, who'd probably left her false teeth in a glass at home, had stopped by just to check on her neighbor.*

That kind of courage shamed Fannie enough that she led Helen back to the front door, assuring her that she really was fine. Then, she grabbed a flashlight and stepped outside to watch and make sure that Helen and her dog made it home safely.

Once assured of that, Fannie locked her door and windows and turned in for the night to get whatever sleep she could, faithful pot and mixing spoon beside her. They weren't a husband, but then those kitchen items didn't snore either.

Fannie snuggled into her handmade quilt, closed her eyes, and prayed the words she had memorized from Psalm 91:4. *"He shall cover you with His feathers, and under His wings you shall take refuge; His truth shall be your shield and buckler."*

Fannie repeated the verse that she'd committed to memory. *"He shall cover you with His feathers, and under His wings you shall take refuge."*

She repeated it again, several more times.

And God did exactly that, as Fannie trusted and drifted off.

CHAPTER 25

Monday morning, Fannie had just dropped some letters off at the post office when she spotted Foster's car in the parking lot. It was her day off from working at the quilt shop, and she'd been busy running errands and was ready for a break—and maybe a little adventure as well. She wondered if Foster might be too.

Fannie waited until he got out of his vehicle and started moving toward the building. His slow walk and slumped shoulders revealed a lack of energy.

She approached him with a smile, followed by a cheerful, "Good morning, Foster. How are things going?"

"With our missing persons case or life in general?" he asked with a distant stare.

"Either. Both."

Foster brought his hand up to his forehead and began rubbing his temples. "To tell the truth, neither one is going so well."

He looked tired. Fannie noticed dark circles underneath Foster's eyes, and she asked if he'd been getting enough sleep.

"Not really. It's hard to sleep when I'm thinking about a case that is still unresolved. I lie in bed at night, mulling things over, and nothing comes to me. At least nothing I've been able to prove." Foster yawned. "I think Chief feels it too. He's been restless, and when I pace, he paces right along with me. I'm convinced that my trusty hund feels my despair."

"Know what I think you need, Foster?" Fannie asked.

"What's that?"

"A little outing. Something that might help to take your mind off the baking contest and those missing contestants."

"What would you suggest?"

"Have you heard of the Miller Manor in Walnut Creek?"

His lips parted slightly. "Well, yeah. I think most of the people living in our area know the manor is there, perched on a hill overlooking the Walnut Creek Cheese Store."

"Have you ever been inside it?"

"Nope, but the description on the brochure I was reading a while back about the place made me wish I could take a peek at the inside of that stately looking home." Foster gave his right earlobe a tug. "There's no reason I would ever rent the house just for me, even if I had the money. So it's doubtful that I will have an opportunity to see what the inside looks like."

Fannie gave his shirtsleeve a little tug. "How about now?"

"Huh?" Foster's fingers went from his earlobe to the base of his neck. "That's a nice thought, Fannie, but I don't have a key. And even if I did, I can't just go walking in there like I own the place. On top of that, there are probably people who paid good money staying there right now." He squinted while looking at Fannie. "What made you even bring that topic up?"

She smiled up at him. "Because I have an offer to go there, and the home is vacant today."

Foster blinked a couple of times in succession. "Seriously?"

"Absolutely."

"Do you know the owners? Is that how you got an invitation?"

Fannie shook her head. "I know the housekeeper in charge of the home, though. Her name is Marie, and she's a friend of mine. In fact, Marie has been to my quilt shop many times. I did a favor for her not long ago, and now she wants to do something nice for me in return." Fannie gave Foster's shirtsleeve yet another gentle tug. "So will you go there with me?"

"Of course! And I'd be happy to drive us there." He gestured to the postal building. "First, I need to get some stamps. And I have one other small errand to run. Then I'll be free to go."

"No problem," she said. "I'll take my horse and buggy home, and you can pick me up at my house when you're done."

He gave her a high five. "It's a date! Uh...I mean..."

"That's okay, Foster. I know what you meant."

———

Walnut Creek, Ohio

Foster pulled his car up to the backside of Miller Manor, turned off the engine, and set the brake. He couldn't believe he was actually on this property, let alone about to go inside. And it was all thanks to Miss Fannie and her friend.

He looked over at Fannie sitting in the passenger seat, as prim and proper as ever. "Are you sure your friend is going to meet us here?"

"She said she would, and I wouldn't be surprised if Marie's not already inside."

"Okay then, let's go knock."

Foster was planning to go around and open the car door on Fannie's side, but she was too quick for him and had already gotten out by the time he'd made it halfway around his vehicle.

She smiled up at him as they approached the back door of the manor. "I'm excited. How about you?"

He gave a nod. "Excited and curious. Every time I've driven on the highway below and looked up on the hill where this home sits, I've wondered what it must look like inside."

"Same here." Fannie reached out her hand to knock, but the door swung open before her knuckles made contact.

A tall English woman with dark brown hair and blue-green eyes greeted them. And after Fannie said, "Hello, Marie," she introduced Foster.

He was quick to extend his hand and pleased when Marie told them that while they took a self-guided tour, she would be in the kitchen going through the silverware and dishes, checking for any that might need to be replaced. She added, "When you two come back to the kitchen, if you have any questions, I'll be happy to answer them."

"Thank you," Foster and Fannie said in unison.

"Should we start down here?" Fannie asked Foster after they'd left the kitchen. "Or would you rather go upstairs or down to the floor below us?"

He shrugged. "It doesn't matter to me. Why don't you decide?"

"Okay. Let's begin at the top and work our way down."

When they came to the grand staircase that encompassed both sides of the upper level entry, they chose the left side and Fannie began the climb. Foster brought up the rear. Climbing this many stairs was not something he was used to doing, and he was a bit winded by the time they reached the top.

After Foster paused long enough to catch his breath, he said, "That brochure I read stated that there are two large king bedrooms on this floor, each with an additional queen-size bed. There are also two full-size bathrooms, one of which is shared between one of the king rooms and another bedroom that has two single beds in it." He pulled a hanky from his pants pocket and wiped the moisture on his forehead. "Oh, and there's also a spacious sitting area up here, with a nice bench and balcony access."

Fannie's eyes widened. "Wow, you must have a photographic memory, Foster."

"Not for everything. I just remember certain things that have piqued my interest, like chairs and benches and beds."

Foster and Fannie walked through each of the rooms on the third floor and then made their way back down to the main floor, using the opposite stairs from the set they had gone up.

"What's on this floor for us to see?" Fannie asked Foster. "I bet you remember every detail you read about this section of the home too."

"I might have missed a few details. My brain is like a sponge, but one that's been around for a while." He took a few steps. "Guess we'll find out soon enough."

They moved into the living area, featuring two great rooms. One included a fireplace and a grand piano, and both rooms had chairs and couches. Foster was tempted to try out the piano, just to see how it sounded, but he held himself in check, since he'd never had a piano lesson in his life.

Moving on, he saw that there was also a den with an extensive library, as well as a desk and sofa. He made sure to point these things out to Fannie.

From there, Foster followed Fannie into the primary bedroom, complete with a bathroom suite that included a large tub with jets, a nice walk-in shower, and the biggest walk-in closet Foster had ever laid eyes on. "Why, I could get lost in here and never be able to find my shoes," he commented with a chuckle.

Fannie giggled. "And if I took a bath in that big, deep tub, I might never be able to get back out. Or want to," she added.

Next, they walked out onto the private balcony that featured a beautiful view of the northern valley. Foster inhaled and released his breath slowly. "If I lived here, I'd set up a lounge chair and relax on the balcony for as many hours as possible each day. With Chief lying on the floor beside me, of course," he added with a grin. "Or swimming in the pool."

"There's a pool too?"

"You think they'd build all this and then pass on a pool?" Foster scratched his head. "Well, I think there was something about a pool in the brochure I read. Maybe I'm wrong, though. I do remember there's a tennis court just down the hill from the manor. I could have been thinking of that and not a pool." He chuckled. "Some days I don't know up from down."

"I understand your reasoning," Fannie said with a wistful-sounding sigh. "This would certainly be a great place to kick off my shoes and unwind after a long day at the quilt shop."

"Maybe we'd better go back in and see the rest of the house before we both get too relaxed and start dozing off out here in the hot sun."

"You're right," she agreed. "It is rather warm. With fall just around the corner, hopefully we should have some cooler days soon."

This time, Foster led the way, although he wasn't sure what they should see next. *Maybe the kitchen and dining area*, he thought. As Foster recalled, the brochure he'd picked up had said the kitchen was quite impressive, and they hadn't really taken it all in when they'd talked with Marie before the tour began.

They passed a formal dining room and found Marie, still in the fully equipped kitchen, with all the cupboard doors wide open, along with the drawers that held the silverware. "What do you think so far?" she asked, looking at Fannie.

"The whole house is wonderful, and the view of the valley from the balcony is simply amazing!"

"I agree," Foster said, looking at the central island with stools. There was a casual dining area with table and chairs. Either place to eat looked inviting. If this place was his, he'd probably sit at the table here in the kitchen for most meals. Or maybe the sunroom that the brochure stated had heated floors and private patio access.

"On this main floor, there's also two half baths and a laundry room," Marie said, dispersing Foster's thoughts.

"I understand why people would be inclined to rent this house while they are on vacation," Fannie said.

Marie nodded. "Did you make it down to the lower level yet?" she questioned.

Foster and Fannie both shook their heads.

"Why don't you check it out?" she suggested. "Only, please don't turn on the large screen TV or mess with any of the home theater equipment and other electronic items."

"Oh no," Fannie was quick to say. "We both know better than to do something like that. Besides, I wouldn't have the faintest idea how to turn on any of that fancy equipment. Nor do I have a desire to watch anything that might be on TV."

Foster didn't comment, but truthfully, he thought it might be kind of interesting to see how it all worked. However, his "old school" principles took over, and he discarded any thoughts about home theaters or fancy electronics. *I'd probably mess something up if I did turn anything on,* he reasoned.

"This place is astonishing!" Fannie declared after they'd finished the tour of the lower level that included a large bedroom with a king-size bed and two single beds, as well as a full bath. In addition to the home theater room, they'd seen a ping-pong table, pool table, and a few pieces of exercise equipment.

Foster opened the outside door and took a quick peek. The rear patio he saw featured a gas grill and outdoor furniture with an umbrella for shade. *Another place I would enjoy taking a nap,* he thought.

There was no doubt about it—this home had everything anyone would want or need for a large family or group to rent while visiting Walnut Creek and the surrounding towns.

"I concur about this astonishing place," Foster said. "I can only imagine how much the doctor and his family must have enjoyed living here. How nice it is that even more folks have an opportunity to enjoy it now."

When Fannie and Foster came up from the lower level a short time later, they returned to the kitchen to thank Marie for allowing them to tour the manor.

"Oh, you're very welcome." She offered them a pleasant smile. "I'm glad it worked out so that you could both come by today. Starting tomorrow, this lovely home will be rented out for several weeks to come."

They said their goodbyes and exited the home the same way they'd come in. On the way out, Foster mentioned the four-car garage. "I wonder if the family who lived here actually owned four cars."

"Maybe so," Fannie replied. "A big garage like this would be helpful when entertaining guests as well."

When they got into Foster's car, Fannie turned to Foster and said, "Did touring the Miller Manor help to take your mind off the missing persons case we've been trying to solve?"

"Yeah," he replied. "For a little while, at least. But now I'm trying to figure out how many extra jobs I'll have to take to even spend one night there."

"It would have to be a very special occasion to rent something like that. Like a graduation, reunion, or honeymoon."

Fannie couldn't believe she'd said that and quickly changed the subject.

"Would you like to go somewhere for a bite to eat before you take me home?" Fannie asked.

"That sounds nice, but I need to be somewhere this afternoon."

"Oh, okay. . .I understand." Fannie couldn't help feeling a bit disappointed. She'd had such a good time looking at the beautiful manor with Foster and wished their time together didn't have to end so soon. *But Foster has things to do,* she reminded herself. *And I had planned to make some more posters today. The ones I had put up before, letting people in Sugarcreek and the surrounding towns know that there are some missing persons who need to be found are probably gone now or tattered and need to be replaced.*

CHAPTER 26

Sugarcreek

Even though his partner in crime solving disagreed with his assessment of the Blustery Sisters' involvement in the disappearances they'd been investigating, a nagging voice remained in the back of Foster's head that would not let him rule them out. No matter how hard he tried to ignore the gnawing suspicion, that voice kept repeating, "They did it! They did it!"

It wasn't that he had any solid evidence or that he had uncovered some kind of double life that the women were leading. It was just a constant dripping of those ominous words playing in his ear, "They did it!"

He had to override Fannie on this. These three women were the culprits—he just knew it. That's why he had stopped in at Faith and Hope's house, just to see if he could trip them up. Sometimes people would loosen up when they were in familiar surroundings, and that's what Foster was counting on.

Foster figured he would ask them a few more questions just to see if they changed any of their answers, and he could also study their demeanor.

Faith was the only sister at home, however, but that was fine with Foster. Separate the suspects and one might rat out the other. That was a lesson Foster had learned many times over while on the police force. Stepping into their home, that voice warned him that he was, in fact, talking to the culprit. It was hard to ignore such clarity and urgency.

"Why, Foster Bates. You're making house calls now?" Faith asked, her smile exhibiting much more friendliness than he believed they had between them.

"Hello, Miss Faith. Sorry for stopping by with no advance notice, but I was in the neighborhood and wanted to ask you a few additional questions, if you don't mind."

"Not at all, Detective. But did you want to wait until my sister Hope gets home?"

"I really just need to talk to you."

"Oh?" she said, as her eyebrows rose. "In that case, may I offer you a chair?"

Foster thanked her and took the hand-hewn rocker positioned across from her.

"I don't really know any more than I've already told you, Mr. Bates," Faith began. "But I'm happy to help you out in any way I can."

"Good. And I shall try to make this as painless and brief as possible. Now then," he continued, taking a pen and small notepad out of his shirt pocket. "Expand on your thoughts about Dorothy Dexter."

"What do you mean?"

"Well, you said you had never met her before the contest. Do you still stand by that statement?"

"Why wouldn't I? It's the truth."

"She's lying!" Foster heard it as clear as day. He pressed on.

"You never met her before in your life?"

"Nope."

She did it! She's lying!

The voice was so loud, Foster wondered if Faith might've heard it herself. *I'm sure she didn't,* he reminded himself and went on.

"Did you think you and your sisters would have a better chance of winning the contest if Dorothy Dexter was out of the way?"

"Of course not!" Faith looked down while she spoke. Foster figured she was probably insulted by the question he'd asked.

Yet the voice urged him on. *Yes, she did! She did indeed.*

Foster wrote down her answer, as well as noting the admonishment his internal radar was clearly sending him. He'd share these notes later with Fannie. *This will convince her once and for all of the Blustery Sisters' involvement. Fannie could be headstrong at times, but she understood intuition and knew how loudly it could holler into your ear when you're hot on the trail of a perpetrator.*

Today, it was the loudest he'd ever heard as he asked Faith a few new questions.

Foster was getting more than he expected. Since neither Hope nor Charity were around, Faith seemed less guarded and open to answering his questions and getting trapped in her lies.

In his previous interviews, the three sisters usually tended to stick together, covering one another's tracks. But getting to interview Faith alone was proving to be most profitable.

After about twenty minutes, Foster decided he had gone about as far as he could go with his questioning, at least for the time being. He had plenty to share with Fannie about the encounter. She would know exactly what to do. To a crime solver, instincts were everything, and even though Fannie's instincts had been telling her that none of the Blustery Sisters were the perpetrators, Foster's instincts were unabashedly screaming their guilt at him.

Once I tell Fannie all about this, she will come over to my way of thinking, he reasoned.

———

"I heard it, Fannie," Foster announced when he dropped by Fannie's house after he'd left Faith and Hope's home. "Yes, indeed, I heard it as clearly as you're hearing me right now. Every time Faith answered one of my questions, there it was, right in my ear saying, "She did it! She did it!"

Fannie tilted her head in a doubtful-looking gesture.

"I'm telling you, Fannie, I couldn't shut it off. My gut knows one of them, if not all three, is involved. I'm going to have to override you on this and go with my gut."

Fannie paced a few steps, and Foster wondered if she was trying to assess their opposing views. Was she wondering why her instinct should step aside for his?

"Shouldn't both of us trust our instincts until the truth is uncovered?" Foster questioned.

"I realize you've had a lot more experience at sniffing out perps than I have," she said. "But you have to admit that my instincts have been proven right a time or two, as well."

Foster had to agree. "But I've solved far more cases than you."

"I've read more mystery books."

"I've got the trench coat and hat."

"I've got my kapp."

"So in other words, we're at an impasse?"

"It would seem so, yes. . .unless. . ."

Fannie's eyes widened and she broke into a fit of laughter.

"What's so funny?" Foster asked, a bit perturbed with her flippantness at such a serious case-cracking moment.

"Foster, my friend, I believe you just met Peggy."

"Peggy?" Foster mentally ran through their list of suspects. There wasn't a Peggy among them. Had his crime-solving partner been holding out on him? Had she uncovered a new suspect she hadn't told him about yet?

"Who's Peggy?" he asked.

"The Blustery Sisters' pet parrot. It sounds to me like she's been overhearing some of their discussions and is now repeating it all and implicating *them*."

"They have a parrot?"

"Yes! That voice wasn't coming from your head, Foster! It was coming from Peggy's cage!"

Foster's shoulders dropped like a bale of hay falling from a loft in the barn. He had been so close to solving the mystery with his laser-focused instincts. But to his chagrin, that had all flown the coop now.

Poor me, he thought. *Now it's back to square one.*

CHAPTER 27

Foster was out of leads and dangerously close to running out of hope.

What's wrong with me? he asked himself over and over as he paced the floor in his office. The baking contest seemed to be progressing a little better than Foster and Fannie's investigation. Contestants were still unaccounted for, and the detective duo were still a long way off from announcing they'd found the culprit behind all the mayhem.

I've solved tougher cases than this! What am I missing?

Indeed, Foster had solved plenty of tougher cases. Throughout his career he had brought drug dealers, carjackers, gang members, and even murderers to justice. Why couldn't he solve a simple baking-contest mystery?

But that was then. This is now. I'm not as sharp as I used to be, he reminded himself. *Or as tough in a fight. Or as fast in a chase. Most of the time, I'm just going through the motions. Too tired, too old, and too technologically outdated.*

Foster was still using his old flip phone. Fannie broke into a fit of laughter when she'd seen it, telling him that even most Amish wouldn't carry one of those if they were allowed to carry a cell.

"Sergeant Foster Bates," Foster said aloud, even though no one was around to hear it. "The decorated Chicago cop who solved major crimes and trained recruits to follow in his footsteps. Where'd that guy go?"

"He gave up," Foster mumbled as his arms hung loosely at his sides.

"But what do you expect? I was stuck in a thankless job that had taken the lives of too many of my buddies and policewomen too. So, I surrendered my badge because it's a losing battle. We get cursed at, spit at, and shot at. And all for what? For people who don't think they need us, and for a paycheck that keeps shrinking?"

I'm glad I left the department. I got out while the getting was good.

———

Fannie closed her quilt shop for the night and rode her bike home by way of Foster's office. She could have taken a shorter route, but she wouldn't have been able to see if Foster was still working. To her delight, his car was parked out front, and a light was still on inside the building.

She parked her bicycle, making sure to lock it in the bike rack that Foster had also set up out front for the convenience of his Amish clients, and made her way inside.

Seeing Foster standing near his desk, Fannie strode right up to him and asked, "Why am I not surprised to find you here still working?" She smiled, admiring her detective partner's dedication. "So anything new?"

"Nothing worth the sleep I'm losing," Foster muttered. "In fact, I was just thinking of shutting down."

"It is after ten o'clock. You should probably call it a night and go home and get some rest."

"I meant shutting down for good."

Fannie was tired, but that quickly gained her attention. "You can't quit," she protested.

"Why not? What good am I doing anybody? Former contestants are still missing, and I don't have a clue where they are."

"That's why you've got to keep going until you solve this case."

"Fannie," Foster said. "The whole town is mocking me. I've heard them laugh behind my back, doubting if I ever was a policeman."

"You've got a badge and a retirement check to prove that." She briefly touched his arm. "Come on, no one's laughing at you. Don't you think you're acting a little paranoid?"

He groaned while crossing his arms. "Sometimes it comes in handy."

Fannie had her work cut out for her. Foster needed a serious dose of encouragement, but would he even listen to her? Fannie wasn't sure, but she had to try.

What did one say to a man who was doubting his own purpose? And from everything Foster was saying tonight, she knew that was exactly what he was doing.

"I don't get it, Fannie. Why can't I make the pieces fit?" Foster's words were rushed as he uncrossed his arms and held them behind his back. "What happened to my police instinct—my sixth sense for finding the bad guys—my nose for sniffing out foul play?"

"None of us are as good as we used to be. You should see my latest quilt," Fannie said, trying to lighten the mood.

"I've aged out of the game, Fannie."

She heard the tension in his voice and was on the verge of saying more, when he spoke again.

"I can't pretend anymore. Criminals are slipping through my fingers like my nighttime muscle ointment, and I can't do a thing about it."

"Maybe some of your physical strength has diminished, but this case doesn't call for you being strong physically. Your brain and your instinct are what are needed to solve this case, and if you ask me, those are in perfect working order. Why, look at all the contestants you've already found, the suspects you've ruled out, myself included. And if the situation ever changes and requires more of your brawn than your brain, there's no doubt in my mind that it'll be there. The speed, the agility, the strength—they'll all be there for you at the very moment you need it."

"I wish I had your confidence," Foster said.

Fannie stayed a while longer just to make sure Foster was in a better mood. At around ten thirty, she told him she'd keep him in her prayers and headed for home. Fannie was worried about her friend. She had never seen him that low before. But checking in on him and praying for him was about all she could do to help matters. The rest was up to God.

A good night's sleep was what Foster needed all right, because the following morning, he was back on the case with as much determination as ever. Which was a good thing, since there was a ruckus going on at the Three Sisters Bakery.

By the time word of it reached Foster and he was able to drive over there, the fray was going full throttle. Several police cruisers were already there, the blue lights on their light bars swirling.

"There she is! That woman right there! She's the one who said it!"

The elderly English woman standing beside one of the officers pointed directly at Hope.

"You're sure she's the one?" the policeman asked.

"Yes, Officer, I'm positive. I was standing in the checkout line, getting a custard-filled doughnut like I do every morning, and I heard her say it as clearly as I hear you right now."

Hope stood near the pastry case with eyes wide. Foster couldn't help wondering what she must be thinking. If she was guilty, would she admit it and apologize?

The other customers in the bakery stopped whatever they were doing and tipped their heads. No doubt they wanted to hear the details. Something big was going down, and Foster was sure they didn't want to miss a thing.

"Now tell me again what the lady allegedly said," the officer prompted.

"There's no 'allegedly' about it. I heard that woman right over there say, 'I wish I could make the other contestants in the contest disappear.'"

"I see."

The officer wrote down a few notes, and Foster stepped forward.

"Excuse me, Officer. Would it be okay if I questioned the witness? I'm Foster Bates, private investigator." He flashed his identification. "I'm working the missing contestants case."

"Mr. Bates, I've heard a lot about you," the young officer said. "Please, go right ahead."

Foster turned to face the elderly woman. "Are those the exact words you heard? You're sure of it?"

"Not a doubt in my mind," the woman said, with the confidence of someone who'd already taken an oath to tell the truth, the whole truth, and nothing but the truth. "And since the Three Sisters Bakery would benefit from less competition, I'd say that woman is a prime suspect."

"So what if I do want to win this contest at any cost?" Hope said, bypassing all good sense to wait until she'd thought through the weight of her words. "And so what if I had the motive and the means to do something that would ensure our win? Sometimes in life one has to take matters into their own hands and..."

Hope blinked rapidly, and the skin around her eyes tightened as she looked around to see the other customers looking in her direction. Then she gave a nervous laugh when the policeman hovered his hand over his handcuffs.

"That's almost as good as a confession," the officer said.

"Officer, please, I can explain." Hope spoke with an emotion-choked tone. "You see, my sisters and I say a lot of things. But we don't mean anything by it. And I can assure you that I wasn't saying I hoped they'd actually disappear. I just meant I hoped they would drop out of the contest. My sisters will fully vouch for me."

Hope looked around the bakery, but her sisters were nowhere in sight.

"Well, they were here just a minute ago," she said, trying to buy herself a little more time. But the policeman continued, "Sorry, ma'am, but I'm going to have to ask you to come down to the station with me."

"But Officer," Hope pleaded. "You have to believe me. I had nothing whatsoever to do with whatever happened to the other contestants!"

Hope knew that many in the crowd, faithful customers all, had also been hurt by the sisters' gossip over the years. So she wasn't surprised when they suddenly got caught up in the moment and started chanting, "Lock her up! Lock her up!"

The policeman, a victim of their gossip himself, gave his regrets for what he was going to have to do.

"Sorry, Miss Hope," he said, taking Hope's arm and leading her away. "But you'll need to come with me down to the station for further questioning."

"I'm telling you, you've got the wrong person!" Her mouth went dry, and she looked at Foster, hoping he would intervene on her behalf. But the detective just stood there with furrowed brows.

Does Foster think I'm guilty too?

"We've got your quote, that's what we've got, Miss Hope. A witness clearly heard you."

"That wasn't a confession!" Hope shouted. "I was just shooting off my mouth. Ask anyone in town. I always shoot off my mouth. It—it's my gift."

"You can tell it all to the judge." The policeman gestured to Hope, then pointed to the door. "Now come on. Let's go."

Frustration beyond anything she'd ever felt welled in her soul, and

Hope decided then and there that she would not go peacefully.

There were flailing of the arms and kicking of the legs, as well as repeated demands that they call the bishop, who, she said, would be more than happy to vouch for her.

When Foster stepped forward and took hold of Hope's arm, escorting her out the door, she was shocked to see that the bishop was outside holding the door of the Sugarcreek Township Police car open for her.

As the police car drove off, Hope saw Faith and Charity standing in front of the bakery front window, slowly shaking their heads. Hope knew that this time, they were really getting a big lesson in why the Bible gives so many warnings about the tongue, like the words of James 3:8: "No man can tame the tongue. It is an unruly evil, full of deadly poison."

Her words hadn't felt like poison when she spoke them, but looking out the window of that police car with a drizzly rain coming down and seeing its flashing lights swirl round and round, she knew that each word she had spoken that day and had spoken so many times prior had indeed been laced with the most potent poison of all. And now she herself was tasting it.

———

Foster Bates followed the police to the station to see what more he could learn. Since he already had a connection with the case and as a demonstration of professional courtesy, he was allowed to sit in on the initial interrogation with Hope. But even though Hope had indeed said that she wished the other contestants would disappear, it was determined that those words alone didn't provide enough evidence to hold her.

After being questioned for almost an hour, Hope was released with a warning to "not go on any sudden trips." More investigation would need to be done, and Hope was still considered a person of interest.

CHAPTER 28

Foster gathered the item he needed, tucked it in his jacket pocket, and drove to the Amish blacksmith around the block from Fannie's Quilt Shop. He didn't know why he hadn't thought of the blacksmith before now, since he'd driven past his shop almost every week.

He was hoping the Amish man, who was obviously skilled at welding things back together, could reattach the pin to the back of his police badge. It had broken years ago, but Foster had never taken the time to have it fixed. But today, it was going to get done, one way or the other.

"Good morning," the blacksmith said when Foster exited his car and approached him. "Name's Isaiah. What can I help you with?"

"Morning, Isaiah," Foster said. "I am Foster. Foster Bates."

"The private investigator?"

"That's right. You've heard of me?"

Isaiah gave a nod. "Fannie Miller stopped by with some posters about the missing contestants. But now, if you are thinking I was involved in any way, I assure you my hands are clean." The elderly man looked down at his fire-blackened hands. "Well, you know what I mean."

"Don't worry," Foster assured him. "You are not a suspect. And I am not here on official business. I was hoping you could help me fix this. . ."

Foster reached into his pocket and pulled out his police badge and handed it to him, followed by the detached pin.

Isaiah looked over both pieces. "You got a story behind this?" he questioned.

"Broke it in a street scuffle with a thug who didn't want to go where I was taking him."

"No other injuries?"

"Only to my pride. I retired a few weeks later. Getting too old for that kind of nonsense."

"One loss convinced you to quit?"

"One? Goodness, no. I have been in dozens if not hundreds of scuffles. Won some and lost some. And I have the scars to prove it."

"So what was different about this last one that made you call it quits?"

Foster thought about his response before answering. "Well," he said, choosing his words carefully, "usually my adrenaline is running so high I don't even feel the kicks and hits. But that time I did. I felt every one of them, and it slowed down my reflexes. For a cop, that could get you killed. So I knew my policing days were over."

"Our bodies tell us when it's time to retire, don't they? My hands have been trying to get my attention for years, but I've been ignoring their advice."

Foster nodded empathetically and watched as Isaiah heated up his tools and began to work on the badge.

"So how many years did you serve?"

"Twenty years, four months, one week, two days, and thirteen hours."

"Not that you were keeping score, huh?"

"Oh, I was definitely keeping score. Didn't want to stay one minute longer than I had to. There'd been too many changes over the years. It's best to leave it to the young kids to handle them now."

Isaiah looked up from his work and nodded. "I hear you, but unfortunately, I don't have that option. What I do is a dying art. Not a lot of the youth have taken it up. Guess it's just not exciting enough. These days I mostly make shoes for horses."

"Well, if I ever get a horse, I'll know where to come." Foster chuckled.

"A horse would save you a lot of money on gas."

"It's tempting, believe me," Foster said.

"You ought to go over to the horse auction and get yourself one," Isaiah said in an almost coaxing tone.

"I did go, and they sure had some beautiful ones over there."

Isaiah nodded, then he pressed Foster's badge pin against the back of his badge and secured it using his red-hot welding iron. When it had adhered and cooled down, he rubbed a cloth over it to take off the smoke and ashes and bring back the shine.

"Here you go," Isaiah said, handing the badge back to Foster. "Good as new."

Foster nodded approvingly. "Beautiful," he said. "Looks like it did on the first day I pinned it on my uniform. So what do I owe you?"

"It's on me. Consider it my thanks for all you did and will continue to do to keep us all safe."

Foster smiled and tipped his hat to him. He hadn't expected such kind words. But it sure did feel good.

———

"Well, it's long overdue," Fannie said when Foster stopped in at her quilt shop afterward to show off Isaiah's handiwork.

"I'd say he did a great job," Foster said. "It looks brand new. I can't believe I waited so long to get it fixed. Something I wore nearly every day for twenty years. I should have gone to see the blacksmith sooner."

"Well, the important thing is that it's fixed now. Foster, always remember that your past is your foundation. If you lose everything you've learned from the past, what will today and tomorrow have to stand on?"

Foster knew Fannie was right. His time on the force was something to be proud of, and it had shaped him to become the man he was now. The man who might even buy a horse one day and work the land. Only time would tell.

"And now that this badge has been properly repaired, I can move on," he said with renewed confidence.

"To solve this case once and for all?"

"No doubt in my mind."

Fannie smiled. "Or mine, either."

CHAPTER 29

Fannie took in a deep breath when she saw Michael entering her quilt shop the following morning. He had come off rather testy in their previous encounter, and she wasn't sure what to expect when it was just the two of them. "Michael! I'm surprised to see you. What brings you to Fannie's Quilt Shop today?"

Michael greeted her with an unexpected smile then said, "Well, I'm hoping you can help me, Miss Fannie. You see, our anniversary is coming up, and in the past, I've sure gotten into trouble when I've forgotten the date."

"I should think so," Fannie said, unable to resist.

"I'm a slow learner, I guess," Michael confessed, "But I was hoping I could find an Amish-made quilt with a heart, or something like that, to buy for her this year. I've got some leftover money from selling some sports equipment. I'm guessing it will be enough."

"Well, I think Melissa would absolutely love a gift like that, Michael," Fannie said. "I could even embroider your names on it, if you'd like."

"You could do that?"

"It's no bother at all," Fannie said as she walked him over to a rack of hanging quilts. "I'd suggest one with the double hearts, but I'm certain the perfect quilt is in here just waiting to go home with you. Take a look and let me know if you need any help."

Michael scooted the quilts along the rack, stopping at every double-hearted one. But then, he noticed something a bit out of the ordinary.

"Excuse me, Fannie," he said. "These all seem to have names already embroidered on them." His shoulders drooped.

"Yes, I know. That's why they're marked down. Sometimes you can get lucky and find the right two names."

"So are you saying they're used?"

Fannie shook her head. "No, brand new. They were ordered but just never picked up."

Michael nodded. "Oh, I see. They were gifts for weddings that never happened?"

"Yes, and anniversaries never celebrated. They're beautiful, aren't they? But here they sit. Apparently, more work went into ordering the quilt than into the marriage. So these lovely creations end up here on the clearance rack." Fannie pulled out a few samples and read the names. "Randy and Sarah. . .David and Annette. . .Steve and Monica."

"That's sad." Michael dropped his gaze to the floor.

"It is indeed. These quilts will last for generations. But the couples for whom they were made couldn't make it past the order form. . . ." Fannie's voice trailed off as she gestured to the quilts. "Well, feel free to look through them. Maybe you'll find your names. But if you don't, you can always have your names added." She stepped aside to give him a chance to look at his leisure.

***

Michael thanked Fannie for the help and continued to look through the quilts. He knew Melissa would love a genuine Amish-made quilt. He also knew it had been a while since they had exchanged any kind of anniversary gifts. They usually just ordered takeout and exchanged the television remote between them.

But this year the occasion seemed to warrant more effort. After all, it was their tenth. He knew that he truly did love Melissa and told himself that she loved him. But work, friends, night classes, book clubs, and other responsibilities and activities had encroached on their "couple" time. They'd grown cold toward each other. Maybe this Amish quilt was just the thing they needed to warm things up.

After looking through the entire rack and several others, Michael approached Fannie again.

"I'll take one of the king-size quilts with the double hearts," he said. "And if you're sure it's not too much trouble, would you embroider 'Michael' in one heart and 'Melissa' in the other?"

"Sure thing." Fannie gathered her embroidery thread. "I'll have it ready for you in a bit. I just know Melissa is going to love it!"

"I hope so," Michael said. "Maybe it'll remind us that sometimes we need to put our marriage at the front of the line."

———

Just then, the bell rang, announcing a new customer. Fannie looked up to see that Foster had entered her shop.

"Well, look who's here!" she said. "Foster Bates, what brings you into my quilt shop?"

"Hello, Miss Fannie," he said and glanced in Michael's direction. "Hello, Michael."

"Hello, Mr. Bates." Michael offered Foster a flash of a smile, but it didn't quite reach his eyes.

As far as Fannie knew, Michael only knew Foster in his official capacity as a private investigator, so she wondered if his guard might be up a bit.

"Michael's here buying an anniversary quilt for his wife," Fannie explained.

"I'm sure she'll be pleased." Foster moved closer to where Michael stood. "How many years?"

"It's our tenth. Two of them good." Michael laughed and said it was a joke. Then he admitted that there was a lot of truth in the statement.

Foster seemed compelled to offer some encouragement to the confused and obviously hurting young man. "Marriage isn't easy," he said. "Life can throw a lot of things at you that you never expected. You've just got to pick up the pieces and do your best to keep going."

"Yeah." Michael gave a brief nod.

It didn't take Fannie very long to embroider the two names onto the quilt, and Michael seemed quite pleased with the result.

"Would you like me to gift wrap it for you?" she offered.

"Thanks, but I've taken up enough of your time as it is," Michael said.

"It won't even take me five minutes." Fannie started the process before Michael could leave.

Foster told Fannie he'd wait outside until she finished up with her customer. He whispered that he wanted to give the two some space, should Fannie want to talk to him privately, which of course she appreciated.

"So, tell me, Michael, if you win the baking contest, do you still plan to use the money to adopt a baby?"

"Yes, we sure do. Although," Michael said, "there's no way on earth we're winning this thing. But. . .if by some fluke we *were* to win, we're in total agreement."

—————

When Michael walked out of the quilt shop, wrapped gift in hand, Foster nodded and said, "Good luck in the contest, Michael."

"Thanks."

"And happy anniversary," Foster said. "Enjoy your quilt."

Michael nodded and started to get into his parked car.

"It's worth it," Foster called.

"Yeah. It was a little more than I had to spend, but Fannie volunteered to embroider our names on it without charging me extra. I think Melissa will love the way the quilt will look on our king-size bed."

Foster moved toward Michael's car. "I was referring to your marriage. It's worth saving."

"I know. Sometimes we make it harder than it needs to be. We argue a lot. Especially over finances. I just hope she doesn't get mad that I spent this much today."

"I'd say it was money well spent. Look, Michael, everybody's been where you're at. My wife and I were broke plenty of times. Trying to make ends meet on a cop's salary. You haven't lived till you've gone sofa diving to find enough change to buy milk for your kid."

"Melissa and I don't have any children," Michael said.

"Decided to wait, huh?"

"Life decided for us. But we've accepted it. It's just one more thing we've failed at."

Foster wanted to continue their conversation, but Michael got into his car and drove away.

When Foster walked back into the quilt shop, he told Fannie of his exchange with Michael and how concerned he was for the young couple. She filled him in on all the miscarriages that Melissa had suffered and their deep desire to become parents. Foster's heart went out to the couple even more.

Fannie also let him know her plans for the following day.

"Would you like to ride with me over to Charm tomorrow?" she asked.

Foster quirked an eyebrow. "What's going on in Charm?"

"The horse auction. Have you ever been?"

"Not to the one in Charm. You in the market for another buggy horse? Patches can't cut it anymore?"

"Well, he is getting up in years."

"I know the feeling," Foster laughed. "Sure, I'll go. I can get some more cinnamon rolls before we leave town, and we can discuss the case on our way over there. When are we leaving?"

"An hour past coffee."

"Nine o'clock. I'll be waiting by my office door."

Nine o'clock was a bit late for Fannie, but she had acquiesced. She knew Foster would be in a better mood with enough sleep and coffee in him. So at nine o'clock exactly, Fannie pulled up in front of the Foster Bates Private Detective Agency.

Foster took a few minutes to leave his office and secure the deadbolt lock behind him. But soon they were off, warm cinnamon rolls in hand, heading to Charm, the little town that definitely lived up to its name. Fannie hoped he would enjoy the day.

Charm, Ohio

The Charm horse auction always drew a good crowd, and Fannie had a bit of trouble locating an empty hitching rail to park her buggy. But she finally did, and the two began making their way to the auction area, which wasn't hard to find considering the mesmerizing melody of the auctioneer.

"Now, that's one good-looking horse," Foster said as he and Fannie took their seats around the auction arena. Indeed, the horse currently up for auction was turning heads as the aggressive bidding began.

"Even so," Fannie said, "when you're looking for a new horse, you need to look beyond appearance. You have to consider temperament, strength, adaptability to circumstances, and obedience."

Sitting there watching the Amish, Mennonite, and tourists bid on the various horses was intriguing to Foster, and it gave him a good education on the process.

Foster enjoyed the rapid cadence of the auctioneer. Fannie explained that some of them had begun training while still children. She stated that some even went to auctioneer school to refine their skills.

"How in the world can they talk that fast?" Foster asked. "It doesn't seem possible."

"Obviously, you've never seen the Blustery Sisters going full throttle."

Foster laughed, along with Fannie, and he continued to sit back and enjoy the "Amish rap" concert, as Fannie, a huge fan of auctioneers, called it.

Jeb, the bishop's son, was sitting a few rows in front of them. When Fannie noticed him, she called out his name, but the young man didn't turn around. "He probably didn't hear you over the auctioneer," Foster said.

"Perhaps," Fannie said. "Before we leave, I'd like to talk to him."

"About the case?"

"What else?"

When Fannie said she'd finally seen a horse she liked, she signaled her bid at six hundred dollars, and then things got really interesting. Two or three others entered their offers, and it became a battle of the pocketbook.

Six hundred, twenty-five, fifty, seventy-five, seven hundred. . . Who was going to blink first?

Even Foster bid on the horse, just to wear out the other bidders and increase Fannie's chances of getting him. But when it came down to just he and Fannie bidding against each other, he quit and let her take the lead and the win.

Fannie paid for the horse from money she had been saving and arranged for its delivery to her home. As for her former buggy horse, she'd told Foster that the faithful animal would now be retired from the road and put to work elsewhere on her property.

As they made their way back to Fannie's buggy, they passed by several venders selling a variety of goods. One item caught Foster's eye. It was a black felt Amish hat. He made the purchase outside of Fannie's view and waited until he could put it on without Fannie seeing him.

When Fannie looked Foster's way, she saw him walking toward her. *Now, where's that fine-looking Amish man been hiding all my life?* she thought.

She couldn't help blushing when she realized it was Foster. She had never seen him looking so ruggedly handsome before, and she forever captured the sight in the camera of her mind.

"It looks good on you," she said when she realized he'd caught her staring at him.

"Does it fit me?" he asked.

"Oh, yes," Fannie gushed. "It's a perfect fit."

For Fannie, the words held deeper meaning. She always thought Foster would make a good farmer and would fit right in with the Amish life. But Fannie didn't go there. Not yet. Maybe never.

But where she wasn't going to go, Foster was apparently already there.

"I could see myself working a farm," he said. "If my body didn't have so many miles on it. Just don't have the energy for it these days."

"What if you had someone helping you with it?"

"Like a farm hand?" Foster asked.

"Or someone like that. Someone who knew their way around farm tools and horses. Then you wouldn't have to do it all alone."

"That does make it a little more doable," he said, pointing to the top of his head. "But tell me the truth. You really do like the hat?"

Fannie smiled. "I really do like the hat."

After spending the day at the auction, Fannie and Foster had dinner at the Italian Nights restaurant that had just opened in Charm. Over a delicious meal of chicken marsala, they discussed the case a little more, and then Fannie shifted the conversation in a more serious direction.

"How often do you think about that terrible night?" she asked.

"Which terrible night?" Foster asked, avoiding the obvious. "I've had plenty of nights in my life that I wouldn't want to relive."

"The night you got the news about your wife and son losing their lives."

There it was. Fannie put it right out there. That was one thing about Fannie Miller that Foster truly loved. She went right to the heart of a matter, even if this time it happened to be *his* heart.

He knew Fannie's intentions were absolutely pure. She truly cared, and so she deserved the truth.

"I think about that night all the time," Foster said. "When I'm lying in bed, or eating breakfast, or out on the lake fishing. I think about that night when I look at the calendar and realize it's another anniversary of that terrible day. So yeah, it's pretty much always in my mind."

"Have you talked to God about it?"

"A lot. . .especially when it first happened. I asked Him, Why us? Why my family?"

"And. . .?"

"Silence. Only silence. It makes me wonder if there even is a . . ."

Foster didn't go on, and a moment passed before Fannie asked, "Do you have a Bible, Foster?"

"I have hers. It's packed away in a box of her things."

"She'd probably want you to take it out and read it, don't you think?" Fannie asked with a smile that offered him encouragement.

"She read it every night," Foster said. "I don't think she ever missed."

"It must have been important to her." Fannie placed a gentle hand on his arm. "Foster. . .the Bible is how God talks to us. As a friend, I would encourage you to look for your answers in God's Word. I read mine every morning before I start my day. It helps me see things in a different light. And it reminds me how much I'm loved. . .no matter what I happen to be feeling at the moment."

"Well of course that works for you. You're Fannie Miller. Who doesn't love you?"

"We all have our days when we feel unworthy of anyone's love, or we feel forgotten and lonely, wondering if we matter to anyone. But then the Bible reminds me that God's love is eternal, unfailing, and unconditional. He loves you too, Mr. Foster Bates."

"I'm a hard man to love, so I've been told over the years. Maybe I'm the exception."

"There are no exceptions," Fannie said. "Loving any of us isn't an easy thing to do. That's why it cost Him His life."

Foster paused a moment to let Fannie's words sink in. "So you don't think I'm hopeless?"

"You are not hopeless, Foster Bates," Fannie said with a note of conviction. "And you are absolutely worthy of love."

Her words felt good to Foster's parched soul. He wanted to thank her, let her know what her friendship had meant to him over the years too. Instead, he opted for, "Tiramisu?"

"Absolutely!" Fannie pulled back her hand and nodded. "I hear they make the best in all of Ohio."

CHAPTER 30

In a tourist community, which both Tuscarawas and Holmes Counties were considered, crime was often committed by strangers passing through. These cases were harder to solve because the perpetrator could check into a hotel, do their dastardly deed, and then check out and leave the area, never to be seen again.

In that kind of a scenario, the perp could hide out anywhere—any city, any state, any country. Foster was well aware of this phenomenon, and the thought of a drifter slipping into their quaint and safe Amish community, simply to disrupt a harmless baking contest, had unsettled him to no end.

It was one thing for such an occurrence to happen in Chicago. Crime could be expected in the big cities. But this was happening where it shouldn't have been happening. The draw of this particular tourist area was its serenity and peace. If people wanted to visit scenes of a crime, get into the mind of a criminal, and learn about their victims, there were plenty of places to do that. London had its Jack the Ripper tours, Chicago had its mob museum. Other big cities offered "after dark" crime tours. There were also tours that a person could take at various police museums across America or at FBI headquarters or even Scotland Yard and Alcatraz.

If the Wild West crimes were of more interest to a person, they could time travel back to the cowboy towns of yesteryear and visit areas where Jesse James did his string of bank robberies or follow Billy the Kid's trail. They could even follow Bonnie and Clyde's path, the Boston strangler, or the Manson family.

What tourists would never see was a brochure for a tour of Amish Country's most notorious criminals. That was not to say there hadn't been some notable crimes. It was just not an everyday occurrence. Folks didn't normally read headlines about kidnappings, bank robberies, mob takeovers, and such in Amish Country.

Headlines usually covered upcoming farm tool and horse auctions, buggy races, flea markets, and bake sales. That was what this community Foster loved so well was all about.

But tourists did visit it. A lot of tourists. And they were from all over the world. So on any given day there was no telling who was staying in their hotels, shopping at their stores, or eating at their restaurants.

Sure, Foster thought as he drummed his pencil against the desktop, *you might have a name on the credit card charges or hotel registrations, but who's to say that was even legit?*

So Foster had his work cut out for him. If he had learned anything working the Chicago crime scenes, it was that nothing could be taken at face value. Just because someone's car license was from Wisconsin didn't mean that they were from Wisconsin. The car could have been rented, borrowed, or stolen. Even if their government ID looked in order, that too could have been stolen or altered.

This was a lesson that Fannie had learned the hard way. She'd told Foster once about a time when she'd sold a quilt to a sweet elderly lady who had happened into her store. The lady said she was from another state where an Amish community had been established. She'd even tossed out names of people who Fannie was familiar with—either she knew their mother or father, cousin, or had shopped at their stores.

Fannie said that she'd enjoyed talking to the woman so much that she had barely paid attention to the other customers in her store. Two men who had been looking through her quilts moved closer to her cash register and stood there while Fannie talked to the elderly woman.

When the lady asked if Fannie had a certain type of quilt, Fannie said she was more than happy to take her to the back and show her quilts that were almost finished but hadn't been put on display yet.

Fannie had gone on to tell Foster that the lady oohed and ahhed over Fannie's fine workmanship and artful designs, to which Fannie had blushed quite humbly.

Then, the woman's cell phone rang. She answered it and told Fannie she needed to get going because there was an emergency at home.

"Oh dear, you go on," Fannie had said. "I can hold the quilt that you liked so much, if you want me to."

"No, I don't know when I'll be able to get back," the nice woman had responded. "But I certainly do admire your work," she'd added.

The woman left, leaving Fannie feeling on top of the world. She told Foster that she'd considered all the nice people she had met over the years and felt that she had done the right thing by opening her quilt shop.

The worst part of Fannie's story, though, was when she'd told Foster that when she had remembered the other customers she had in her store that day and hurried to wait on them before they left for lack of service, she discovered that the two men waiting near the cash register had already left. The elderly woman was nowhere in sight either. Nor were about three dozen quilts that had been folded up on a display table. The quilts that had been hanging on a spin display had also disappeared, along with all the cash in her register that had been filled with that day's income.

Fannie had ended her story by telling Foster that everything was gone, including her belief in the goodness of all people. She had bought the woman's story, hook, line, and stinker.

And what a stinker it had been, Foster thought, as he looked across the room and stared out his front window at two senior citizens passing by his building. *The gait looked real, and the silver-streaked hair, but who knows these days? Anyone could fool anyone. . .or be fooled.*

His thoughts returned to Fannie's story. She'd said that the woman who had tricked her didn't live near an Amish community at all. The police investigation showed that she was from another country quite well known for its out-of-control crime, identity thefts, phone bank operations, and lack of empathy toward innocent victims.

Fannie had also told Foster that she couldn't believe how easily she had been fooled. "And this, after years of reading mystery novels. How could that have happened to me?" she'd asked.

It just goes to show you, Foster thought, *that blind trust isn't always a good thing. That elderly lady knew all the tricks in the book, and poor, unsuspecting Fannie fell for it, while that woman's goons cleaned her out!*

"Never again," Fannie said she had vowed. And it never did happen again. Unless, of course, it was happening now.

Could it be that she, as well as Foster, were missing valuable clues in the baking contest mystery that they both should have picked up on? Was someone distracting their attention from learning who they really were? Were Michael and Melissa Taylor really just a struggling married couple who had suffered losses in life? Or were Foster and Fannie being gullible? Maybe there was a lot more to their story.

And what about Jeb, the bishop's son? Was there more to that young man than anyone knew, not even Bishop John or his wife?

And then there were the Blustery Sisters. Could their "innocent" gossip and cinnamon rolls be a cover-up for a major criminal operation going on in the back room of the Three Sisters Bakery?

What if Hilo is playing everyone in town for a fool? Foster's blood felt like it was on the verge of boiling. *Could Hilo be on the take, accepting bribes to read the wrong name when the winner is announced?*

Or the judges? Have they misled me and are working a major scam behind the scenes? Are they also on the take?

Then a new, very disturbing thought popped into Foster's head. *What about me? Does anyone, even Fannie, think I might be an imposter? Have I really gained her trust, or does Fannie believe I might be manipulating her interest in crime solving just to stay one step ahead of any evidence she uncovers?*

Foster figured Fannie had a lot to think about, what with the finals being so close. When she should be practicing her biscuit making on this peaceful, quiet day in their unassuming county, was she sitting in her quilt shop, biting her nails because their mystery had still not been solved?

———

Wanting to gain control of her emotions and her concerns about the baking contest, Fannie decided to do what she always did when her thoughts were racing. She would get busy and make a to-do list. She was between customers, so there was time.

Fannie had discovered over the years that a thorough to-do list could work miracles at stopping her mind from feeling so overwhelmed. Once she was able to break a stressful situation down into manageable increments, it didn't seem so impossible and overpowering.

Selecting her favorite pen from her desk drawer, she prepared to write. Her first thought was, *Where in the world do all the pens go after they've been placed in the pen drawer?* She could have forty pens in there, and the next time she opened the drawer to find one, the pile had dwindled down to just four or five. How could she expect to find missing contestants in a baking contest if she couldn't even keep track of her pens?

At least her favorite pen had survived the alien abduction. She chuckled and proceeded to write.

Fannie's To-Do List:

1. *Pick up additional colors of quilt thread at the general store.*

2. *Refold and straighten all quilts in shop.*

3. *Put beef roast on counter to thaw out for supper this evening.*

4. *Stop by Foster's for update on missing persons cases.*

5. *Buy more lace, buttons, and other notions for quilting store.*

6. *Buy more mace, just in case.*

7. *Ask Foster where I can buy a nightstick.*

8. *Get fitted for new burgundy Amish dress that can accommodate a bullet-proof vest.*

9. *Buy more pens.*

10. *Buy more ink for fingerprint kit.*

11. *Read my daily devotions.*

12. *Finish reading crime novel.*

13. *Solve the crossword puzzle in this morning's newspaper.*

14. *Solve at least one more missing persons case.*

15. *Remember to keep my eyes on the prize.*

16. *Remember to keep my eyes off the private eye.*

"There now," Fannie said to herself. "I think that about covers it."

———

Back at his house that afternoon, Foster was still doing a good bit of thinking, but that's about all. Time was running out for him and Fannie to solve the case, and they couldn't waste a minute.

He decided that it might be best if they separated their investigative duties and each pursued their own leads for a while. *But what fun would that be?* he thought, and immediately got back to thinking clearly. Separating would provide them with the focus they may have been lacking. And it would certainly allow them to cover more ground, interview more witnesses, and process the evidence with more single-mindedness and clarity.

He decided he would bring the proposal up to Fannie tonight over supper. Maybe they would go to a neighborhood charity barbeque, and then as they sat at a picnic table and ate their plate of shredded pork, hamburger bun, beans, and coleslaw, they could discuss the best way for them to proceed, seeing how time was getting short.

Yes, that would be the perfect plan. Foster wondered what Fannie might wear to such a meeting. Would it be the light blue dress that accentuated the color of her eyes? Or the darker blue that he liked equally as much?

And would her lips be that same color of cherry that made her skin tone appear so fresh and tanned?

He knew none of that had anything to do with her investigative skills or even the intuitive nature with which she approached each case. But they were just as important as his assessment as to what he should wear.

The brown shirt, or the black one that she had complimented on numerous occasions? And should he wear the boots that added an inch or two of height as well as a nice aroma of leather? Or should he opt for his more relaxed loafers?

These were significant considerations that anyone in the business of crime solving needed to consider. It was covered in basic training and in most crime novels.

After all, Sherlock Holmes had his trench coat and pipe. Some detectives had a defined moustache. And Foster Bates had his...Hawaiian shirt? He eyed the item in question, hanging in his closet all by its lonesome. It was a retirement gift from his officers. Giant pink flamingos standing on one leg—dozens of them graced the shirt from sleeve to sleeve. Even the collar got in on the action.

Would he? Could he? Should he dare to wear it to their important meeting?

Of course, he should, and he could, so he would.

And he felt sure that Miss Fannie Miller would absolutely love it.

CHAPTER 31

Faith sat at her desk in the back room of the bakery, going over the books. It was difficult to concentrate with so many other things on her mind. She was worried about the reputations she and her sisters were earning in this town. When it became clear that Foster had been scrutinizing some of what he'd called their "suspicious behaviors," they'd looked for ways to deflect the heat off of them. The best way to do it, Charity had told Faith and Hope, was to do what they did best—gossip.

Admittedly, they excelled at gossip and spread it with the ease of applying buttercream frosting to a six-tiered wedding cake. They could have filled their daily conversations with the latest political or national news or the Amish community news they'd read about in the Plain people's newspaper, *The Budget*. Or they could even talk about their personal lives. But none of that was as much fun or of as much interest to Faith and her sisters as pure, unfiltered, no-holds-barred, tall-tale tattling. The bigger the scandal, the less evidence was needed to back it up.

So Faith, along with Hope and Charity, started all kinds of rumors. And each one got the attention off them, momentarily anyway, and they'd all agreed that they were fine with that.

Still, Faith couldn't help but wonder why Foster wasn't looking into the missing contestants themselves. Did he know for sure whether they were missing?

What if one of the "missing" contestants was out of town, secretly getting a tummy tuck? Faith asked herself. *And what if another "missing" contestant was taken to jail on another crime?*

She tapped her pen on the surface of the desk. *And I have to wonder if the missing couple had simply arranged a romantic rendezvous and don't want anyone to know about it.* Faith clamped her lips shut, hesitant to continue down that line of thinking.

The potential scenarios were varied and eyebrow raising, and she and her sisters had openly discussed each one at length until the reputations of most of the missing contestants had been sufficiently tainted. *It might seem as though none of us care that innocent people who had merely entered a baking contest were getting caught in a web of suspicion,* she thought. *But we do care, because it's making it that much harder for Foster to find the real culprit. And anyway, we're all just speculating. Isn't that what detective work is all about?*

Faith thought back to the conversation she'd had with her sisters over supper last night, when they'd talked about Foster's ridiculous suspicions about them. She could still see the fire in Hope's eyes when she'd stated firmly, "I am an upstanding member of this community! Taking me down to the station for questioning? How dare that man drag my good name through the murky waters of his investigation! I can't go shopping or out to eat or even to the flea market without people scurrying past me like I'm some sort of a criminal."

"And these people aren't strangers," Hope had added. "They've known me for years. Known all of us. How could they allow one false accusation to change their opinion? How can one tiny morsel of gossip erase all the good I've done—all the good we've done for this town?"

Faith was indignant, and her sisters echoed her outrage.

"We must stick together!" Hope said.

"One for all, and all for one!" Charity said with a nod.

"We will not stand by and watch our blood kin be accused of having anything whatsoever to do with the disappearances of the baking-contest contestants," Faith stated firmly. "There are plenty of other people who should be considered suspects first. If Mr. Bates needs names, we will be more than happy to oblige him!"

"As far as I'm concerned, the whole town should be investigated!" Hope said. "Anyone could be involved."

"Except for us," Charity added. "Because we have alibis! We can vouch for each other's whereabouts every minute of every day. We are almost always together."

"That's right!" Hope agreed. "Ever since the day each one of us was born, we've been together."

Faith's thoughts returned to the present. "The nerve of that man to cast aspersions on us like this!"

———

"Good morning, ladies," Foster said the following day when he entered the bakery.

"Oh, it's you," Hope said, her words almost dripping with ice.

"Is something wrong?" he asked, stepping up to the pastry counter.

"It most certainly is!" Charity stated with hands on her hips. "We're disappointed that you consider the three of us as suspects."

Foster gave a slight chuckle, trying to warm the moment. But it remained the same frozen tundra he had walked into.

"You've got it all wrong, ladies," Foster said. "For a while I didn't believe you were involved in the disappearances in any way. But some rumors have reached my ears that have, well, made me rethink my opinion."

"Rumors?" Charity said. "What kind of rumors?"

"The kind of rumors you ladies are known for spreading about other people," Bishop John said as he made his way through the cloud of people and joined them. "It may be a game to you, but in the end, gossip usually backfires on those spreading it." Foster couldn't resist adding, "Look at it like this, ladies. It's like the daily breakfast rush at your bakery, and you three are left with egg on your faces."

Their eyes widened, and Charity opened her mouth as if she wanted to say more. But Foster and the bishop were on a roll, and it had nothing to do with cinnamon.

One by one, he covered each rumor they had started regarding the baking contest and missing contestants, dispelling many of them.

"As it turned out, the man you three had suggested might be serving time in jail had actually gone into seminary on short notice and forgot to officially drop out of the baking contest. Guess he had a higher calling on his mind," Foster added. "And as for the lady you all surmised was off getting a tummy tuck, it turned out that she had actually donated a kidney to her brother in Montana and was in the hospital recovering."

Hope appeared to be on the verge of saying something, but Foster took the lead again.

"And as for the couple supposedly on the secret rendezvous? That didn't happen the way you sisters had speculated either. In reality, the couple secretly eloped and are still on their honeymoon." Foster paused to collect his thoughts.

"There's a lesson here, ladies, but I don't think you see it: Gossip *isn't* harmless. It taints reputations, including the reputation of the person telling it. No wonder the wise avoid it."

A flush of color swept across the women's cheeks. Faith spoke up. "I guess the truth is, we seldom see things that are right in front of us, and unfortunately, they don't make eyeglasses for that kind of visual impairment."

Charity and Hope nodded, as if in agreement. They were finally getting it.

Still, the Blustery Sisters seldom saw things that were right in front of them.

"You wouldn't spread rumors about yourselves, would you?" Foster questioned.

"Of course not!" The tips of Faith's ears had also turned crimson. The importance of the truth was dawning on her too.

"We're not bad people," Hope was quick to say. "Don't forget we bake cinnamon rolls for you."

"I never said you were bad people." He shifted his weight from one leg to the other. "Still, some of the things I've heard about you from others have piqued my curiosity. And it made me wonder if I need to be more thorough."

"But you know us, Mr. Bates," Hope reminded him. "You're not going to believe other people's gossip over what you already know about us, right?"

"Well, as you ladies well know, gossip can be quite convincing. I'm going to have to check things out to be sure," Foster said. "But only because it's my job."

He moved toward the door, and in so doing, his shoulder bumped a small sign on the wall, causing it to fall to the floor.

Charity bent down to pick it up, and Foster noticed that there was a carousel painted on it, along with the saying, WHAT GOES AROUND COMES AROUND.

The Blustery Sisters are finally getting a taste of their own meddling, he thought before going out the door.

———

"Why do you suspect the Blustery Sisters?" Fannie asked Foster later that night when they met for ice cream. It had been a very hot day with temperatures reaching well above one hundred degrees, with a cold front predicted to move in later. In the meantime, the humidity made for very oppressive conditions, and once the temperature started to drop, that could also mean a thunderstorm. Fannie figured a double scoop, rocky road ice-cream cone and a tall glass of ice water were exactly what both of them needed to take the edge off both threats to their comfort.

"Well, to be honest, each of the sisters has been on my radar since the beginning. But Charity rings the most alarms."

"Charity?" Fannie waved a hand, hoping to dismiss Foster's statement. "I assume you've got something to back that up?"

"Just a hunch," Foster said, causing Fannie to tilt her head slightly and raise an eyebrow of doubt.

"Sorry, my friend. But I don't think I concur," she said.

"Duly noted. But I've learned a thing or two about human nature over the years. Sometimes people who spread lies about someone else are doing it to get the suspicion off themselves. And those sisters have sure spread an awful lot of lies."

"That's true." Fannie nodded.

"And Charity most of all."

Fannie couldn't argue against Foster's reasoning. At one time or another, just about everyone in town had had their reputations skewered by Charity and her sisters. Community leaders, store owners, neighbors, and former friends had all been trashed by their tongues. Why should the baking contestants be any different?

"All right, I see your point," Fannie acquiesced. "So what do we do?"

"We don't get sidetracked."

Fannie glanced at the clock. It was getting late, so she told Foster she was going to have to call it a night. The ice cream was long since gone, as was the sun, and it was time they both got their rest. They would continue their investigation tomorrow or whenever they acquired more evidence.

———

Tomorrow came much too early for Fannie. Loud knocking on her front door woke her from a sound sleep. Fannie jumped out of bed, threw her coat over her night clothes, and went to the door. Whoever it was, they were sure in a panic.

"Fannie Miller!" A familiar voice shot through the door. "I need to talk to you right now!"

Fannie was more than willing to do that if the voice would just give her time.

When she reached the door, she swung it open, ready to handle whatever life-or-death crisis was on the other side.

"Fannie Miller!" Bishop John stepped into Fannie's home without an invitation.

"My goodness, Bishop John," Fannie said. "What is it? Has something happened to someone in our community?"

Fannie held her breath and steadied herself for whatever horrible news was coming. The bishop wasn't an emotional person, so the urgency in his voice caused her great concern. Had another contestant disappeared? Had a body been found? Had a mysterious fire broken out at the Three Sisters Bakery? Had the police been called to Michael and Melissa's home? What could have possibly gotten him in such a stir?

"Fannie," he said, a rush of red flooding his cheeks. "Did you go to the horse auction in Charm?"

"Why, yes, I did," Fannie said. "Why?"

"And were you with that man, Foster Bates?"

"Jah, but we were there on business," she said. Then added, "More or less. I was there to buy a new buggy horse, and we also discussed the case of the missing contestants."

Fannie wanted to be honest with the bishop. Foster and Fannie were both crime solvers and good friends. But her official reason for having gone to Charm was to look for a new buggy horse. And she found him.

And anyway, none of that would have caused such anxiety in the bishop, Fannie told herself. So what was he driving at?

The bishop continued. "And did you happen to talk with my boy Jeb while you were there?"

So that's what it was. If Fannie had any reason to suspect the bishop's son, that was getting multiplied now.

"Well, did you?" Bishop John pressed.

"I did," Fannie said.

Bishop John closed his eyes as if to edit his words carefully.

"As you know, Miss Fannie, my son Jeb has his challenges. Doesn't always know what he's saying yes to. I sure would hate for him to confess to something that he had nothing to do with."

"We wouldn't want that either," Fannie assured him. "Even if we were to question him as investigators, we would just be doing our job."

"And as a father, I would just be doing mine to be present at any such questioning."

The bishop bid Fannie a good day and left. Fannie knew she was going to have to find some way out of this mess. Casting any level of suspicion on the bishop's son, who had already faced enough challenges in life because of his social anxiety disorder, was sure to make her presence in their upcoming church services more than awkward. Church members were already physically divided, with men sitting on benches on one side and the women on the other. Would the bishop go so far as to have everyone sit on one side and Fannie all alone on the other? Fannie hoped not.

She looked out her window and saw the bishop's buggy turn out of her driveway. *I've got to talk to Foster!* Fannie hurried to put her dress on and practically ran out to get her bike.

With her heart pounding, she pedaled as fast as she could. She needed to tell him about the bishop's early morning visit. About his overreaction to her talking to Jeb. That could be a clear sign of guilt. But then again, it could be a clear sign of a protective father's love. Maybe Foster, with all his experience, would be able to tell the difference between the two.

At least, Fannie sure hoped so.

CHAPTER 32

Foster was in a hurry to get to Yoder's Hardware Store and back home before the predicted storm hit the Tuscarawas County area. He needed to pick up a new ladder so he could change the light bulbs on his ceiling fans.

It was normally a twenty-minute drive from his home, but he made good time that day because most people with any sense had stayed home.

Once he got the new ladder loaded into his vehicle, Foster was on his way back home, taking in the lightning show that pierced the darkening sky.

Foster remembered some of the car wrecks he had seen due to storms that hit the Chicago area, and he reminded himself to slow down. He didn't want to be one of the storm-caused casualties reported in the next day's news.

His drive home took him by the Main Street Grill. Had the weather been better, he might have been tempted to stop in for a tasty steak, but then he remembered that they were closed on Mondays anyway.

Might as well keep on driving and eat at home, he told himself.

But then he noticed there was a light on at the Main Street Grill. Foster had never seen a light on at the restaurant on a Monday. Had someone broken into the restaurant when no one was around? If so, Foster was glad he'd shown up when he did.

Foster turned out his car's headlights and slowly drove up to the rear entrance of the restaurant. Sure enough, the rear door was open. Foster thought about placing a call to the local police but talked himself out of it. *What if it's just Nick stopping by to do some paperwork or take care of something while the restaurant was closed?*

The cop in him kicked in, and before he knew it, Foster had stealthily approached the back door and entered. He had only taken a few steps inside the kitchen area when someone spoke from the shadows.

"Sorry, we're closed," the voice said.

When a figure stepped forward, Foster recognized him immediately. "Jeb?"

"I'm surprised you remember me," the young man said.

"The restaurant's closed on Mondays, isn't it?" Foster asked even though he knew the answer.

"Yeah," Jeb said. "Nick asked me to check on things for him while he's out of town."

Foster took a few steps closer. "He did, huh? He gave you a key?"

"It was unlocked. Good thing I checked. Nick must have had to leave in a hurry. But everything looks good, except for you coming in and scaring me half to death."

"Sorry. I saw the light on and figured I'd better check it out."

"How 'bout that, huh?"

"What?"

"I think like a detective," Jeb said.

Foster smiled, then walked to his car. He took his time starting it, waiting for Jeb to lock up and be on his way. Then, when he was sure all was well, Foster turned the key in his ignition and headed for home.

———

It had been raining for hours, and Fannie had run out of buckets and towels for the leaks that had sprung in her ceiling. There were so many, she had to start setting out large vases and old coffee cans at strategic locations in the various rooms and hallways of her home.

Fannie gritted her teeth. *This is not good. Not good at all.*

She had been told by countless roofing salesmen who had stopped by her house, at the worst possible times, that her roof was in dire need of replacement. But Fannie's personal needs were always listed last on her to-do list, preceded by the needs of everyone else in her life. Foster had offered to help her in any way he could, but Fannie knew he didn't have a lot of extra money either. She also knew the bishop and her Amish community would help if they knew about the leaks, but Fannie kept the matter to herself. After all, the leaks were only a problem when it was raining. Otherwise, everything was fine. More than fine, compared to what other people were dealing with. She'd read the headlines of the newspapers as she passed them in the grocery and general stores. The world was a mess of confusion, inflation, and crime, and some of that had crept into Amish Country.

She shook her head slowly. *Such a shame. Whoever thought it would happen to us here in Sugarcreek?*

A leaky roof was nothing compared to losing a job. Or dealing with health issues or being at war. It wasn't nearly as serious as any number of stressful things people were facing these days. So Fannie gave thanks to God for her good health, her home, her quilt shop, and her family and friends. And then, as she watched a brand-new leak break through the roof above her and droplets of water splattered on her forehead, she simply brought in another empty vase, set it in place, and went about the rest of her day.

Blessings come in all shapes and sizes, she told herself. *Even a leaky roof can bring us a blessing if we keep our hearts open! Besides,* she added, temporarily forgetting all about Noah, *how long can it rain?*

Bishop John looked up from his Bible and saw Jeb standing in the doorway of the spare bedroom the bishop used as an office.

"Looks like a storm's coming in," Jeb said. "The fish will be bitin' for sure now, Daed."

"They do like storms," the bishop said without looking up from his notepad. "But I'm still working on my sermon for the service this Sunday. And I don't think either one of us should be out there until this storm passes over. We'll do something together later."

Jeb's shoulders sank, and he lowered his head. It was a promise he'd heard before.

"But I thought you said. . ." Instead of saying more, Jeb lowered his gaze to the floor.

"Look, I love fishing. You know that. But sometimes these sermons come easy, and sometimes they don't. And sometimes a storm interrupts life. Sorry, Jeb. Next week, I promise."

"But that's what you said last week." Jeb pulled his long fingers across his forehead.

Bishop John took a slow, deep breath. "Now, Jeb, you know where my responsibilities lie. We'll fish, I promise, but it'll have to be after I deliver this sermon I've been working on for hours."

The bishop did not wait for Jeb's agreement on the matter. He turned his thoughts back inside the Good Book, jotting down more notes for a sermon about setting priorities.

———

Jeb clenched his fingers in the palms of his hands. *My daed is so wrapped up in his study that he doesn't notice I'm still standing here, watching him hard at work.*

Jeb continued to watch as his father thumbed through the Bible and wrote down notes. It was obvious to Jeb that Daed's sermon was finally coming together. Jeb recognized that look on his face. His dad was in his zone now, and there was no chance of disturbing him. It appeared as if the sermon was practically writing itself, coming as fast as his dad could write it down.

But Jeb also knew that he was one church member who had already heard the sermon his father was preparing, this one on priorities. He'd heard it today and every day of disappointment in the past. And as always, that message was coming through loud and clear before he ever stood before the other church members. *Dad cares more about his position as our church bishop than he does me.*

With a sigh that came from deep within, Jeb turned and left the room. *Forget about goin' fishing,* he told himself. *It's getting kinda late in the day, and the weather's too nasty anyway. I'll just go off by myself, like usual, and find something else to do. If only. . .if only I mattered.*

CHAPTER 33

Storms had never really bothered Fannie before. She had grown up in areas where spring and winter storms were common. She had even survived not one but three tornadoes that had touched down in areas near her home. So high winds and approaching funnel clouds were usually met with measured calmness as she found shelter.

But this night was different. Fannie's sense of safety had been breached by the mysterious occurrences in the baking contest, and she flinched every time she heard the shutters slam against her house because of the high winds.

It wasn't so much the wind that was unnerving her, but what the wind could be hiding. Was that a scream she just heard? And what about the turning of her front doorknob? Was the wind doing that too, or was there an intruder outside her door trying to get in?

Even the walls of her house were in on the "scare Fannie" operation as they made creaks and squeaks the likes of which she had never heard before.

She thought about calling Foster, but that would involve running out into the storm to the phone shed and placing the call. With lightning striking all around, that certainly didn't seem like a safe thing to do.

So Fannie did the only thing she could do. She climbed into her bathtub and took one of her handmade quilts and hid under it, head and all. It didn't take away the sound of the storm. Or the flashes of lightning, not totally anyway. But under there she could pretend that she was at a Fourth of July picnic and the flashes were simply fireworks, which she had always loved. And the booms and blasts of the thunder were cannons going off, celebrating the nation's birthday. That's all it was. There wasn't an F-4 barreling down on her or a serial killer coming up to her doorstep trying the doorknob and windows.

Everything could be explained away under her quilted theater, and she could be at peace. Sort of.

At least it worked for a while.

Fannie wondered if she should have entered the baking contest in the first place. Did she really need a first-place ribbon so bad that she would put herself and her community through everything that was happening? Sure, her intentions were innocent, but what about everything that had already happened and what might still happen.

Some of the disappearances remained unsolved. Contestants feared unknown dangers and were turning on each other with false accusations and suspicion. The contest could even jeopardize the relationship she had with her dear friend, Foster Bates. He had already named her a suspect, hadn't he? Never mind that she'd had to take a lie detector test to prove her innocence. How did that better their friendship?

Fannie wished she could go back in time. Back to the moment when she had first learned about the Tuscarawas and Surrounding Counties Baking Contest. Only this time, she would ignore the newspaper advertisements and would most certainly never have put any posters up to advertise the big event.

Perhaps she would even throw away her aunt's biscuit recipe. Yes, they were delicious, but were they worth all the grief they were causing her and her beloved community?

Just then, she heard a trashcan roll down her driveway, making a racket that sounded like a car being flipped and rolled down the street.

She turned on her battery-powered radio and listened to the weather updates. The storm was directly over her area, and the weather report was continuing to warn people to get to a safe place.

Fannie let those words tumble around in her brain. *A safe place*, she thought. *What safe place? This quilt? How's that going to protect me if my house falls down?*

She remembered all the advertisements she had seen for storm shelters and made herself a mental note to call one of them at daybreak.

That would be a safe place, she thought. *But what do I do in the meantime?*

Then, Fannie recalled her go-to scripture, Psalm 91:4, that always brought her peace: "He shall cover you with His feathers, and under His wings you shall take refuge."

Even on a night like this, Lord, when a storm is raging all around me?

Fannie repeated the verse again, this time out loud.

When some contestants are still missing, finalists are being falsely accused, and fear of the unknown keeps us awake at night. The words of the verse returned to her mind. They seemed to have embedded themselves deeply into her brain.

Fannie peeked out from under the quilt and looked around. There was no lighting. She listened for the next clap of thunder, but it never came. She braced for the gusts of wind to rush against her door and windows. But it had been stilled.

Fannie smiled. The storm had finally passed.

———

When the sun rose the following morning, Fannie got dressed and was about to head over to Foster Bates Detective Agency to see how he had fared in the storm, but she remembered the promise she had made to herself.

She slipped on a sweater, went out to her phone shed, and placed a call to Henry's Portable Storm Shelters, to get an estimate at least. The man she spoke to gave his first available date, which, after the storm, wasn't for several weeks out.

"I'll take it," Fannie said. She hung up the phone and dodged the puddles, as she headed over to check on her closest neighbor, Helen. And then on to check on Foster.

———

"What did you say?" Foster asked when Fannie showed up at his office. He was still a bit shaken up by the storm and wasn't sure if he'd heard her right. "Did we just live through a tornado?"

"Well, they're still assessing it, but we might've. I passed a lot of damage on my way over here." She pulled out a chair and sat down.

"Yeah, me too. That crazy storm sure did make a racket!"

"I've survived several tornados in my lifetime, and if the one we had last night didn't touch down, it sure came close."

"I'm glad to see you're okay. Was there any damage at your place?" Foster asked, leaning forward with both elbows on his desk.

"Just a lot of things knocked over. Nothing major, I don't think. I checked on my closest neighbors this morning too, and no serious damage was done to their places either."

"That's good, and you're obviously safe—that's really the important thing."

"I'm glad you are too. God was watching over us."

"Well, I was sure asking Him to. For both our sakes."

"Thank you, Foster. I don't take that lightly. It means a lot whenever someone says they were praying for me."

"Well, my safety was riding on that prayer too."

"And God obviously heard it. Above the wind and the chaos, He heard it."

"He did indeed," Foster said.

Fannie smiled. "He always does."

They sat quietly for a few minutes, then Fannie asked Foster about Chief. "How did he respond to the storm?"

"He didn't like it one bit. He whined a lot, paced back and forth, and ended up sleeping at the foot of my bed." Foster scrunched up his nose. "At one point, that poor dog got so scared, he tried to crawl under the covers with me."

"Did you let him?" she asked.

"No way! After a hot summer like we had, and Chief being outside more than usual, he might have some fleas. The storm was bad enough. I sure don't need a bunch of flea bites to deal with."

But then Foster remembered the elevator mirror he mistakenly shot and decided Chief could have used a little grace and mercy shown to him too.

"And speaking of grace and mercy," Foster said, "when I stopped for a cup of coffee and a few cinnamon rolls at the Three Sisters Bakery before coming to work, Charity was quite talkative, and she filled me in on something she heard on the news channel this morning."

As though eager to hear, Fannie leaned forward with her hands clutched together. "What all did Charity tell you?"

"She said the reporter had mentioned the baking contest and stated that the windstorm had caused some damage, but not enough to call off the baking finals. There were a few downed trees and debris strewn around, but nothing that couldn't be quickly cleaned up." Foster reached for a half-eaten cinnamon roll and took a bite. "It should only take a few days of cleaning, and I bet the area will look as good as new."

Fannie reached up and readjusted her head covering, which felt like it had slipped back on her head. Apparently, in her hurry to get over to see Foster, she hadn't been thorough enough in securing the pins that held her kapp in place.

What else could happen to try to sabotage this contest? Fannie wondered. *Luckily, we're not over an earthquake fault, and we're too far inland for a tsunami. I sure wouldn't want to experience either one of those.*

But the storm had passed, and Fannie was trying to get back to being her positive self. She knew it was just a matter of time before all the missing persons would be present and accounted for, the finals would take place, and maybe, just maybe, she would be awarded the first-place ribbon. And of course, the twenty-five thosuand dollars. But it was the ribbon that she wanted most.

In her mind, she pictured her aunt Selma sitting out in the audience when Fannie's name was called, even though her dear aunt was no longer alive. She imagined the shocked-then-pleased look on her face as the audience erupted in applause. Fannie pictured herself grabbing Aunt Selma's hand and making her accompany her on stage to accept the award. Nothing would make Aunt Selma happier, and nothing would make Fannie happier than to make one more memory with her dear sweet aunt.

Even if Fannie didn't win, she knew that Aunt Selma would be proud of her for having entered the contest year after year, believing in her baking skills enough to have tried.

And if that was enough for Aunt Selma, Fannie knew it was enough for her too.

Hilo wasn't thrilled with the rainwater that had flooded the front entrance of the theater. How was he supposed to get to the rehearsal area for the pre-show run-through? They had decided to host the finals inside the theater that was on the same property as the restaurant and Carlisle Inn. The spectators that had come to the conference center to watch the preliminaries had nearly filled the room to capacity. So it was decided that they needed a bigger facility to accommodate the crowd that was expected to witness the finals and cheer the baking contestants on.

Not wanting to mess up his tuxedo pants, Hilo rolled up the pant legs to his knees, waded across the newly formed pond caused by the storm, and entered the building.

"I see you survived the storm, Hilo," the show's director, Bernie Caldron, said.

Bernie had worked with Hilo before, and the two knew each other quite well.

Hilo, having had his mailbox blown over in the storm, was still a bit shaken. He didn't need this, not on the night before the finals. Nobody did. But him, most of all. It was his face that was going to be on camera. Those very visible bags were going to be under his eyes due to lack of sleep. The power had gone out at his house, and he wasn't able to plug in his CPAP machine. He was a mess of nerves and frustration today.

"You've got to pull yourself together before tomorrow," Bernie told him. "The rehearsal starts in a few hours, and those who have come to watch it will be eager to see it. Even more so on the day of the big event. That will be broadcast live. Maybe not in Hollywood or California, but certainly in Cleveland, Toledo, and Akron. Some might even be watching from the Chicago area and other parts of Illinois, since there are popular Mennonite and Amish communities there. As well as Mennonite friends from Indiana, Pennsylvania, Tennessee, Kentucky, and other Amish communities across the United States and Canada."

Hilo was aware that Michael and Melissa, the Blustery Sisters, and even Fannie had done several podcasts about the contest, and the local news stations had covered it as well. The contest was getting the most publicity it had ever gotten in its ten-year history. In other words, this was no time for Hilo to fall apart. Who knew what kind of opportunities could open up to him after his emceeing of this special event? The national rodeo championships? The annual quilter's convention? The Emmys? The Oscars? The Grammys? Anything was possible. That old

THE RISE AND FALL OF MISS FANNIE'S BISCUITS

adage of being in the right place at the right time to be seen by the right people couldn't have been truer than it was that day. For everyone in the contest. Especially Hilo.

"So just get out there and do your best," Bernie said. "That's all I can demand of you, and that's all you can demand of yourself."

At those inspiring words, Hilo thrust his chest out. He stood a little taller, and he felt a thousand times more confident than when he'd walked into the building.

What am I really afraid of? he asked himself. *What's a couple of under-eye bags between friends and fans? They'll understand. We had a storm here last night. We've had to deal with missing contestants and feuding finalists. Life doesn't always go as planned, but if we're adaptable and professional, we can make it through anything.*

Hilo thanked Bernie for his sage advice, straightened his bowtie and cummerbund, and turned to walk into the staging area for the rehearsal.

"Hilo. . ." Bernie called out.

Hilo stopped and turned back, eager for whatever additional words of wisdom Bernie might wish to add.

"Before I say the word 'Action!' and you step out onto the stage, I would highly suggest. . ."

Bernie paused just long enough for Hilo to press him.

"Suggest *what*, Bernie?" he asked in hurried desperation.

"I'd strongly suggest that you roll down the legs of your tuxedo pants before the rehearsal recording starts. Dressy short pants went out with George Washington."

CHAPTER 34

Bright and early Saturday morning, cars began arriving at the Ohio Star Theater. Local news crews parked over to the side with their trailers and equipment. Contest staff and a steady stream of locals and tourists continued to arrive early, no doubt trying to ensure the best seats.

The annual Tuscarawas and Surrounding Counties Baking Contest had always drawn a good-sized crowd, and this year it seemed was the biggest turnout yet. In all its history, the only year the contest had been cancelled was in 2020, due to the COVID pandemic. The event was enthusiastically supported by the community and tourists alike. This was the tenth anniversary of the beloved contest, and the celebratory spirit was in high gear.

Hilo, the perennial emcee, did his microphone check for the sound engineers, and everything seemed to be in tip-top shape.

Fannie tried to keep her mind on the competition. But she was also still trying to fill in the final pieces of the contestant mystery. Truth be known, she wanted to win both contests—the one for her homemade biscuits and the unspoken one between her and Foster. Which sleuth would break the case first? There were still questions to be answered and loose ends to tie up.

When Fannie saw Foster arriving, she made a beeline straight over to him.

"Any news?" she asked, looking around to make sure no one was eavesdropping, especially one of the Blustery Sisters.

"Nothing yet, but I'm keeping my eyes and ears open."

"Well, at least I'm no longer a suspect."

Foster hesitated a moment too long before answering.

"I'm not, right?" Fannie pressed.

"Of course not," Foster said as beads of sweat formed at his temples.

Foster smiled, appearing to be a bit uncomfortable. "You were never on the short list, and I crossed you off as soon as I could. I knew you weren't involved."

Fannie gave Foster a look that she hoped said a lot more than she had time to get out at the moment.

"The important thing is you're in the clear."

"So who all are still suspects?"

"Well, one of the Beiler Sisters, for certain."

Her eyebrows rose. "Which one?"

"I'm still determining that."

"But Foster, I told you I am sure they are not guilty." Fannie clutched Foster's arm, nudging him to continue. "Who else is on your list?"

"Michael or Melissa are also still suspects, but I don't think both. Just still trying to piece it together and figure out which one it could be."

"I see." Fannie let go of his arm.

"And there are a few other people too."

"Could you repeat that?" Fannie asked. "Your voice was so low I could barely make out what you said."

Foster moved closer and spoke into Fannie's ear. "I said, 'There are a few other people too.'"

"In other words, we're no closer to solving this mystery than we were before we started?" She gave a huff.

"Well, you're in the clear, and that's a good thing." Foster gave Fannie a mischievous wink, and then he asked if the judges had arrived yet.

"I think so," Fannie replied. "They're probably getting their makeup done." She rolled her eyes.

———

Foster couldn't help but smile. He couldn't imagine Fannie wearing makeup. Although her lips did look like the color of cherries sometimes.

Get your thoughts in perspective, he scolded himself. *This is no time to be thinking about things like that.*

"I saw equipment trucks. Is this being televised?" he asked.

"Of course," Fannie said, striking a pose. "How do I look?"

"Lovely, Miss Fannie," he said. "Perfectly lovely. But aren't you worried about being on camera? I mean, isn't posing for cameras against your Amish beliefs?"

Fannie's cheeks turned crimson. Now it really did appear as if she was wearing a little makeup. She had asked for the compliment, but when it came, it seemed like she wasn't prepared for it. By the looks of her wrinkle-free dark blue dress, it appeared she had spent an unusual amount of time ironing it. Fannie's kapp was on just right too. Perhaps dear Fannie had not expected such a nice response from her friend.

"Well, I did ask them to only film my biscuits, if possible. Or at least, whenever feasible, refrain from showing my face," Fannie said. "They agreed to oblige me with that. That'll make Bishop John happy too."

———

There was still an hour before the finals would begin, and Fannie stood in the lobby next to Foster with her arms folded. As guests continued to file into the building, she went over the case once more in her mind. It was a shame they weren't any closer to naming the perpetrator behind all the missing persons cases, and she knew that Foster didn't like it one bit.

She bit the inside of her lip. *And neither do I.*

A few holes had been closed, and a couple of people were off the hook, including Fannie, who was glad she was no longer considered a suspect.

Dorothy Dexter had finally shown up with her daughter, so that was a good thing. Apparently, the elderly woman had an undiagnosed multiple-personality disorder and had taken off to the beach for a few days under the alias of Cindy Harris. She'd come home several days ago with no recollection of even having been a contestant in the baking contest, but Dorothy's daughter had refreshed her memory. Foster and Fannie had spoken to them both a few minutes ago and wished Dorothy well. Fannie hoped that the poor woman would get the help she needed.

Foster had crossed Dorothy off his list of missing contestants, once again telling Fannie that he felt sure one of the Blustery Sisters had been trying to frighten everyone with those threatening notes so they would drop out of the contest.

"I believe it may be Charity," he whispered to Fannie. "She tried to bribe me the other day with some of her homemade cinnamon rolls and even included doggie treats for Chief."

Fannie shook her head. "The only thing that proves is she wanted to impress you with her baking skills. Charity is looking for a husband, don't forget, and I'm quite sure she has both of her blue eyes set on you."

Foster shrugged. "Guess you could be right. But she's not my type. Her cinnamon rolls, on the other hand. . ."

"Laugh if you want, but I know I'm right." With her chin held high, Fannie thrust her shoulders back.

Foster pointed to Bessie Carson, who'd just entered the building. "Look over there, Fannie. I thought you had said Bessie was missing and that you were sure foul play had been done."

"Yes, I did say that. Because ever since the preliminaries, no one seemed to know where she was."

"Well, let's go find out."

Foster led the way, and Fannie followed. When she approached Bessie, Fannie was quick to ask where the woman had been.

Bessie twirled her finger around one of her reddish-blond curls and grinned. "After I failed to make the finals, I was feeling rather down until I met up with Pearl, my old high school friend, who'd seen my name in the newspaper article about the contest." She grimaced and tugged on the collar of her bright pink dress. "For whatever reason, possibly a little too much rum cake, the two of us decided to put on our boots and go on a little hiking adventure in the higher-elevation Pennsylvania woods.

"Luckily," Bessie continued, "I got over the loss and got back in time for the finals. I really wanted to be here to support the winner, whoever that might be."

Foster's eyes widened, and Fannie was almost at a loss for words. She couldn't imagine that anybody who'd already lost the preliminaries would worry about hurrying back to congratulate the grand prize winner, unless. . . unless she had a hand in determining said winner. Could it be that the whole reason Bessie left town was to have an alibi?

Fannie tilted her head from side to side, weighing the issue. If that had been Bessie's plan, she'd pulled it off rather neatly. *Maybe some of the other contestants who either dropped out or simply didn't show up had a viable excuse too. An excuse so buttoned down, it would be difficult, if not impossible, to disprove.*

One by one the suspects were getting cleared, and all the missing people were showing up.

But there was still one last mystery. What of the red envelopes with the ominous messages? Someone had obviously written them with the intent of threatening the people who'd received the notes.

Foster gave a tug on Fannie's dress sleeve. "Look, Michael and Melissa have arrived. Think I'll go have a talk with them. Maybe under the pressure of the moment, they'll slip up. Maybe one of them is guilty of writing those frightening notes."

Fannie was about to say that she would go with him, when she spotted the Blustery Sisters with their heads together across the room. *I wonder what those three women could be talking about. Is it possible that Foster might be right about Charity? Could she have written the notes?*

Or maybe Hope or Faith is responsible for the notes. They have stated many times how badly they wanted to win the big prize money.

Foster had only taken a few steps toward Michael and Melissa, and Fannie was on the verge of going over to talk to the sisters, when Bishop John, holding tightly to his son's arm, called their names.

Fannie halted her footsteps, and so did Foster.

"What is it?" Foster asked when the bishop approached.

He reached up with his free hand and rubbed the back of his neck. "It seems that my son, Jeb, found himself cornered in a story and couldn't find his way out. I brought him here today to speak to you."

Foster's brows squished together. "What do you mean?"

John gave the boy a nudge. "Go ahead and tell them what you told me earlier today."

Jeb's chin quivered as he lowered his head. "I wrote the notes in the red envelopes."

Fannie's mouth dropped open. "Why would you do such a thing, Jeb?"

"I dunno," he said haltingly. "It was just a prank, you know. Didn't mean no harm." Jeb scrubbed a hand over his flushed face. "I'm. . .I'm really sorry."

"Nobody was hurt physically, Jeb," Foster stated, "but those notes seemed threatening, and the people who received them were understandably frightened."

"But how did you get the notecards?" Fannie asked. "They were in our swag bags. Only those connected with the contest recieved them."

Jeb explained that Nick, who had far too many of those types of gifts around his house from catering all sorts of events, told Jeb he could have whatever he wanted out of this year's baking contest swag bag. Jeb had chosen the notecards and a nice ball point pen—a decision that resulted in Jeb being the one who would ultimately "regret this."

"I'm sorry," Jeb repeated. "If there's some way I can, you know, make it up to everyone, I sure will."

"I'll certainly come up with some things you can do right now," Bishop John said before either Fannie or Foster could comment.

Fannie heaved a sigh. "Is that all the mysteries?"

"I believe it is. All the missing contestants are present and accounted for, and the red envelope mystery is finally solved," Foster replied.

"So I guess the only thing left to do now is get on with the finals and declare the winner of the Tuscarawas and Surrounding Counties Baking Contest," she whispered to Foster after the bishop and his son had gone.

"Ladies and gentlemen," Hilo said into the microphone, causing an ear-piercing screech to blast jarringly out of the speaker.

Foster whipped his hands over his ears and said something under his breath that may or may not have been appropriate. Fannie wasn't quite sure, so she opted to give him the benefit of the doubt.

Hilo moved the microphone a few feet away from one of the speakers and tried again. This time his emcee voice came through smooth and clear.

"Thank you for coming tonight to witness the crowning of the best baker in all of Tuscarawas County and the surrounding areas."

As Hilo continued, Foster let his mind wander to how much he hoped that Fannie would win. He knew how much the title meant to her. But he also knew that he couldn't do anything to help Fannie. She had to stand on her own in the contest.

He couldn't risk the slightest appearance of having pulled any strings, no matter how much he hoped Fannie would win.

The finalists took their places at their stations. Fannie couldn't help but pace with excitement. The Blustery Sisters were slightly crouched in a starter position, and Fannie wondered if Michael and Melissa, being well-practiced in disappointment, were trying their best not to get their hopes up too high.

Then the moment came.

"Contestants, start your ovens!" Hilo said, drawing a chuckle from the audience. "Let the baking begin!"

With that, he snapped a colorful dishtowel before him, and the race was on.

Flour was flying, eggs were being whipped into a frenzy, and pots and pans were performing their own heavy metal concert, the likes of which had never been heard before in Amish Country. At least as far as Fannie knew.

She glanced to her left and noticed that Michael and Melissa had some challenges working together as they tried to spread out the dough for their wedding cookies. Wedding cookies were an interesting choice for their entry in the finals, given their marital history, but Melissa had mentioned to Fannie that the recipe was a cherished recipe of her mother, and she thought they might have a good shot at winning with it.

But not if they couldn't work together, Fannie thought. Every time Michael pulled the pan toward him, Melissa pulled it back toward her. It made the process take that much longer, but Fannie hoped it was a good reminder to them of how futile this kind of "working together" could be.

The other bakers got busy slicing and dicing and mixing and fixing. Faith, Hope, and Charity had some trouble rounding the curves of their devil's food cake when it came time to frost it. Fannie hoped that, like Michael and Melissa, the sisters would also see the benefit of working together.

She glanced at the judges and noticed that they all seemed to be paying rapt attention to every detail and taking meticulous notes on each finalist, including her, so she tried to tune out what was going on around her and focus on the details of making Aunt Selma's buttermilk biscuits.

The Blustery Sisters, baking sheets in hand, made a quick pit stop to review their recipe, allowing Fannie to overtake them in the prep lane and take the lead.

Apparently, the audience loved it, for there were spontaneous cheers, a few jeers, and a whole lot of oohs and ahhs.

———

Foster's ears rang with all the noise going on, and his mouth began to water. The food looked so good he could almost hear his stomach growling in three languages, as his father used to always say. But the dish he wanted to sample most was those Fannie Miller biscuits.

"Finalists," Hilo said, "you have only five minutes left on the clock. At that time, I will tell you to return your ovens to their starting positions, drop your spatulas, and add the final trimmings to your cakes and other baked items. The question remains: Finalists, will you be declared the best baker in all of Tuscarawas and the surrounding counties, or will you have to return next year and take another crack at it?"

Foster leaned slightly forward with his hands clasped tightly together. It wouldn't be long now before the winning name would be announced. It was all he could do not to get up and start pacing.

———

Fannie couldn't believe she was only a few minutes away from finding out if she would be the grand prize winner. She couldn't believe that she had made it into the finals. Her heart wished her grandmother was still alive to see this—the one who'd passed down her cast-iron pan to Fannie. Or her dear aunt Selma, who had perfected the recipe over the years and taught her how to knead the dough just right and gently brush on the melted butter during the baking process to give the biscuits that perfect golden-brown color. And she especially wished her competitive cousin Annie May, who always told her that she'd never amount to anything, could be here to witness her acceptance speech, should she win this special baking contest.

But Fannie was happy that her good friend Foster Bates was present. If anyone would be happy for her, she knew he would be. And tonight, that's what mattered to her most.

"Two minutes!" Hilo said, as Fannie and the other contestants quickly finished up their masterpieces. This was their last chance to impress the judges, and everything had to be perfect.

Fannie glanced at the Blustery Sisters again, as they put the final touches on their devil's food cake. Michael and Melissa had arranged their wedding cookies in an impressive design on a doily covered platter.

And Fannie let out a huge breath of relief after she added a last brush of butter over her biscuits.

With only ten seconds to go on the clock, Fannie started to run her tray of biscuits over to the judges' table, but then was cut off by the Blustery Sisters, who were balancing their devil's food cake between them. The aggressive move threw off Fannie's balance and left her standing there a little disoriented. Meanwhile, the seconds continued to tick off the clock.

Michael and Melissa passed Fannie with their wedding cookies. But at this point it was every man or woman for themselves.

Foster wasn't sure what to do. He knew he had to help out his friend, but would it be allowed?

Apparently having witnessed what the Blustery Sisters had done, Nick motioned to Foster that it would be okay for him to help out his friend.

With only five seconds to go, Foster jumped to his feet. He looked at Fannie and then over at the judges' table, assessing the distance between them. Breathing in enough air to get him there, he grabbed the tray of biscuits from Fannie and took off running across the room, with the speed and dexterity of a man half his age—a man he used to know and admire, but who had been missing, just like all those contestants he had been searching for.

But now he'd found himself. Foster was back. His strength and energy came flooding in at the very moment it was needed, just like Fannie had said it would.

With three seconds left on the clock, Charity broke away from her sisters and turned back to cut off Foster on his way to the judges' table, sending him flying in one direction and Fannie's tray of perfect biscuits flying in the other.

In spite of her apparent intentions, Foster somehow managed to whip around midair and hit the ground feet first, catching the biscuits before they hit the ground.

"Time's up! Surrender your spatulas and flour sifters!" Hilo shouted, just as Foster placed the tray on the judges' table, after scooting the devil's food cake over a bit. Michael and Melissa's wedding cookies, and the couple themselves, somehow managed to stay above the ruckus.

Foster shifted his weight from one leg to the other, as Hilo nodded to the contestants and said, "Let the final judging begin!"

Nick Landers took a bite of the devil's food cake, and Foster could tell by the way the man's lips moved that he was shifting it around in his mouth. After a long, dramatic pause, he gave his assessment.

"Smooth, but not too rich. A delight to the senses, but not overpowering. Excellent," he said.

The Blustery Sisters clapped and squealed with delight.

Foster heard Betty Campbell concur with Nick, noting the exceptional creaminess of the frosting.

Alice Trumble said she was equally impressed, stating, "This is exactly what a devil's food cake should be—heavenly!"

"That's three for three," Hilo said.

Things were looking good for the Blustery Sisters, but there were two more entries to be judged, and it was all Foster could do to remain firmly in place beside Fannie. He wanted to go get the first-place ribbon and hand it to Fannie herself.

Next, the judges sampled Michael and Melissa's wedding cookies.

This time, Alice was the first to give her judgment. "These cookies have perfect symmetry, and they aren't dry or crumbly. In fact, they're quite wonderful."

Nick was equally impressed. "These cookies are magnificent. They are so elegant and tasty, they could be served at a royal wedding."

Quite a high compliment, Fannie thought as a knot formed in her stomach. Her hope of winning was vanishing as quickly as steam rising from a teakettle.

"All the ingredients in these cookies work together in perfect harmony," Betty said, looking at Melissa and her husband. "Well done, you two."

Fannie was happy for the couple. But now her biscuits were up, and she held her breath. She also held Foster's hand to steady herself. And that's what she would tell anyone who asked her about it.

Hilo lifted the microphone to his mouth again. "And now," he said, "the final entry, number three, is Miss Fannie's homemade buttermilk biscuits."

Nick scooped one of the biscuits out of the tray and took a bite.

"Oh, my!" he exclaimed. "Oh, my, my, my! These are absolutely delicious! They're light and fluffy and perfect!"

Betty sampled one next, and a look of supreme delight swept over her face. "This is no ordinary biscuit. Why, this is a masterpiece!"

Alice finished her bite and looked toward Fannie. "For a biscuit to stand out in the company of a decadent chocolate cake and chic wedding cookies is no easy task. But you, Fannie Miller, have pulled off the impossible. It would be a sin to cover such a biscuit in dollops of jam or a ladle of gravy. This biscuit deserves the spotlight!"

"All three of these entries are wonderful. This is going to be our toughest competition yet," Nick said as the three judges discussed the entries among themselves.

When Fannie thought she couldn't wait another minute, Alice handed a white envelope to Hilo.

"Drum roll, please," Hilo announced from the stage, as he prepared to open the envelope that held the winner's name.

A drumbeat sounded, and along with Fannie, the audience members seemed to be holding their breath as Hilo ripped open the envelope.

"And the winner is..." He paused—no doubt for dramatic effect. "The grand prize winner of this year's baking contest is..."

Melissa held Michael's hand; Faith, Hope, and Charity locked arms with one another; and Fannie held her breath as Hilo continued.

"Miss Fannie Miller!"

The cheers and screams went out into the theater, and Fannie figured it could probably be heard for a three-mile radius. And that was just hers.

Fannie let loose and hugged Foster until she noticed people staring at them. Then she quickly made her way up to the microphone.

After tapping the microphone a few times to make sure it was on, as she had seen so many others do in moments like this, Fannie proceeded.

"I want to thank my fellow finalists for all their hard work and talent," she said. "It's been quite a journey. None of us knew how it was going to turn out, but thankfully, we're all safe and accounted for. And we're richer for the experience." Holding up the check, while trying not to feel proud, Fannie added, "Well, me most of all. Wow! That's a lot of zeroes!"

"I can't thank all of you enough for your friendship and kindness over the years. I especially want to thank the judges for bestowing on me this great honor."

The crowd chanted, "Fannie! Fannie! Fannie!"

Fannie smiled and then lifted her arm to hush the audience.

"You know, I've been doing a lot of thinking about what I was going to do with the money if I won. To tell you the truth, this is what I really wanted." Fannie held up the first-place ribbon. "And I know exactly what I'm going to do with this."

Again, everyone cheered.

"But the prize money presents me with some options. I could travel, expand my quilt shop, or use it to help change someone's life." Fannie's throat vibrated and her chest expanded as she said her final words. "I have decided on the latter."

CHAPTER 35

As Foster sat in the theater, listening to Fannie's acceptance speech, he recalled the conversation he and Fannie had the night they'd eaten at the Main Street Grill. She'd asked him a poignant question: What was the one thing he wanted most out of life? His answer came quickly and easily: a fishing boat. A fishing boat had been part of his dream of moving back here. But the expense of buying a home and renting office space for his investigative business had taken all of his savings. After that, it seemed he couldn't manage to save two dollars, much less enough greenbacks for a fishing boat.

"Why do you want to know?" Foster had asked Fannie.

"You can find out a lot about a person by knowing their dreams," was her response.

So when Fannie said what she'd said at the microphone, those words about using the prize money to change someone's life had caused Foster's heart to race.

Could it be? Would his partner in crime solving be planning to use her prize money to buy him his own fishing boat? Foster could barely wrap his mind around such an incredibly generous gift and act of pure selflessness.

He closed his eyes and pictured the striped bass and catfish practically leaping into his shiny new red boat. Or was it blue with a red racing stripe? It didn't matter. What mattered was that he had the best investigative partner and friend in the whole wide world. And Miss Fannie *was* the generous type.

A hush came over the crowd as Fannie continued to speak. The entire audience seemed to hang on her every word.

"And so, in keeping with my desire to use this money to change someone's life, I would like to present this check to. . ."

Foster puffed out his chest and even felt the heat of blush on his cheeks, thinking about what he was going to say concerning such a thoughtful gift. And when she needed her own roof repaired. Was this really happening? His eyes met Fannie's, and he sheepishly shook his head a bit, hoping to signal to her both his excitement and disbelief.

But Fannie looked slightly beyond him.

"Michael and Melissa. . .Would the two of you join me up here?"

Michael and Melissa? Foster repeated mentally what Fannie had said. His mind raced, searching for answers. *They're going to be presenting my boat?*

All heads turned toward Michael and Melissa, the couple they had just witnessed losing the competition to Fannie. Looking more than a bit confused, Michael and Melissa hesitated then made their way to the stage to join Fannie. Foster wondered if they had any idea what Fannie was about to do. Foster certainly didn't. He could almost feel his fishing boat leaving the dock without him.

"Michael and Melissa," Fannie said as they stood beside her, "I know that it has been a dream of yours to become parents, and I also know how difficult your journey has been. I want to help change that, if you will allow me. I would like to present the two of you with this check for twenty-five thousand dollars, to put toward your adoption expenses. You see, I discovered that, if you had won, you'd both decided that would be where the money would go. I want to help make it happen." Fannie paused a few seconds as if to take control of her emotions. "I also believe that God will help you every step of the way to be the best parents you can be."

Michael and Melissa pressed fingers to their quivering, smiling lips. Through tearful words, they thanked Fannie for her unbelievable generosity.

The audience was now passing around tissues to dry their eyes, and even Foster had to grab a few. *This is better than any fishing boat,* he thought.

What a selfless act dear Fannie has made on behalf of this childless couple.

Lifting the microphone to his mouth again, Michael added, "Fannie, before we can accept this check, there is one condition that we would have to insist upon."

"What would that be?" Fannie asked, curiously.

"Foster Bates and Fannie Miller. . .the two of you have to promise to be godmother and godfather to any child we bring into our home."

Fannie looked out into the audience at Foster, and when he bobbed his head, she did too. Then Fannie clearly stated, "Foster and I would be honored."

———

"Well, that sure went different than I thought it would," Charity exclaimed as she drove her two sisters home from the theater where the big announcement had been revealed.

"It sure did," Faith agreed from the front passenger seat. "I never expected that Fannie would give away the grand prize money to people she barely knows."

"It didn't surprise me that much," Hope put in from the backseat of the car. "Fannie Miller is a kind and generous person. What surprised me the most was that she won the contest with her buttermilk biscuits. I really expected us to take first place."

"Same here," Charity interjected. "We own a bakery and bake all sorts of delicious goodies, so I thought—"

"I admit, I was disappointed that we sisters didn't win the prize money," Faith interrupted. "But if we had to lose to someone, I'm glad it was selfless Fannie."

Charity emitted a deep sigh as she drove the vehicle up her sisters' driveway. "That huge sum of money isn't the only thing Fannie won tonight."

"What do you mean?" Faith questioned. "As far as I know, that check was the only winner's prize."

"I believe Fannie won Foster's heart, which means I have no chance with him at all." She turned off the engine and sat with her fingers clenching the steering wheel. "So much for trying to gain the investigator's attention. Guess the cinnamon rolls and doggie treats I made for him and Chief didn't impress Mr. Bates that much."

"Quit feeling sorry for yourself." Hope reached over the seat and gave Charity's shoulder a squeeze. "It's not like Foster is the only male in Sugarcreek. . .or any other town here in Tuscarawas County."

"Hope is right," Faith said. "There are plenty of unattached men in the area. You just need to be patient until you find the right one." She gave Charity's arm a little nudge.

Charity's shoulders drooped as she tried to form her lips into a smile. "I suppose you're right, but I really had my sights set on Foster Bates."

"You know," Hope said, "things might not work out between Fannie and Foster, and if they don't, maybe he will take a serious look at you."

"You really think so?" Charity brightened a bit.

"Anything is possible if the Lord has a hand in it," Faith said.

What is going on? Charity wondered. *Hope sounded hopeful, and Faith was suddenly full of faith.*

Charity clasped her hands in a prayer-like gesture, bowed her head, and closed her eyes. Her situation with Foster was definitely something she would be praying about. And she added a thankful prayer for the changes she was hearing in her sisters too.

Berlin

When Michael and Melissa arrived home that night, Melissa's adrenaline spiked as she collapsed onto the couch. "I still can't believe it, Michael! Why would Fannie Miller, who we didn't know until we signed up for the baking contest, give us her prize money so we could adopt a child?" Her thoughts scattered, feeling too excited and confused to think straight.

He took a seat beside Melissa and clasped her hand. "The only thing I can say is that she obviously has a tender heart and truly wants to help us become adoptive parents and see the child gain a family. That's the kind of attitude all Christians should have, and I'm sorry to say that we have both been remiss in that area—especially when it comes to our marriage." Michael tipped Melissa's chin and stared lovingly into her eyes. "I'm sorry for all the things I've said and done to hurt you. I've taken you for granted, and we have both wasted too much time quarreling over so many stupid things." He paused for a minute, and his voice cracked when he spoke again. "I really have no excuse for my bad behavior except the stress I felt over not being able to give you a child."

Melissa swallowed around the lump in her throat and swiped at the tears rolling down her hot cheeks. "I forgive you, Michael, and I'm sorry too. I've had a bad attitude and said many hurtful things to you as well." She nearly choked on the sob rising in her throat. "I can't believe how close we came to getting a divorce, more times than once, and I'm so thankful we finally went to see a Christian counselor."

"Me too." Using his thumb, Michael wiped her tears away, and then he pulled Melissa into his arms and gave her a tender kiss on the lips. "I love you very much, and if it's God's will for us to adopt a child, then I'll try to be the best Christian father I can be."

She smiled and cried some more, only this time with happy tears. "And with the Lord's help, I will commit to be the best mom I can be."

"Let's pray right now," Michael said, bowing his head and reaching for Melissa's hand. "We'll ask God to guide and direct our lives, and if it be His will for us to adopt a son or daughter, it will happen in His time, not ours.

Sugarcreek

The following day, as Foster approached his office, he spotted Bishop John heading up the sidewalk in his direction. The bishop waved, and Foster waved back, then he paused and waited to see if the man wanted to chat.

Sure enough, the bishop made his way over to Foster with a hearty grin. "Well. . .well. . .that Fannie Miller sure surprised us all last night, didn't she?" he asked. "That woman is one of the most selfless people I know."

"Yes, she certainly is," Foster agreed. "She needed a new roof herself, but she just gave the money away. But that's her heart. Michael and Melissa were long overdue for some happiness. And speaking of happiness, I think I'm going to do a little fishing this afternoon to celebrate closing another tricky case. You and your boy want to join me?"

"I wish we could," the bishop said. "I love fishing. Even have a good fishing boat. But I haven't had a lot of free time these last few years. Had to squeeze in my Tuesday trip to the lake the day you stopped by to talk to me."

"As far as I'm concerned, if a person's too busy for fishing, they're just too busy." Foster gave the bishop a wide grin.

John reached under his straw hat and scratched his head as if letting the truth of those words sink in. "You know, on second thought, we will join you. I can't think of anything more important than fishing with my son and giving him my attention." He thumped Foster's back. "And I will enjoy spending time with you too, my new friend. Maybe we can even get Fannie to join us."

Foster shook his head. "I think she has plans to show off her first-place ribbon around town."

Just then, he heard the *clip-clop* of a horse's hooves, followed by the sound of a horn from a passing car, as Fannie's buggy sped past them. At that moment, Foster saw it—on the back of the buggy in full prominent view and against all regulations—Fannie's first-place ribbon flapped in the breeze. It was right above a HONK IF YOU LOVE FANNIE bumper sticker.

The bishop chuckled and shook his head. "I love her spirit," he said, "but it's a full-time job keeping that woman in line."

Foster smiled. "Tell me about it."

As though understanding the excitement of the moment, Bishop John said he would be letting Fannie know that she'd need to remove both items from her buggy by the end of day.

"I am sure Fannie will happily agree," Foster responded as he waved when she sped past his office.

———

A week later, Fannie had gone into town with her horse and buggy to pick up a few things. It had been such a busy week with the finals and solving the cases and all, that some of her daily chores had taken a back seat. Now she was determined to hurry home to catch up, at least getting some groceries in the house. And maybe a few extra buckets, just in case it rained again and she had more leaks.

But as soon as Fannie neared her house, she was surprised to see cars, wagons, and horses and buggies parked up and down her driveway and into the yard.

What's going on? she asked herself.

As she got closer, she saw them. Dozens of Amish and English men were scaling the rafters, putting a new roof on Fannie's home. Even the Beiler sisters were there, along with other women of the community. And up on the tallest rafter stood Foster Bates!

"Foster! What are you doing up there? You get yourself down from there right now!"

"Can't do that, Fannie. We're fixing your roof."

"But...I..." For once in her life, Fannie was speechless.

"What goes around comes around," the bishop called out to Fannie. "Think I'll preach on that next Sunday." Then he gave Jeb, who was working right next to him, a hug.

What goes around comes around, Fannie repeated to herself. *It does indeed.*

———

The following day, Fannie stopped by Foster's agency to thank him once again for helping her solve the mystery of the Tuscarawas and Surrounding Counties Baking Contest. "As always, Fannie, I couldn't have done it without you."

And he was right, for it was through their combined efforts and investigative skills that one by one each of the missing persons was either found safe and unharmed and exactly where they had said they would be or in a situation they were perfectly capable of handling on their own. The bottom line? All were accounted for.

"Well, partner, we did it again!" Foster said with a wink, and looking as though he was quite pleased. "You and I make a pretty good team, I'd say. Do you concur?"

"I concur."

"I concur! I concur!" came a voice from the other room.

When Fannie went to investigate, she immediately found the issue. "Hey," Fannie said, "what's Peggy doing here?"

Foster gave a sheepish grin. "Yeah, well, that's a bit of a long story."

"Of course it is," Fannie said. "But do go on. I'm all ears."

"Well, you see, after all the good things that happened after the contest, the Blustery—I mean Beiler—sisters decided to turn over a new leaf and quit gossiping. But until they knew they had successfully kicked the habit, they didn't want Peggy around repeating everything she overheard to Bishop John or anyone else. So they gave her to me for safe keeping, until they are fully recovered from the transgression of gossiping." He pointed to the parrot. "Now how do you say no to a bird like Peggy?"

The parrot let out an ear-piercing squawk and said, "Foster did it! Foster did it!"

Fannie and Foster laughed.

"You're right about that, Peggy!" Foster said. "I sure did it—I took you in for a while, so you'd better behave yourself."

"I think it was very nice of you to do such a thing. You're always surprising me, Foster Bates."

"And you're always surprising me, Fannie Miller. So where do you want to go for supper tonight?" he asked. "My treat."

"Is this a date?"

"Of course not," Foster said. "We need to debrief."

"Go over our tactics for the next case we solve together?"

"We'll see if we need to brush up on any of our skills."

"And we've got to eat."

"Right. But it's not a date."

She shook her head. "Far from it."

"Good. Shall we take your buggy?"

"Of course."

"I do love riding in your buggy, and as you know, the price of gas has gone up again."

"Of course it has."

EPILOGUE

Walnut Creek

Ten Months Later

Excitement filled Fannie's heart as she walked into the banquet room at Der Dutchman, where a dinner party for Michael and Melissa was being held. It was in honor of their three-week-old baby boy, Jesse Raul, whom they adopted from an international adoption agency.

The wide smile on Foster's face let Fannie know he was equally excited about being here and getting to meet his and Fannie's new godchild.

After greeting little Jesse and his new parents, Fannie presented them with a beautifully handmade baby quilt.

"Oh, this is lovely. Thank you so much," Melissa exclaimed.

Michael nodded his agreement. "We appreciate your kindness."

Foster stepped forward and gave Michael a toy police badge and police uniform onesie. "It's never too early to start training your little guy in police work," Foster said with a deep chuckle.

"Thanks," Michael and Melissa said in unison. "We love it!"

The bishop, along with his wife and their son, Jeb, stopped by to drop off a hand-hewn wooden highchair that John said he had built with Jeb's help.

The Beiler sisters were there too, and they presented the infant with gifts and the promise of a job when he turned sixteen.

The entire town seemed to have gotten infected with Fannie's generosity, and everyone had been trying to do whatever they could to help the young couple celebrate their new addition.

As for Fannie and her relationship with Foster? They still planned to solve crimes together whenever possible and be the best friends to each other they possibly could be.

Foster even built Fannie a nice display case to keep her ribbon in, which she exhibited at her quilt shop. Foster had stated that everyone who came in needed to know that Fannie Miller was the maker of the absolute best biscuits in all of Tuscarawas County and the surrounding areas.

"And there is no mystery about that!" he'd added.

Fannie was content with the way things were between her and Foster Bates—just good friends who would stay in contact and put their heads together when another mysterious case came along that needed her input. Was it wrong to look forward to that?

MISS FANNIE'S
BUTTERMILK BISCUITS

- 2 cups flour
- 4 teaspoons baking powder
- ½ teaspoon salt
- ¼ teaspoon baking soda
- 4 tablespoons shortening
- ¾ cup buttermilk

Sift dry ingredients together in large bowl. Add shortening and cut into dry ingredients with fork or pastry cutter until dough is pea sized. Add buttermilk and mix until dough is soft. Form biscuits with hands. (May dip hands in a little extra flour if needed to keep dough from sticking.) Place biscuits in greased pan. Bake at 475 degrees about 12 minutes. Makes 16 2-inch biscuits. Serve with butter and jam or pour gravy over biscuits. Enjoy!

New York Times bestselling and award-winning author **Wanda E. Brunstetter** is one of the founders of the Amish fiction genre. She has written more than one hundred books translated in four languages. With over twelve million copies sold, Wanda's stories consistently earn spots on the nation's most prestigious bestseller lists and have received numerous awards.

Wanda's ancestors were part of the Anabaptist faith, and her novels are based on personal research intended to accurately portray the Amish way of life. Her books are read and trusted by many Amish people, who credit her for giving readers a deeper understanding of the people and their customs.

When Wanda visits her Amish friends, she finds herself drawn to their peaceful lifestyle, sincerity, and close family ties. Wanda enjoys photography, ventriloquism, gardening, bird watching, beachcombing, and spending time with her family. She and her husband, Richard, have been blessed with two grown children, six grandchildren, and two great-grandchildren.

To learn more about Wanda, visit her
website at www.wandabrunstetter.com.

Martha Bolton is a prolific author of eighty-nine books, an Emmy nominee (Outstanding Achievement in Music and Lyrics, 1988), a Dove Award nominee (Children's Musical, 1999), and a "with" author on three *New York Times* bestselling books. She was nominated for a Writers' Guild Award for her work on the Emmy-winning *Bob Hope—The First Ninety Years*. She was Bob's first full-time female staff writer and wrote for his television specials (over thirty hours of primetime programming and fifteen years of his personal appearances and special events). As a staff writer for Bob Hope, Bolton had the opportunity to write scripted lines for a virtual Who's Who in entertainment, sports, and politics.

Bolton also wrote for Phyllis Diller for many years, and her series of books for those over fifty include *Didn't My Skin Used to Fit?*, *Cooking with Hot Flashes*, and *The Whole World Is Changing and I'm Too Hot to Care*. She has also written for many Christian comedians such as Mark Lowry (including parodies and cowriting his Piper the Hyper Mouse series), Chonda Pierce, Jeff Allen, and numerous others.

Martha's stage work includes writing the script for "The Confession," based on Beverly Lewis' bestselling Confession trilogy; cowriting both "Half-Stitched," based on Wanda E. Brunstetter's bestselling book *The Half-Stitched Amish Quilting Club* and "Our Christmas Dinner" with director/composer Wally Nason; "Josiah for President"; and "The Home Game" for Blue Gate Musicals. Both *Josiah for President* and *The Home Game* have accompanying novels penned by Bolton.

THE RISE AND FALL OF MISS FANNIE'S BISCUITS
THE MUSICAL
IS COMING TO THE STAGE

A collaboration between bestselling authors Wanda E. Brunstetter and Martha Bolton, this delightful show from Blue Gate Musicals reunites Fannie Miller and Foster Bates, who were introduced in the popular show *Stolen*. The result is an intriguing musical comedy mystery.

Fannie Miller has finally made it to the finals in the Tuscarawas and Surrounding Areas Baking Contest. She's thrilled—but other contestants are disappearing mysteriously. Convinced that something's amiss, she calls her old friend Foster Bates, a retired police officer and part-time private eye. Join them as they investigate the cast of colorful characters and stir up a plan to solve the case.

April 3 – August 2, 2025
The Bird-in-Hand Theater – Paradise, PA
https://bird-in-hand.com/stage/

July 2025
The Blue Gate Theater – Shipshewana, IN
https://www.thebluegate.com

This hilarious musical whodunit will keep you guessing until the very end.

COOKBOOKS FROM WANDA!

Wanda E. Brunstetter's
Amish Friends Outdoor Cookbook
Grab this must-have cookbook for nature lovers and adventurous cooks who want to cook outdoors on the backyard grill or a campsite fire. Amish cooks have shared over 250 recipes divided into sections by method: stick, pie iron, foil packet, cast iron, grill. Also included is advice for prep work, packing a cooler, maintaining cast-iron tools, and much more. Encased in a lay-flat binding and presented in full color, home cooks of all ages will be delighted to add this cookbook to their collections.

Comb Bound / 978–1-63609–831-9

Wanda E. Brunstetter's
Amish Friends Comfort Foods Cookbook
Why do we turn to food when our emotions are on a rollercoaster? Why do things like mac and cheese or chocolate chip cookies bring us comfort? Well, this book won't answer the psychological questions, but it will deliver those foods that help you through a bad day or add to a celebratory occasion. Over 270 recipes from Amish and Mennonite cooks are divided into traditional categories from main dishes and sides to desserts and snacks, encased in a lay-flat binding, and presented in full color.

Comb Bound / 978–1-63609–973-6

Other Fiction Works by Wanda E. Brunstetter

Amish Cooking Class
The Seekers (Book 1)
The Blessing (Book 2)
The Celebration (Book 3)
The Amish Cooking Class Trilogy (All 3 books in 1)
Amish Cooking Class Cookbook

Amish Greenhouse Mystery
The Crow's Call (Book 1)
The Mockingbird's Song (Book 2)
The Robin's Greeting (Book 3)
The Amish Greenhouse Mysteries (All 3 books in 1)

Amish Hawaiian Series with Jean Brunstetter
The Hawaiian Discovery (Book 1)
The Hawaiian Quilt (Book 2)
Amish Hawaiian Adventures (Book 1 & 2)
The Blended Quilt (Book 3)

Amish Millionaire with Jean Brunstetter
The English Son (Book 1)
The Stubborn Father (Book 2)
The Betrayed Fiancée (Book 3)
The Missing Will (Book 4)
The Divided Family (Book 5)
The Selfless Act (Book 6)
Amish Millionaire (All 6 in 1)

Brides of Lancaster County
A Merry Heart (Book 1)
Looking for a Miracle (Book 2)
Plain and Fancy (Book 3)
The Hope Chest (Book 4)
Brides of Lancaster County Collection (All 4 books in 1)

Brides of Webster County
Going Home (Book 1)
On Her Own (Book 2)
Dear to Me (Book 3)
Allison's Journey (Book 4)
Brides of Webster County Collection (All 4 books in 1)

Creektown Discoveries
The Walnut Creek Wish (Book 1)
The Sugarcreek Surprise (Book 2)
The Apple Creek Announcement (Book 3)

Daughters of Lancaster County
The Storekeeper's Daughter (Book 1)
The Quilter's Daughter (Book 2)
The Bishop's Daughter (Book 3)
The Daughters of Lancaster County (All 3 books in 1)

The Discovery – A Lancaster County Saga
Goodbye to Yesterday (Book 1)
Silence of Winter (Book 2)
The Hope of Spring (Book 3)
The Pieces of Summer (Book 4)
A Revelation in Autumn (Book 5)
A Vow for Always (Book 6)
The Discovery Saga Collection (All 6 books in 1)

The Friendship Letters
Letters of Trust (Book 1)
Letters of Comfort (Book 2)
Letters of Wisdom (Book 3)

The Half-Stitched Amish Quilting Club Series
The Half-Stitched Amish Quilting Club (Book 1)
The Tattered Quilt (Book 2)
The Healing Quilt (Book 3)
The Half-Stitched Amish Quilting Club Trilogy (All 3 in 1)

The Hochstetler Twins with Jean Brunstetter
The Lopsided Christmas Cake (Book 1)
The Farmers' Market Mishap (Book 2)
Twice as Nice Amish Romance Collection (Books 1 & 2)

Indiana Cousins
A Cousin's Promise (Book 1)
A Cousin's Prayer (Book 2)
A Cousin's Challenge (Book 3)
Indiana Cousins (All 3 books in 1)

Kentucky Brothers
The Journey (Book 1)
The Healing (Book 2)
The Struggle (Book 3)
Kentucky Brothers (All 3 books in 1)

A Mifflin County Mystery
The Protector (Book 1)
The Peacemaker (Book 2)

Prairie State Friends
The Decision (Book 1)
The Gift (Book 2)
The Restoration (Book 3)
The Prairie State Friends Trilogy (All 3 books in 1)

The Prayer Jars
The Hope Jar (Book 1)
The Forgiving Jar (Book 2)
The Healing Jar (Book 3)
The Prayer Jars Trilogy (All 3 books in 1)
The Prayer Jar Devotional: Hope
The Prayer Jar Devotional: Forgiveness
The Prayer Jar Devotional: Healing